MURDER IN THE PINES

A.J. RIVERS

Murder in the Pines
Copyright © 2024 by A.J. Rivers

All rights reserved. Without limiting the rights under copyright reserved above, no part of this publication may be reproduced, stored in or introduced into retrieval system, or transmitted, in any form, or by any means (electronic, mechanical, photocopying, recording, or otherwise) without the prior written permission of both the copyright owner and the above publisher of this book.

This is a work of fiction. Names, characters, places, brands, media, and incidents are either the products of the author's imagination or are used fictitiously. The author acknowledges the trademarked status and trademark owners of various products referenced in this work of fiction, which have been used without permission. The publication/use of these trademarks is not authorized, associated with, or sponsored by the trademark owners.

PROLOGUE

D**ELILAH'S BREATH CAUGHT IN HER THROAT. HER HEART PLAYED** an upbeat tempo, closer to techno music than its usual rhythm. It rippled through her body, vibrating her very bones. She knew this was going to happen. Well, she didn't know, but she had a feeling. Something was going to happen. The feeling, solid in shape, crept into her mind. She felt the weight of it like a stone as she left the gas station and pulled back onto the road, heading to her cousin's house.

They hadn't seen each other in months. But family always came together for baby showers, birthdays, and funerals. The baby shower was bringing everyone out of hiding. Even their Aunt Rachel, who had become a recluse after her husband died. When her mother called and told her Rachel was coming, she was excited. It had been years since she'd seen her, and she couldn't wait. Though that feeling had dissipated.

All she wanted now was to get out alive.

She ducked behind a tree. The distant whistling of her attacker floated closer on the light breeze. Her heart pounded faster. She was smarter than that. She should have been. Why didn't she just keep driving? Keep moving? Why didn't she just drive until she found a more well-lit road? She should never have stopped.

She knew better, but...

The urge to blame herself for everything was something she had been working through in therapy. Those techniques weren't working now.

Beads of sweat threaded down her back as she hid behind a tree she knew wasn't big enough to conceal her. She needed to catch her breath. Rest her legs. Try to come up with a game plan. But her mind was blank. She couldn't even think of an exit strategy. She didn't know the woods like he did.

"Now, now... Delilah, running around these woods will not get you to where you want to be. Home with your family. Doesn't your cousin have a baby shower tomorrow? You don't come out now, you won't make it."

Delilah knew that was a lie. Everything he said up to that point had been a lie. She wasn't going home. She wasn't going to make it to that baby shower. Not if she kept running.

She needed to get back to the road. Off in the distance, she heard cars driving by. The road was close. Delilah hadn't been paying attention when she started running. She just knew she needed to get away. Getting away from the road seemed like the smartest thing to do at the time. But now, shrouded in darkness, she was having second thoughts.

She needed enough space between them so she could loop around and go back. Her keys were still in her car. She stayed low to the ground and moved over to another tree. The sound of crunching leaves sent a shiver down her spine. He was always too close.

"Delilah..."

Bile rose up her throat. The way he sang her name. Sickeningly sweet. Innocent. Like a child wanting to get her attention. His voice did not match his actions. Even while running through the forest, she still felt his hands wrapped around her neck. Squeezing the breath out of her lungs. The grin on his face became brighter as she started to lose consciousness. He smiled at her as she was fading.

He had gotten so much pleasure from it. His dark eyes getting darker and darker. His smile growing wider as she closed her eyes.

A loud car door slamming got both of their attention. Delilah had opened her eyes, and he had looked behind him. It was the perfect opportunity. She silently thanked her guardian angel as she kicked him and ran into the forest. There was no path, no trail. Just trees. She ran. Her lungs burned with every breath. Pain licked up her leg. She had twisted her ankle, though that seemed like it had been forever ago. She gritted her teeth with every step. Blocking out the pain. If he caught her, the pain would be much worse.

She ducked behind a larger tree, resting her head against it to catch her breath.

"Delilah? I know you're still here! You can't get out. You'll never make it past me."

She heard the smile on the edge of his words. She knew he was right. There was no other way out. She either had to keep running forward or make it past him in some kind of way. Inches away from her feet, there was a thick branch that had fallen from one of the trees. Her fingers wrapped around it. It was thick and heavy and could do some damage if she hit him in the right spot. If she did, she could make it out. If she didn't, at least she would go out fighting. She'd get some of his blood on her hands so people would know it was him.

She braced herself, squeezing the branch in her hands. When he got close enough, she'd swing. She'd make it out of the forest and back to her car.

She'd make it home...

CHAPTER ONE

Riley Quinn

"**H**ELLO, MR. GILL. IS EVERYTHING OKAY?"
This was the first time he had called me since the last time we talked about the cameras that he keeps on his property. People, mostly teenagers, were always going onto his property and messing with his things. He got the cameras because he felt like the police weren't doing anything about it. He had a point; we weren't. Ever since I was a kid it was well known that Mr. Gill was a strange old man who stayed away from the people in town as best he could. We would go onto his property to mess with him; the officers at that time felt like it was a rite of passage. It was something all teenagers did, but that didn't make it right.

It made me sad to think about the hell we caused that poor man when I was younger, and now, if I could do anything to make it right, I would.

"Are they there now? Okay, we're on our way."

I hung up the phone and grabbed the keys from Zelina's desk. She looked up from her book. "What's wrong?"

"Kids messing with Mr. Gill."

"We going to scare them?" She flipped her file closed and set it on her desk. She jumped to her feet. Z loved scaring children. It may seem like a strange thing to say because she's a cop, but it makes her happy. She would be great in one of those scared straight programs.

"I don't know about scaring them, but we could teach them a lesson as long as you don't go overboard. You know how you are."

She sighed. "Fine. I'll behave."

"Did you two hear?"

I spun around just as Officer Rainwater rounded the corner and stopped a few inches away from me. Beads of sweat snaked down the side of his face.

I shrugged. "Hear what?"

Zelina walked over and stood next to me.

"Tory Craster confessed to more victims. I heard that they are getting a crew together to dig up just outside of town."

"I'm not surprised. I figured there had to be more," I said.

He nodded. "Me too. But I also heard it wasn't just in town either. He was a truck driver. He's got bodies from here to Wyoming to New York; at least, that's what they're saying."

I shook my head. It wasn't surprising, but it still made me angry. I knew there had to be more. What really pissed me off was how much we trusted him. I can't believe that no one saw the warning signs; he was so good at hiding in plain sight. He was a model citizen; a helpful and happy person who everyone trusted. We had no idea of the dark secrets he kept.

"Still didn't confess to that girl you were looking for," he said. "Sorry. He's confessed to a lot, but not her."

"That's odd," said Zelina. She folded her arms across her chest and leaned back on my desk. "I mean, if he's in a confessing mood, then why not confess to everything? He seems eager to talk. He hasn't shut up since he was arrested. So why not? Why is he refusing to talk about her?"

That made me curious, too. Once the jig was up and we uncovered all those bodies on his property, he couldn't talk his way out of it. It was clear he was a serial killer, so he stopped denying it. He started talking and hadn't shut up in weeks. The sick thing about him was that he remembered all the girls' names. He took pictures of them to keep, which we found under the floorboards of his home. But even without the pictures, he remembered the girls, where he took them, and when and where he buried them. He always smiled when he recounted what he had done.

But there was one girl who was still missing. Cynthia Harmon, a high school student, disappeared a year ago, and I still believe he had something to do with it. She looked like his type, but Tory would not claim her. He reiterated every time I talked to him that he knew nothing about Cynthia, and he didn't kill her.

"Sorry. You're going to have to try to pin that on someone else. It wasn't me."

Something about the way he wouldn't claim her didn't sit right with me. I wanted to call him a liar; after all, he'd lied about his entire life to the entire town of Pine Brooke. But it felt like he was telling the truth. Why would he confess to killing over a dozen young women and keep insisting that this one was different?

I sighed. "Well, if he talks about Cynthia, please let me know. I'd love to be able to tell her mother something."

Rainwater nodded. "I get that. Will do."

"You joining the dig?" asked Zelina. We both knew the answer before he said it.

A smile bloomed on his lips. "Of course."

Officer Rainwater was a great officer—always there if you needed help. Whenever we were short-staffed, he was the first person to sign up to help. If they needed volunteers to dig, even if he didn't want to do it, he'd sign up.

"Steve, you gonna help with the dig?"

I glanced up and saw Officer Blaese. He stopped short near my desk.

"The dig for the bodies that kook murdered? I'll pass. That's way too much sadness, not to mention the smells."

He had a point. However long they had been buried there, it was bound to smell horrible. I didn't think I could do it either.

"Makes my stomach turn just thinking about it. Still pissed about it. How could he?" mused Rainwater.

That was the general consensus around town. How could he do it? So many people trusted him and believed in him. Invited him over for dinner. Hung out with him when he wasn't working. He was part of so many lives, yet no one really knew him.

Officer Blaese shook his head. "So disappointing."

"Yeah," I said. "It is. But it's a reminder that anyone is capable of anything. You guys done for the night?"

Rainwater nodded while Blaese shook his head. "Nope, got the night shift. I'm going back out on patrol. I just needed to take a bit of a break."

"Alright. We'll see you guys tomorrow." The officers went their ways while we walked out the door. On the ride to Mr. Gill's home, we discussed what we were going to do to scare the kids. At first, I wasn't sure they would still be there, but as we reached the edge of town, we saw them. Two boys in varsity jackets stood near the front porch throwing things at the house.

I jumped out of the car. "Seriously?"

The two boys spun around, their eyes as wide as saucers. I glanced at Zelina, her eyes burrowing a hole into the boys.

"We—"

"Yeah, we know." I looked up at the house and saw the front curtains move. A second later, the front door opened. "Now, we could arrest you idiots, but I don't think that would do anything."

"Arrest us for what?" I recognized the annoying voice. Carl Larson was on the football team and was known to be a spoiled brat. "Everybody does this."

"That doesn't make it okay. You are ruining this man's home for no reason. You are just a bunch of spoiled kids who have been getting away with this for far too long. So we can either arrest you or you can do community service. Bear in mind before you answer that if we arrest you for destruction of property and vandalism, it will go on your record. That won't look good on your transcripts, especially if you're trying to get out of here."

The two boys were perfectly still and quiet. Carl stared at me. The other boy, with short black hair and wide eyes, stared at Zelina, who hadn't said a word.

"What kind of community service?" Carl finally asked, with his arms crossed. He was clearly the leader.

"You two have to come up here every day after school and help Mr. Gill clean up his property. And we want a list of your friends that were here with you tonight but had the good sense to run away."

Carl sighed. He traded glances with his friend; they looked like they wanted to argue, but a mean look from Zelina quashed it. "Fine."

Zelina took out a pad and pen and quickly wrote up two tickets for the boys. "We'll be stopping by your homes in a week to make sure you're holding up your end of the deal."

"Seriously?" Carl groaned.

"Seriously," Zelina said. "Unless, of course, you want to come downtown. I'm sure your parents would love to get a call."

The kids grumbled and accepted the tickets. Zelina kept an eagle eye on them as they slunk away back to town, while I walked to the front door. Mr. Gill stuck his head out from behind the door.

"Everything's okay now, Mr. Gill. They're gone. But they and their friends will be back every day after school to help you clean up your house, cut your grass, and whatever else you need to be done."

He stepped out onto the porch. "I don't need any help. I got it. Been doing it for a long time."

I smiled. "I understand that. But everyone needs help every now and then. And this is the least they can do, so let them do it. Besides, Doctor Elwood said to take it easy on your back, didn't he?"

This time it was Gill's turn to grumble. He sat down on a wooden bench on the porch, beckoned me over to sit next to him. "Fine. I guess I'm getting a little old."

I snorted. "A little?"

He chuckled. "Well... maybe *really* old."

Zelina walked up and leaned against the railing. "So, how have you been?"

He shrugged. "I have my life. Can't complain. At least it isn't worse. Did you find the man you were looking for on the tape?"

I nodded. "We did. Arrested him and everything. Freed the girl he was holding. He'll be going away for a long, long time."

"No trial?"

"Not yet. But he confessed... to a lot," I said.

The old man shook his head. "So much depravity in this world. How could someone do that to those girls?"

I wished I had an answer to his question. But I didn't know. How could he do that to those young girls? To his wife? To his son? Boston was broken up after he learned about his mother. She had never run off and left him. She wanted to take him with her, but his father just couldn't let go. He killed her and then buried her near the front steps of his cabin. He stepped over her every time he walked in.

Boston posted bail and left town, and I doubted he would ever come back. I wouldn't. I'd leave, maybe change my name, and just disappear. Interestingly enough, he took Tiffany with him. At least, that was the rumor. She disappeared the same day he left town. All of her stuff packed and gone with her. Technically, he still should have stayed in town if Tiffany's mother wanted to press charges, but she didn't. She actually said it was just as well.

"Maybe it's better this way. She'll have a second chance without all of the whispers and prying eyes. Maybe she'll call one day when she's on her feet."

She was probably better off than being in the town where her brother murdered several people. Nobody looked at her the same after that, and probably never would. It wasn't fair to her or her family, but it was how small towns were. Once you were known for something, you could never be anyone else.

We talked to Mr. Gill for an hour. He seemed happy for the company and a little sad when we left. I hoped the teens coming up here to help him would be good for him and them. I didn't want them to make things worse.

Zelina drove us back to the station, where I got in my car. "See you in the morning." She drove off, heading in the opposite direction of her home. A smile tugged at my lips as I wondered where she was going.

I was on my way home, stopped at a stop sign when Cynthia's case, my last conversation with her mother, began playing over and over in my head. So instead of turning left, I went right—through a maze of streets—until I got to her old house.

It hadn't been sold yet. Everyone in town knew what had happened there. Her father killed himself in her old bedroom. I doubted anyone from town would buy it. It would have to be an outsider who thought living in a small town was a good idea. And no one in town would tell them about what happened until after they bought the house and settled in.

The beige house with the red door had good curb appeal. The two-story home had a full-length front porch featuring a comfortable-looking swing. It was the perfect house for the perfect suburban family. Well, maybe not too perfect.

Camille Harmon had sent us the key to the house when we were looking at Tory Craster for Cynthia's murder. She didn't want to come back to town to look through the house.

"Do whatever you want with it. It's doing me no good now."

She sounded like a broken woman. A woman who had been defeated and now had nothing left. Her daughter was gone, and her husband killed himself. Hard to pick up the pieces after that. I eased into the house. There was a musky, damp, smell as soon as I walked in. The windows had probably been closed since she left. I sighed. It was still furnished. The living room had a beige sofa and a loveseat...their family photos were still on the walls.

I used the flashlight from my cellphone to get a better look.

The photos on the wall were all her husband's. Camille and Cynthia were nowhere to be found in them.

So she took the pictures of her and her daughter with her, but left her husband's.

I tucked that tidbit of information away for later. It was strange. You would think that if she was leaving and both of them were dead, she would have wanted pictures of both her husband and her daughter.

Why leave just him behind?

She could have still been angry at him for killing himself, and leaving her behind to deal with everything. That would make me angry.

I headed down the hallway into the kitchen, and then up the stairs. I walked through each and every room, including the bathroom. I'd already been through here before, but this time I really took my time, trying to imprint every square inch into my memory.

Cynthia's room still had some of her stuff in it. Mirror, books, and other knick-knacks. I looked up at the ceiling fan. It didn't look like it was strong enough to hold his weight as he hung himself.

Maybe the closet.

Inside the closet, there was a beam he could have used, but he was a tall man. He would have had to sit down and stay there while he strangled himself.

My forefinger tapped against my thigh as I walked out of the room and into the primary bedroom. Still furnished. Pictures of Mr. Harmon still present. She took nothing of his. I looked in their closet, and his clothes were the only ones there.

"Huh." My voice echoed in the empty house.

I strolled out of the house and locked the door behind me. There was something strange about it... about what was left there. I walked back to my car.

I needed to look at the pictures of the suicide scene.

CHAPTER TWO

Logan Elwood

"I UNDERSTAND."

"How could you possibly understand anything? Are you in heart failure?"

I took a deep breath. The trick to dealing with older patients was being patient. Try your best to understand them and what they're going through. Some days were harder than others. Today was a harder day.

Mr. Carson was in heart failure and had been for a long period of time. Because of his age—over seventy—it was unlikely that he would get a heart transplant. He knew that.

"You're right. I don't know what it's like to have heart failure. You got me there. But I know that it only gets worse if you don't take the medication. If you don't take better care of yourself." His wife was in the waiting room. He had insisted that she stay there. That he could do the appointment on his own. She had looked so rejected at his words.

Her face fell instantly. Made me feel sorrier for her than I already did. He didn't seem like a reasonable or easygoing person to get along with even before he was sick.

"I don't care. I'm sick of the pills. I'm sick of all of this. I just want it to be done."

"I know. But the odds of you getting a heart transplant are pretty…" I looked into his eyes, and only then did I understand what he had meant. He wasn't sick of waiting for a transplant; he was sick of life. Of everything. Of waiting, taking the meds, and the pain. He wanted to be done with it all. His glassy eyes stared into mine, and my heart fell into my stomach. That was why he didn't want his wife to join the appointment. He was ready to die and didn't want her to know. I sighed.

"I just want it all to be over. I don't want any more medication."

I nodded slowly. "You have that right." I took a deep breath. "Have you talked to your wife about this?"

He glanced at the door. "She doesn't understand. She wants me to keep going. Not to give up, but she doesn't understand how hard it is. It's hard for her too, but in a different way. I can't keep living and suffering for her."

I understood that living your life for other people was dangerous and a surefire way to be miserable. He needed to do what was best for him. I didn't like the idea of it myself, but I respected his right to make that choice.

"I can't help you commit suicide. I prescribed the medication, but if you choose not to take it, that's on you. That being said, you need to make sure your wife understands and is prepared for what will happen. Make sure your affairs are in order and that you have a DNR."

"I do. I did all that the last time I was at the hospital. It's already done. Along with my will and all my important matters."

"Good. I hope you understand what you are doing."

"I'm just tired. So tired, and it's not getting better, so I think it's time to go."

I nodded. His heart failure was progressing even with the medications and treatments prescribed. While we were able to slow down the deterioration of the heart muscle, we couldn't stop it or reverse the damage that had already been done. It was left untreated for too long. Short of a heart transplant, all we could do now was continue slowing down the deterioration, keep him comfortable, and manage his pain.

It was a bleak diagnosis for someone who had once been so active and filled with life. He had the right to die on his terms. While I agreed with that, I could not do anything to help him. "You still have to pick up the prescription even if you aren't taking it."

He nodded slowly as he stood up. "I understand. Don't want to get you in trouble." He held out his hand, and I took it. He still had a firm handshake. "Thank you."

I walked him out. Nicole eyed me as the two left. When the door closed behind them, I leaned against the wall.

"Something tells me he's ready to slip out the back door and turn out the lights," she said as she sat back down at her desk.

I nodded.

"I thought so. I mean, there's really nothing else we can do for him. His blood pressure is low, and the medication isn't really helping with that. And he's lost weight. He's close to a hundred and fifteen pounds."

"I know. He's ready to go, but his wife isn't ready to let him go. I think it's one thing if he dies of the disease, but it's another if he dies because he didn't want to keep fighting."

Nicole shook her head. "I'd hate to be a fly on the wall during that conversation."

"Me too." It was still morning, and I was already hoping for the day to end so I could go home and spend time with Dani. Explaining to her why Jamie wasn't there with us anymore was a hard conversation—one I wasn't sure I had explained correctly or that she understood most of what I said.

"She wants you to go live with her," I had explained to her.

"Why? I like living here with you, Miss Bonnie, and Uncle Isaac."

"I know you do, but Jamie thinks that she can take better care of you than we can."

"Why?"

I didn't know how to answer that question. I wasn't sure why she thought that. I didn't think she could. She barely took care of her own kids. I didn't want Dani to hate Jamie even though I did, and my brother Isaac felt the same. But I had wanted her to understand her aunt's intentions. She still didn't.

Hell, I didn't understand what made her think she had more of a right to my daughter than I did. That didn't make any sense. But she was insistent on taking Dani from me.

The day dragged, as usual, when I had a lot on my mind. I kept thinking about Jamie in between taking care of my patients. I knew she was still in town. I hadn't seen her, but I felt it deep in my bones. She was still there and watching us. Waiting for me to slip up so she could have a reason to take Dani.

When the day was done and we locked up for the night, I went straight home. As soon as I walked in, the smell of spices and meat cooking enveloped me. My mouth watered instantly. I set my stuff down in the foyer and rounded the corner into the kitchen. Isaac stood at the stove with Dani at his hip, staring into a large pot.

"What's going on here?"

"Uncle Sac is making dinner. It smells really good." She detached herself from Isaac and ran over to give me a hug, her face bright and happy. "How was your day?"

"Long. Yours?"

"Also long… and annoying. But I did all my homework, so I'm done for the day." She ran back to the stove.

"They have homework in second grade now?" I asked.

"I did math puzzles with Uncle Sac! It was fun!"

"That's great, honey," I said, then directed my attention to Isaac, who still hadn't spoken. "Brother? And how was your day?"

"Boring. I don't know what to do on my days off. If I were in the city, I would know. But here? I just walked around and then ended up at the diner."

I shook my head; a smile pulled at my lips. I understood what he meant. Knowing what to do in a small town was hard. I had just gotten used to it myself.

"And now you're making dinner."

"And now I am making you guys dinner. Gumbo, following a recipe."

I wanted to mention that it was a little too hot outside for gumbo, but I didn't want to distract him or make him feel like I was criticizing him. I was thankful for any meal I didn't have to make. And it smelled amazing. Isaac was always a good cook. Not that I couldn't cook, I just didn't have the passion for it like he did. He loved it. He always smiled when he cooked. I watched him from the doorway to the kitchen—he and Dani, her eyes wide looking up at him while he chopped chicken thighs.

Bonnie was in the living room with her feet up when I walked in. "Nice not to have to cook, eh?" I asked with a smile.

"It sure is. And he's actually good at it. If he wasn't, he wouldn't be in there."

I laughed. "He was always good at it. How was your day?"

She shrugged. "Quiet, mostly. Did you see the mail?"

I shook my head. "No, I didn't look. Why?"

"I think you got a letter from her lawyer today." She threw her hands up. "I didn't open it, though I was tempted. I left it for you."

"Yay." I leaned back on the sofa. I wasn't in any rush to see what craziness Jamie and her lawyer had in store for me. I didn't care. I didn't want to do it right then anyway. I was ready to eat.

"What's on your mind?"

I blew out a silent laugh. "That obvious?"

She pointed at me. "You've got a vein in your neck that really bulges out whenever you're stressed. It was out all the time when she was here. I was worried about it for a while, but I figured you know better than me how to take care of your health."

I reached up and touched it a little self-consciously. "Thanks, I guess?" I sighed. "It's just one of my patients. He doesn't want to take his medications anymore—or do anything anymore, if you catch my drift. And I'm still worried about her being in town."

She nodded. "That sucks."

"It does," I said with a chuckle. "I do what I can, I try to help people, but… it feels like sometimes I don't really make as much of a difference as I want to."

She nodded her head back to the kitchen, where Dani was happily bouncing around pretending to help Isaac prepare dinner. "You do make a difference, you know. To her."

"Sometimes I feel like… what if Jamie's right? What if I'm not cut out to be a single father? I feel like I'm barely managing it even with you and Sac here."

She leaned over and tapped me on the knee. "It'll get better. It has to. That girl loves you so much. She knows how much you've sacrificed for her to have a good life. She doesn't understand everything, of course, but she knows."

"But Jamie…"

This time she swatted my knee. "Now, you stop that. Don't worry about Jamie. She has no rights, and the court will see that. They have to. No one can be that stupid."

I chuckled. *You'd be surprised.* The fact that she was able to get her lawyer to work for her, and send me mail about *my* daughter was a sign that some people really were that stupid.

"Thanks, Bonnie. Let me know when dinner is ready, please."

"Will do."

I got up, grabbed the mail off the console by the front door, and headed to my home office. I sighed as I eased into my chair. I was exhausted, not from work but from thinking. Constantly thinking about everything all day, nonstop. I stared at the letter on the desk. I took a deep breath before I opened it. It was indeed from Jamie's lawyer, and she was just reiterating Jamie's intentions. Wanting to work this out in a way that doesn't scar Dani or harm her emotionally.

We don't want to get a judge involved. If we can work this out amicably, that would be the best thing for the child.

"No, the best thing for the child is for Jamie to leave us alone," I said under my breath. My hands were squeezing my phone before I knew it. I dialed the only number I could think of: my old lawyer buddy, Ricky.

"Hello?"

"Hey, Rick."

There was a pause, and then Ricky's voice changed. Deeper. Somber. "What happened?"

I sighed as I leaned back in the chair. "She had her lawyer send another letter." I went on to explain everything that had happened since the last time we talked.

"What!" He groaned before adding, "How crazy is she? How can she have more of a right to your child than you do? What made her feel that way?"

"She believes that I'm not raising her right and that Marie would have wanted her to have Dani."

"Marie wouldn't have wanted that. She knew her sister had a few screws loose."

He was right. Marie would never have said it that way, but it was something we all knew. Not that Jamie was crazy, or had mental issues, or anything like that. We just all knew she was strange, and her thought process didn't match that of a normal person.

"She was obsessed with Marie, though," he said after a long pause. "I mean, I like my sister, but I don't have to be up under her all the time. I don't have to see or talk to her every day. But Jamie had to see Marie every day and talk to her a few times a day."

"Yeah, and she went along with it. Although sometimes you could see that it irritated her. She'd roll her eyes every now and then."

"I'm sorry, man. I was hoping someone would talk some sense into her, and it wouldn't have to come to this. But since it has happened, I'm going to call Bert and tell him he needs to give you a call. Now, when he calls you—well, he's a bit eccentric. And he'll have to talk to Dani. He won't take the case if he believes that Jamie is right, and she would be better off with her."

"Understood. I don't mind if he talks to her. I'd welcome it, actually."

"But other than this bullshit, how are things going with you?"

A sigh erupted from my mouth. "Okay, I guess. Work and Dani seem to be the only things that I have time for these days. Nothing else. Still trying to get to know the new town."

"You haven't found some nice small-town girl to cuddle up with at night?"

I laughed. "I don't have the time."

"No one you're interested in?"

Bright blue eyes and dark brown hair flashed in my mind. I shook the thought away before I answered.

"Judging by your silence, I think there is someone."

"I'm not—not really. It's not like that, anyway. We're just friends, I suppose, and that is not why I called you."

"Right. Right. But since we're on the subject, you should go for it. Three years is a long time to be alone."

"I'm not alone. I have Dani and Isaac and Bonnie."

"Yeah, but you can't have sex with any of those people. Not unless you think Bonnie—"

"I'm hanging up now."

Ricky laughed. "But seriously, Marie wouldn't want you to be alone for so long. You gotta come up for air sometime. Start slow, but start. You might feel better."

I bit my lip. He was right. I knew he was right, and yet I still couldn't bring myself to say it. Marie was still a shadow in my life, and I wasn't ready to let her go. I wasn't sure I'd ever be ready.

"Papa, food is ready."

I looked up at Dani in the doorway. She smiled and waved me over.

"I'm on my way." She ran back into the kitchen.

"I got to go, Rick. Isaac is making dinner."

"Oh. I'll have to come and visit you all soon. I miss his cooking."

"Come down any time. Call first, though."

CHAPTER THREE

Jamie Washington

You are my sunshine, my only sunshine…

Jamie tucked her suitcase under her arm while she stuck the key in the door to her hotel room. She could have stayed in a nicer place; she had the money for it, but it was too late. Almost midnight.

The Pines Motel was small and dank, and she didn't want to be there, but she would do anything to get custody of Dani. She had to keep an eye on her.

Logan wasn't raising her right. He wasn't doing what Marie wanted him to do. Raising her out in the sticks in a small town with no family around her. It didn't make sense to Jamie that he could move away from them.

She went from seeing her niece every day to a few times a year. It wasn't enough.

I need more time with Mar—Dani.

She needed more time with Dani. Jamie was her only link to her mother, and she knew that would mean a lot to Dani.

She'd want to know more about Marie, about their childhood, and what her mother was like when they were children. And Jamie needed to be around to tell her everything she didn't know. Or couldn't learn from Logan. She needed her.

Her body vibrated on the bed, rage pulsing in her bones. He had to understand where she was coming from. Jamie knew there was no way that Logan believed he was the better option. He couldn't have. She laid back on the bed, her hands searching her pockets for her phone. There were a few people she could call, starting with her mother, but the thought of that conversation soured her stomach. She didn't want to speak to her. She didn't want to hear her voice, shrill and accusatory.

She rested the phone next to her head. She could have called her husband or her children. It had been a long time since she'd heard their voices, and she didn't feel like hearing from them. But she dialed the number anyway.

"You called. Are you on your way home?"

The hopefulness in her husband's voice annoyed her.

"No, not yet. I'm still trying to get Log to see reason. Right now, he's being unreasonable. He refuses to do what's best for Dani."

"You need to get the police involved. If he's hurting her, then you bringing all this up isn't going to be good. Might make things worse for her at home. Do you want me to come down there and straighten him out? Because I will."

A smile pulled at her lips. "No. I can handle it. I wanted to see if we could agree without having to drag the police into this. I didn't want to make this harder for Dani than it has to be."

"I understand that."

"I swear, ever since she told me about her father's abuse when we walked to school, I can't get it out of my mind. I have to get her away from him. I did contact a lawyer, and I think she has already sent him some paperwork."

"Good. The sooner this gets done, the sooner you two can come home, and we can be a family."

"Exactly. I look forward to that. Are the kids awake?" Even though she asked the question, she hoped the answer was no. She didn't want to hear their little voices nagging her to come home. They might be happy she was gone and not want her to come home. She was happy not to be there with them; of course, the feeling could be mutual.

"They just went to bed. I'll tell them you called."

"Of course. It's so late. I don't know what I was thinking. You should go to bed, too. I'll call you tomorrow."

After a few 'I love you's, she hung up. Her brain relished the silence. If she did get custody of Dani, she doubted she'd go home. Not right away, anyway. It was too loud. Too many people talking, wanting things from her. Demanding she do this and that. She just wanted them to leave her alone. She wanted peace. She wanted Marie back.

Jamie pulled her knees up to her chest and rolled over on her side. It took her hours to fall asleep. Images of Dani and Marie dancing in her head.

She thought about her sister every day since she died on the worst day of her life. There wasn't a moment Marie didn't cross her mind. Before she drifted to sleep, she thought about Marie and how they used to talk when they were younger. Marie was a teenager then, while Jamie was still in elementary school. Marie sat at her desk while Jamie, as always, was sprawled across her bed recounting the drama of the day. Marie always listened to her no matter what she said. She missed that. Since her death, it felt like no one was listening to her anymore. No one cared about what she thought or what she wanted. But Marie had. And so did Dani.

She needed them in her life, and if she couldn't have Marie, she would have Dani.

She woke a little after three in the morning. It felt like no time had passed. Like she hadn't been asleep at all.

"Who do you think you are?"

"How dare you talk to me that way?"

"I wouldn't have to talk to you that way if you weren't such a—"

Jamie sat up and turned on the light next to the bed. The voices were directly outside her door. A man and a woman arguing about something. She hadn't heard the beginning of it, but the end was filled with loud curses and a slamming door. A car door a few minutes later.

She sank back against the headboard. She would not stay another night. Check-in for most hotels was around three or four. She might be able to find something that would let her check in earlier. Maybe a bed and breakfast. Jamie took out her phone and started typing. A few minutes later, she found a bed and breakfast near Logan's office so she could keep an eye on him.

After making a reservation, she set her phone back on the nightstand and tried to go back to sleep.

"Do you know how long you'll stay?" The older woman smiled at Jamie as she waited for an answer. But Jamie didn't know what to tell her. She wasn't sure how long she'd stay in town; as long as it took for Logan to see reason. Hard to put a timeline on someone changing their mind.

"I'm not sure how long I'll be here."

"I see." Her smile faltered for a second. "Well, you can stay here, and if you want something more permanent, there are a few houses close by for rent."

It was like a light bulb went off in Jamie's eyes. "Oh, I hadn't thought about renting a house. It never crossed my mind."

"Yes, there are some with short-term leases." Clara smiled as she searched through a stack of papers on her desk. Near the bottom, she found a card. "Here, this one might be just what you're looking for."

"Thank you so much. That's a great idea. I appreciate it."

"Let's get you signed in." Clara handed Jamie a pen so she could sign the guest book. Once she had her signature, she handed her a key. Jamie stared at it for a long moment. Rubbing her thumb along the edges. It was an old key, like the kind she had seen in Victorian period dramas.

Clara looked at the key and smiled. "We are a little old-school here. I always loved keys like that, so I had the doors changed so we could use them."

The key was black with bronze edges. "Such a cool idea. I love this." Jamie shoved the key into her pocket. "Thank you."

"Your room is upstairs, first door on your right."

"Thanks so much." She grabbed her suitcase and started up the stairs. The bed and breakfast was nice enough. It would do in a pinch. Jamie thought the woman was nice but a little too cheery. She rounded the corner and stopped at her door—Room 4. The key slid into the lock. She entered the room and glanced around. The room was cute, with a king-size bed, dresser, TV, and a sitting area are in the far corner of the room next to the window. The furniture was big and sturdy.

She closed the door behind her and leaned against it.

"Renting a house is a good idea," she said to herself. "I can stay as long as I need to, and if I need to go home for something, I can always come back as long as I pay the rent." She nodded her head slowly as she inched toward the bed. She rolled the idea over in her mind. Over and over again until it settled. It was the right thing to do.

She sat on the bed just as her phone vibrated in her pocket. She rolled her eyes instantly. She knew it wasn't her husband; he was at work. She glanced at the screen and exhaled.

"Yes, Mother."

"What the hell are you doing?"

"What are you talking about?" She knew exactly what she was talking about, but she loved making her mother feel like she wasn't understood. What she was saying didn't make any sense. In a way, it was payback for how her mother had always made her feel. Misunderstood.

"You know what I'm talking about. Don't act like you don't. Why are you bothering Logan?"

"Did he call and tell you that?" Jamie thought she would have had more time before Everly learned of her plans. She would have had Dani with her before her mother knew anything. She never thought Logan would call her mother, seeing as they didn't get along too well.

"No, when I called my grandchildren, the ones you *left behind*, I was told you were in Pine Brooke trying to get custody of Dani. Why?"

The anger in her voice made Jamie squeeze the phone in her hand. "She should be with me. It was what Marie would have wanted. Logan isn't raising her right. Not how we were raised. She'd be better off."

"You can't be serious!"

"You were upset when he took her away too. You were just as angry as I was. He moved her out here in the sticks, and she's so far away from us and her family. Marie needs to be with us. With me."

Her mother inhaled sharply. "Dani. You mean Dani, don't you?"

Jamie blinked. "That's what I said. I'm just trying to do what Marie would have wanted since no one else seems to care."

Everly sighed. "That *isn't* what she would have wanted."

She said it as if she knew something that Jamie didn't. But it wasn't the right time to bring it up. So maybe Marie had hated how they were raised. Maybe it made them too dependent on each other because, for a time, they were all they had. Their mother had been neglectful, too busy trying to reclaim her youth from before she had children. It was a cause of contention between the two. A bruise, black and purple and sore to the touch that would not heal.

But that didn't matter anymore. Jamie was certain she was right.

"You are so selfish. You aren't thinking about what's best for Dani but what's best for you. All these years later, and you still can't let go of Marie."

"She was my best friend. She was my everything. She was all I had."

"You have children and a husband, and Marie is still all you have? Have you told them that?"

"You don't understand."

"No, I don't. If your dead sister is all you have in this life, you might want to take a good look at yourself. Why can't you solve your own problems before you start ruining people's lives?"

Jamie ended the call without a response. She didn't want to talk to her mother or anyone else who could not understand her point of view.

"She just doesn't get it. She never will. Dani belongs with me. Marie—" She took a deep breath and exhaled slowly. "Why can't they see I'm doing what's best for Dani? Why is that so hard to understand?" She sank back on the bed. Her heart pounded in her chest. She rolled over on her side. She was so tired. *So* tired.

"Marie? Are you there?"

The first time Jamie had seen her dead sister was after the funeral. She was home, her eyes red and raw from crying, when she felt a hand on her shoulder. Marie whispered in her ear.

"*I forgive you.*"

It was the one thing she so desperately wanted to hear. She felt relieved, like she hadn't left her. Like she would never leave her. Marie appeared a few times after that. Checking in on her. Talking to her when she needed someone to listen. Then, one night, she appeared and asked her to do something.

"*Please, go check on my Dani. I'm afraid Log isn't raising her like I wanted. She's so far away from family. You should raise her. It would be better that way. That way, you will always have a piece of me with you.*"

Jamie had never considered it, but in the following weeks, it was all she could think about. Raising her sister's child. It was an ideal way to make amends. To fix what she had done. That was all she wanted to do: fix what she had ruined. Of course, no one else ever saw Marie. Just Jamie. But she didn't mind. It was like old times when she and Marie were all they had. Before she met Logan, the sisters had gone in different directions. But Marie was hers and only hers. Marie was the only person she could talk to, and Jamie was the only person she could confide in.

No one else would understand.

"I think that it's possible," her husband had said. "I'm not saying I believe in ghosts and all that. But maybe she has some unresolved business with you. Something she wants to make right. Maybe that's why, and once that is done, she'll go away."

After she'd told him, Jamie could tell by the look on her husband's face that he didn't believe her, but he was trying to. She appreciated it.

He didn't make her feel crazy or stupid for saying she talked to her dead sister. He tried to understand her. He was like Marie in that regard. But she never told anyone else, least of all her mother. She would have tried to have her committed again, and Jamie was never going back.

"You're doing the right thing, Jamie. Don't worry. It will all work out as long as you don't let anyone get in your way. I want you to have Dani. Only you. Just focus on that."

"You're right, Marie. You're right. I won't let anyone get in my way. Dani is mine, just like you said."

CHAPTER FOUR

Riley Quinn

"Hey, you two, we need everybody in on this." Captain Williams pointed at me and Z and waved us over to the front desk, where a woman and a man stood.

"What's up?" Zelina leaned on the desk.

"My sister is missing. She was supposed to get to my house last night, but she hasn't shown up yet."

"Maybe she changed her mind," I said.

The woman's eyes narrowed. "She was on her way. She calls when she stops somewhere so we know where she is. She stopped at a gas station, and she called. She was following the usual route she takes when she comes to visit."

"And she hasn't called to check in since?" I moved closer to the desk. "No one's heard from her?"

"No one. Last night, early this morning, we thought she might have run into trouble on the road, so we retraced her route. Nothing. No signs of her car. And she's still not answering her phone. It's turned off now."

My heart sank a little. Either she turned it off because she didn't want to be bothered by them, or someone turned it off for her.

"Okay."

"I want patrol officers and get a few other detectives to start looking. Maybe she got into an accident and got run off the road…" said Captain Williams.

"Understood."

He walked back into his office and left us there with the anxious family members. Zelina waved at a patrol officer and told him to take down the family's information and help them file a missing persons report. At the same time she did that, I gathered the troops. Once we got all the information we needed, the route she took, the places she stopped, and an image of the car she was driving, we were on our way.

I hated looking for missing people. It was nerve-wracking. Everyone wanted to find the person, but no one wanted to be the one who actually found them. Finding a dead body—seeing one—was a horrific experience. One that stayed with you for a long time. I usually didn't like taking family members with us because what if they were the ones who discovered the dead body? A mother shouldn't have to see their child that way.

But they insisted on coming with us. Delilah Preston was visiting family because her cousin was having a baby shower. It wasn't something she would miss. She and her cousin practically grew up together like sisters. She would have been there no matter what.

I wanted to believe what the captain said. Maybe she got into an accident and was somewhere off-road. I clung to that thought as I followed Zelina to the car. I clung to it with every ounce of strength I had because deep down, somewhere in my bones, I knew this was going to have a tragic end.

We followed the family back to Delilah's last stop. A coffee shop on the edge of town. It was just opening up by the time we got there. The sister, Marissa, sent a picture of Delilah to my phone. We had the family stay in their car while we went in to ask questions. While we were doing that, patrol officers started searching for her car both inside and outside of town.

"I did see her. Yesterday, but I can't remember the time," the manager of the coffee shop told me.

"Did she look distressed or anything?" I asked.

She shook her head. "She seemed fine, upbeat. She said she was going to a baby shower, and she was really excited about it."

I sighed. "Do you have any surveillance cameras outside?"

"Of course. I can send them to the station if you'd like."

"We would love that."

"No problem."

We walked out of the coffee shop and jumped in the car. "Let's try the gas station. They probably have cameras outside, so maybe we can see if someone was following her."

The family followed us to the gas station and again stayed in their car while we went in.

The owner wasn't nearly as chipper as the coffee shop owner, but we finally convinced him to help. "Um... she looks familiar. I might have seen her last night, but it's hard to say. So many people come in here at night."

"Do you have cameras?"

"Of course. I've been robbed twice; I had to get them. You want them?"

"We do," said Zelina.

"Come on back, and I'll make copies."

Zelina followed him to the back room while I stayed near the front door. Another woman emerged from the back just as Zelina disappeared.

"Excuse me?"

She stopped short and spun around. "Yes?"

"Were you working last night?" I held up my phone and showed her the picture.

"Oh yeah, I remember her. She was nice."

"Did you see her inside?"

"No. Last night, I was cleaning up outside. You know, taking out the trash. Sweeping up before I got off. She pulled up soon after I got started. It was a zoo here last night, and everybody had somewhere to go. But she got out of her car, and the radio was playing a song I liked. She got out singing it."

"Was there anyone watching her or following her?"

She shook her head. "Not that I saw, but like I said, it was a madhouse here last night. We had everybody: truck drivers, cop cars, vans, and motorcycles. The works. I saw her walk into the building, but I didn't see her leave. I was doing something... dumping trash, and when I looked up, her car was gone."

"Right."

"But when I saw her go into the store, she seemed fine. Upbeat. She was singing all the way up to the door."

"That's good to know."

She looked around the parking lot. "Did something happen to her?"

"She's missing."

Her back straightened. "Oh... that's horrible. She might have just gotten into an accident or something. The roads can be confusing at night. She might have just got turned around and was too embarrassed to tell her."

A smile pulled at my lips. She might have a point. Delilah could have gotten turned around at night if she wasn't paying attention. She might have headed in the opposite direction. Before I could ask another question, Zelina and the owner emerged from the back room.

"Got the tapes."

"Okay." I turned my attention back to the young woman in front of me. "Thank you so much for answering my questions."

"No problem. I hope you find her."

I nodded and followed Zelina out of the door. I told her what I was told while she was gone. Her fingers drummed against the steering wheel. "Maybe they should go back to the station while we continue our search."

I looked back at Marissa's car. Zel was right; they should go back to the station and wait for us. It would make it easier to do the search if we weren't worried about finding evidence of something horrible happening to Delilah in their presence. I got out of the car and walked over to the car. I knocked on the window on the driver's side, and she rolled it down.

"We are going to keep searching for her, but you should go back to the station and wait for us there. Just in case she calls you, and this is all a misunderstanding."

"But—"

"Marissa, go back to the station and wait for us there. I'll call if we find something. I promise." I kept my voice stern but light. I wasn't trying to be harsh.

Her eyes narrowed for a moment and then softened. She didn't want to go back. She wanted to stay and follow us. She wanted to find her sister, and while I understood that, I would feel better if she went back to the station. If we found Delilah's dead body, she shouldn't be the one to see it.

"Fine. We will."

My back straightened, and she rolled her window up. I walked back to the car. "She wasn't happy about it, but she's going back to the station." Zelina didn't take the car out of Park until Marissa pulled out of the parking lot.

We waited a moment after they had gone, and then we drove in the opposite direction to meet up with the patrol officers who were searching for Delilah on the outskirts of town.

"What do you think happened to her?"

Officer Blaese shrugged while Officer Rainwater stared off into the tree line. "She might have just gotten turned around."

"If she was new to town, I would say maybe. But her sister said she comes home to visit often. She takes the same route every time. I don't think she got turned around," I said.

"Well, that means somebody took her. Tory still in jail?"

The four of us shared a look. I knew he was. We all knew he was. Whatever happened to Delilah could not be blamed on him. Not this time. Not to mention, she wasn't his type. She was too old for him.

"Maybe someone was following her." Rainwater kicked a tree branch out of his way.

"Zelina has the footage from surveillance cameras of the last places she stopped. We still need to look through them, but everyone we talked to said she looked happy and upbeat, and no one was following her."

"Maybe she stopped along the way somewhere."

I looked at Rainwater, who was staring off into the trees.

"Possible." I looked around. "Has anything turned up?"

He shook his head. "Not a thing. We've been getting radio calls from the other officers all over town. We thought we might have found her car, but it wasn't right. The color was right on, but the make and model were wrong. We just got here ourselves, and were getting ready to search the forest."

"Alright, let's get started." The officers took the right side while Zelina and I searched the left side with our flashlights. "Okay. What are we looking for?"

Zelina shrugged. We walked in tandem a few inches apart. "I guess for any signs a car rolled through here. So far, I'm not seeing it. No branches or grass disturbed anywhere on this road. Nothing."

"Yeah, that's what I'm seeing." We walked slowly, looking for broken taillights or shattered glass, but we found nothing. We walked a few miles down the road and then turned around and walked back to our cars. Officers Blaese and Rainwater were walking back.

"Find anything?"

Rainwater shook his head. "Nothing. Nothing out of place or disturbed. Her car didn't run through here."

"Okay. We should keep searching along this road. And we'll go back to the station and put a call out to neighboring precincts to be on the lookout for her car." Even as I said it, something about it didn't ring true to me. Deep down, I knew she hadn't gotten turned around, nor did she get into an accident outside town.

If she had, we probably would have heard about it by now. Or someone would have called it in to us. But there had been nothing. And it worried me that we hadn't been able to find her phone.

After a couple hours, we headed back to the station, driving as slowly as possible, looking for any signs of a car accident. There was nothing. There was some debris on the road, but none of it was from a car.

Marissa was sitting by my desk and stood up as soon as we walked in. Her eagerness was a stab in the heart since we had nothing to tell her. We had found nothing, nor had we heard anything.

I threw my hands up. "We haven't heard anything about your sister. Not yet. I'm so sorry."

Her shoulders sagged. "Right. Okay. What now?"

"Well, right now, I'm going to take you into our conference room and talk to you about your sister. After, I will get us both a large cup of coffee."

"I'll get it," said Zelina. "I'll go to the coffee shop and get us some coffee and a Danish or something. Can't spend the day searching on an empty stomach."

She left while I showed Marissa to the conference room. She slumped into a chair and sighed. I knew that sigh. A sigh of frustration. Of not knowing what else to do.

"I know this is difficult for you and your family, but the more information you can give us, the better our chances of finding her are." I sat in the chair next to her and turned it so I could face her. "What kind of person is Delilah?" I took out my notepad and pen.

"She's the nicest person I have ever known. She always puts other people before herself, which, most of the time, isn't a good thing. I keep telling her to think of herself and do things for herself, but she's so giving. I don't think anyone would ever want to hurt her. I really don't."

"Okay. So she hasn't had any problems with anyone? No one stalking her or wanting to get back at her?"

She shrugged. "No. Nothing like that. She's so well-liked by everyone. I can't think of anyone that would want to hurt her."

"Would she tell you if there was?"

She paused for a moment, her forefinger drawing a pattern on the table. "Probably not. She wouldn't want us to worry. She probably would keep it to herself. That's just how she is. Anything that would make our mother worry about her, she'd keep to herself."

"Your mother worries a lot?"

She nodded. "She does, especially about Delilah. She's the one who lives out of town, so we don't get to see her as often as we'd like. It's hard to know what she's up to unless she tells us."

"So she might be holding something back?"

"I think so. Couldn't say what it was, though."

"Okay. What else can you tell me? Is she dating someone?"

She nodded. "Yes, her boyfriend is named Tyler Rosales. They've been dating for a few years."

"And he hasn't heard from her either?" I asked.

She shook her head. "I haven't even had a minute to call him."

"Okay." I slid the pad over to her with the pen. "Can you write down his information for me? I'll contact him when I'm done to see if she called him."

Marissa wrote down his name and number. Zelina walked in and set a box of pastries and two coffees on the table, along with a bag.

"I didn't know how you took it, so there's creamer and sugar in the bag." She slid a cup and the bag across the table.

"Thanks."

"Who else was waiting for your sister? Your mother and who else?"

Marissa wrote down the names and numbers of everyone who was at their house waiting for Delilah to show up. We needed to talk to them all individually. One of them might know something the others did not.

"Okay, so we are going to send you home—"

"No. I'm staying. You might need me here to identify…you might need me."

I glanced up at Zelina, who shrugged. "Okay. You can stay in the conference room, and if we need you, we will let you know."

CHAPTER FIVE

Logan Elwood

MY HEART STUTTERED IN MY CHEST. THE PAUSE SURPRISED ME and made it difficult to catch my breath. Sweat coated my palms. I had to wipe them on my jeans before I could dial the number. I braced myself for whatever the conversation would bring. Rick told me Bert was eccentric. He didn't say how, but that he was. It made me curious to talk to him. I needed all the help I could get at this point.

"Hello?"

"Who is this?" His voice was harsh, like sandpaper against my ear.

"Um... Logan Elwood?"

"I don't know why you phrased that as a question, but okay. You're Rick's friend."

"Uh... yeah. Sorry, I just don't know how this works, and I'm a little nervous."

"I always say, if you ain't got shit to hide, then there's nothing to be nervous about."

The sound of him chewing echoed in my ear. "Right. It's just... I didn't think she'd be able to sue for custody. The whole thing is throwing me off."

He swallowed. "Well, she would have to show cause for your daughter's removal from your custody. Do you think there's cause? Better yet, explain this whole situation to me. Tell me everything."

"Okay." I started with the death of my wife and moved on from there. I ended with Jamie coming to visit and then telling me that she should take Dani and that I should just give her custody.

"Is she a little looney?"

"I... maybe."

"Right." He sighed. "Okay. I'll need to come down and talk to your daughter and anyone else living in the house. That shouldn't be a problem. Now, what can you tell me about Jamie?"

"What do you mean?"

He sighed. "What kind of person is she? This is usually the time when a person in your position starts disparaging the other person. Talking all kinds of shit about them."

"That's not really my style. She is my wife's sister, and I don't want to bad mouth her if I don't have to. To tell you the truth, I've never really spent that much time with her. When she came over, it was to see Marie, and I kind of steered clear of her best I could."

"Huh. Was there a reason for that? She not like you?"

I shrugged instinctively. I was never too sure. She never came out and said it, and I didn't say it either. But in truth, I didn't like her. The way she clung to her sister was so off-putting and unnerving. Before we got married, every time I wanted to spend time with Marie, Jamie had to be there, or she was always calling her.

Like she just so happened to need something from her sister while we were on a date. Perfect timing. Pretty much every time. "I don't know if she didn't like me because of me or because I was taking attention away from her. Whenever Marie and I were together while we dated, she just had to try to worm her way in."

"What did your wife have to say about that?"

I sighed. "She loved her sister. Their mother was absent for most of their lives. Marie was always there for her no matter what. Sometimes, it annoyed her, but she kept in contact. There were a few times when Marie ignored her phone because she was too tired to talk. But then Jamie would just show up at our front door. She lived thirty minutes away."

"Sounds like she was a little too obsessed with her sister."

I threw my hand up in the air. "That's what I always said. But Marie didn't see it that way. Or maybe she didn't want to see it that way. She loved her sister to a fault."

"And now that sister believes that she should be the one to take care of her child. Hmm..." The sound of papers rustling was loud and went on for a long time. "Okay. Once I talk to your daughter, I will decide whether to take your case or not. I'll see you in a few days."

Before, if I could say anything or ask any questions, he hung up. "Okay. I guess that's that." I leaned back in my chair. It was good to get that conversation out of the way. I just hoped he took my case. Better yet, I hoped he was good at his job. There was no way Jamie could raise my daughter better than I could. She wasn't even raising her own kids. How could she raise mine? I shuddered at the thought.

Barely a couple minutes later, the phone rang again.

"Hello?"

"Yeah, this is Bert again. I just thought of something. Dani needs to see a child psychologist. I'm not saying anything is wrong with her, but it would be a good thing in court to show the judge that she is well-adjusted and thriving living with you. If the judge sees that she is doing well with you, a judge might be less inclined to snatch her away."

"Okay. I'll get on that."

"You might want to do that anyway. Help her process her feelings about her mother not being able to be around. Now on to the next thing."

From the way he talked, it sounded like he had already settled on taking the case without talking to Dani. I didn't want to get my hopes up, though.

"What's the next thing?"

"Rick said you just moved to a new town. How is that going?"

"Well... we both seem to like it. She's made friends at school, and she likes it."

"Okay, what about you?" After a short pause, he added, "I ask because I need to know that you've put down roots. It looks good to the judge. It is important to know that you have a community around you and aren't out there by yourself. If Jamie takes Dani home with her, she'll have her husband, kids, and mother to help her. Who do you have?"

I took a deep breath. The first people to came to mind were Isaac and Bonnie. So that was what I said.

"I see. You guys need to get out more. Meet more people and build a community. Not just because it will look good to a judge, but it will be better for both of you. Fill up your lives with people and laughter.

You don't want Dani to live an empty life because you don't want to let people in. And you shouldn't live an empty life either."

My jaw twitched. "Now you sound like Rick, but yeah... I know." He chuckled, then hung up again. He had a point. I knew that. It was something I had been hearing for years.

Let people in. Don't be so closed off. But it wasn't that easy. I let someone in, and she died. Whoever else I let into our lives would just die and leave us again. It didn't feel worth it. Not now. It probably never would.

But I needed to build some kind of community. I didn't even know how to do that. Marie was good at that. She never met a stranger. She could throw a dinner party together in a matter of hours. She was so warm and inviting. I didn't have that. I never had that. We weren't raised to be nice and warm in my house growing up. We were raised to be successful and to be obedient. I was that. Or at least I used to be.

I guess there was one person I knew. My mind wandered back over to Detective Riley Quinn... but no, that would be crazy. Sure, she was beautiful, and we'd developed a little bit of an acquaintance. I'd even run into her family at the beach the other day. But I doubted anything was going to come of it. It wasn't like we were dating or anything.

Bonnie peered into the office. "Are you alright? You have been in here a long time."

I leaned back in my chair. "I know. It's been a long day. I just have a lot on my mind as usual."

"Have you talked to that lawyer yet?" She leaned against the door frame, her arms folded across her chest.

"Just got off the phone with him. He's a little strange, but I think he's going to take the case. He seems interested. But I'm not sure. He says that I need to build a bigger community around me and Dani. Don't know how to do that, though."

She chuckled. "I think you'll have no problem making new friends once you spend more time outside of this house. And I don't mean at work either."

A smile pulled at my lips. "Noted. I guess I could do that even though I don't really want to. I just want to go to work and take care of my daughter. That's it."

"That's not a full life, and Marie wouldn't have wanted that for you. Take your time, but remember that you can't just spend the rest of your life hiding away."

"I'm not hiding away. I'm busy."

"Not that busy," she chided. "At least stick a toe in the water. It doesn't even have to be your big toe. Stick your pinky in and see what the water's like."

I had to laugh. "I'll work on that."

"Really work on it. Don't just do it to shut me up now."

She knew me too well. That was why I said it. I nodded slowly. Putting myself out there was a scary thought. Not something I wanted to do again. But I could handle being friends with someone. Just friends.

Maybe I could join a club or something. Go to the gym and see if I could meet people. But that made me tired just thinking of it. I sighed. Jamie really knew how to ruin people's lives. Everything was fine before she got here.

Instead of staying home and enjoying my day off at home, I left the house and headed to the diner for lunch. Maybe I would see someone that I could be friends with. The diner was busy as usual. I slid into a booth and looked toward the kitchen. I caught a glimpse of Isaac as he rushed past the doorway.

"You!"

I looked up. I saw a woman with brown skin and curly black hair. Her face looked familiar, but I couldn't place her name. "Hi, um… Zee…?"

"Zelina. I'm Riley's partner."

"Oh! Right, we all had lunch one day."

"Exactly." She glanced around and then slid into the booth. "I'm just here to pick something up for us. We've been going all morning."

"New case?"

"Missing person. We are still searching for her."

"Oh," I said as I leaned back. "Hopeful?"

"For now."

"Anything I can do to help?"

She shrugged. "Not sure. I think we might get a search party together and start searching the woods, but we still aren't sure where she went missing. Or if she is. Maybe she just decided to go for a drive."

Her tone told me she didn't really believe that. It was possible, but she didn't think it was likely. "Well, if you do, I'd love to help."

"Okay. We will. Could use all the help we can get. I'll let you know."

The waitress came over and dropped a large bag on the table. "I'll be back for your order."

Zelina took the bag in hand. "It's nice to see you out and about. You should do it more often." She got up to leave.

"Why do I keep hearing that today?" I sighed, resting my elbows on the table.

"What are you doing here?" Isaac slid into the booth. "Thought you were staying home on your day off."

I shrugged. "I was going to, but people keep telling me that I need to get out more, so I'm trying."

"Yeah. I wasn't going to say anything, but you could use some outside time. Away from Dani time. Out in the world time. You know."

I rolled my eyes. "That's what people keep telling me. I'm actively working on it."

"Who was the hot chick sitting across from you?" He glanced at the door, but Zelina was long gone.

"Really? She's Riley's partner."

Isaac's back straightened. "You mean that hot girl with the blue eyes?"

I nodded. "Yeah, that's her partner. They're working on a case, so she came to pick up lunch."

"I would have taken it to them."

I rolled my eyes and shook my head. Isaac tried to be a ladies' man, but deep down, he was quiet and reserved around women. A smile bloomed on my lips. Maybe he had outgrown it in the last few years. "Right."

He chuckled. "I've gotten pretty good with the ladies. My years of traveling abroad."

I smiled. "Yeah, abroad?"

"Greece, Spain and Rome. Love Rome. Beautiful city, food, and women."

"So you were just getting around."

He shrugged. "Something like that."

"Why did you come back?"

He bit his bottom lip for a moment. "Um... I don't know, Log. I guess I'm looking for a place to put down roots. That would be nice. Spend time with Dani and you."

I smiled. "Good. Stay a little while."

The waitress returned with a menu, but Sac waved her off. "He doesn't need a menu. He'll have the shrimp po-boy with fries and a soda."

"I guess I will," I said.

"They let you add something to the menu?"

He grinned. "Just this one thing for now. And then, if this goes well, then I might be able to add some more items."

He looked so proud. I was happy for him. Putting down roots and making changes to menus. He was doing better than me. "It better be good."

"I don't make food any other way." His smug smile was annoying, but he had a point. His food was always good. He stayed until the plate arrived and then sat there and watched me eat. The shrimp was crispy and tender. There was a sauce that was spicy and tangy with a hint of sweetness. Lettuce and tomatoes rounded it out. The bread was soft and fresh. It was perfect.

"It's amazing. I mean, it's really good."

His grin got wider. "I know, right?"

"What's the sauce?"

"Spicy remoulade."

"It's good. It really sets it all off and brings it together. Man, you outdid yourself with this. I think I'm going to order another one."

He smiled so hard it looked like it hurt. "I got you." He got up from the table, a bounce in his step as he walked back to the kitchen. I finished the sandwich. Sad about the last bite and then happy when he set another one in front of me. When I was finished, I dragged my fries through the sauce on my plate. Salty and spicy.

I paid and then left, stopping by Quinn's Coffee and Bakery to get an iced coffee for the walk home. "How's your day off?" Mrs. Quinn, Riley's mother, stood behind the front counter.

I didn't question how she knew it was my day off without my telling her. That was how it was in small towns. Everyone knew everything.

"Ummm... it's been okay. Nice to relax for a few hours."

"You looked like you needed it. We running you ragged already?" A soft smile danced on her lips.

I smiled. "No, not yet. Although it is a bigger workload than I was expecting for such a small town, it's been nice meeting all of you. Though *some* of you are a bit, uh, strange."

Her cackle was startling. Two people waiting at the counter for their order jumped. She laughed and laughed.

"Yes, we have weird in spades. You ain't seen nothing yet."

CHAPTER SIX

Riley Quinn

THE REST OF DELILAH'S FAMILY ARRIVED RATHER QUICKLY. WE took each member and interviewed them separately, asking them questions about Delilah. No one knew anything that her sister didn't know.

While I talked to the family, Zelina watched the surveillance videos to see if anyone was following Delilah. When I finished, I joined her in the computer lab, where the techs dissected the video. Jose stared at the screen next to Zelina.

"Find anything?"

"Nope," said Jose. "She seemed like she was okay. She wasn't upset or scared. She was just walking in and out of both buildings. No one followed her from the look of it, although—" He rewound one of the tapes and then stopped it. "This guy opens the door for her at the coffee shop. I'm not saying he followed her, but before he goes into the shop, he takes a long look at her as she walks by. And then he stares in her direction. The camera doesn't get to the parking lot, but he stares in her direction as if he's looking at her car or something."

"Maybe trying to remember her plate." I stared at the screen. "Can you make his face clearer? Maybe we can find him. Do a search, figure out who he is."

"Yeah, I'll get started on that. When I'm done, I'll send it to you." He clicked over to the second tape. "On this one at the gas station, I think something caught her eye."

I watched as the tape played from the moment Delilah walked into the building. Seconds ticked by. Just like the cashier had said, it was a pretty busy night with lots of people coming and going. A young girl exited the building and was stopped by a man. They chatted for a bit by the corner of the door, both of them seeming to whisper harshly—and then she followed him out of frame.

A moment later, Delilah exited and she stopped. Her steps stuttered toward her car while her head was turned in the direction the girl and the man went.

Jose paused the video. "I think she might have seen something in that direction that caught her attention and made her pause. Can't see what it was though. Even as she's walking toward her car she keeps looking in that direction. And then…"

The tape continued. I watched as the car with the young girl in the passenger seat drove by. A second later Delilah's car drove past the camera following the other car. "What was that about? Maybe she recognized the girl or the guy."

Zelina leaned forward and stared at the screen while the video was replayed. "Maybe. Or maybe something looked off and she was concerned about the girl's safety."

"Then why didn't she call us instead of following them?" I watch the events unfold yet again on the screen. It could have been an innocent altercation. The guy might have known the girl and seen that she was walking so late and night and offered to drive her home. It was a possible scenario, but judging by Delilah's movements, she didn't think so. And I didn't blame her. We just put away one predator who gave girls rides home. It turned my stomach to think that there could be another one out there so soon, in this small town.

"That's all I got for now. I'll send the copies to you as soon as I can."

"Thanks. And see if you can get an image of that guy's face or any identifying marks on his car. We need to track him down."

"Will do."

Zelina followed me out of the room. "Learn anything from the family?" She sat at her desk. "Oh, and that's your lunch. Shrimp po-boy."

I poked the bag on my desk. "When did that get on the menu?"

"Just added. It's good."

"Okay. And as for info? Not really. Her family didn't know anything, nor did her sister. All pretty much the same: She was a kind and sweet person, and no one would ever want to hurt her. But I got the contact info for a couple of her friends as well as her boyfriend."

"I'll call the friends. You take the boyfriend."

I finished eating, and then I called her boyfriend, Tyler.

"Who is this?"

"This is Detective Riley Quinn with Pine Brooke police department. Is this Tyler—"

"What's wrong?"

"Is this Tyler Rosales?"

"Yes, I'm Tyler. What happened?"

"Your girlfriend is missing, and we need to know if you've seen her or talked to her in the last few hours?"

"Wha-what?"

"Yes, I'm sorry. Delilah is missing."

There was a long pause. "Wait. Delilah? I'm confused."

I was troubled by his response. "Sir, this isn't a joke. Delilah Preston has gone missing. Her sister said you are her boyfriend, and we're trying to track her down."

"Um… no. I haven't seen her. Marissa said I was her boyfriend?"

"Is that wrong?"

He exhaled. "Delilah and I broke up a few months ago. She didn't tell her sister?"

I swallowed. "I guess not. Maybe she was waiting until she saw them." I leaned back in my chair. "Okay. So you two haven't talked in a while."

"Yeah, not since she broke up with me because she wasn't ready to settle down. We talk here and there, but it's not like an in-depth conversation. She moved out of town."

"And you haven't heard from her since last night?"

"Not in weeks."

"Okay. What can you tell me about Delilah? You two were together for a long time. I'm looking for something she wouldn't tell her sister or her family."

"I'm not sure. She never wanted to worry them, but they did talk a lot."

"Were there any hard feelings between you two?"

He let out a loud exhale. "Not on my end; I mean, I was sad, but I understood it. Dee had never lived on her own or away from her family. She wanted to move away, live a little more independently. Put herself first. And that's what she was doing. I didn't like it, but I couldn't be mad at her for that."

"Were you hoping to get back together?"

"I was. She was open to it, but she just needed time to do all the things I got to do in my teens and early twenties."

I sighed. "I get that. Okay. Well, if you think of anything else that might help us, please give me a call. If you hear from her, call me immediately."

"Will do."

I hung up with no answers. I looked up, and Zelina was just getting off the phone. "Anything?"

"One of her friends didn't answer. The other one was too shocked to answer any of my questions. She can't believe Delilah would just disappear like that. She said it was not like her. Someone had to take her, and then that started a spiral of all the horrible things happening to her in this very moment."

"The boyfriend was just as shocked. Also, they broke up months ago, and she hasn't told her family yet. He hasn't heard from her and will call when he does."

"So we have bupkis."

"Pretty much. Anything on the radio?"

"No, patrol units are still searching around town. And we have units in the neighboring towns looking for her car, too." Zel rubbed her eyebrows. "No one can disappear into thin air."

"Okay. I'm going to tell the family to go back to the house with two units just in case she shows up."

Marissa jumped to her feet as soon as I walked into the conference room. "We still haven't found her. I need all of you to go home and wait. If we hear anything, we will let you know." I handed my card to Marissa. "If she shows up or you hear from her, call me."

Marissa opened her mouth to protest, but her mother's hand clamped down on her shoulder. "We need to go home and let the police do their jobs." She pulled her away before she could say anything else. I nodded as they left. Marissa looked so helpless. She wanted to find her sister. She wanted to look for her.

I took a deep breath before I walked out behind them. I went back to my desk, searching for leads. She was coming into town; where could she have gone between the gas station and her sister's home? It didn't make any sense.

Zelina shook her head. Her radio rested on her desk, next to her fingers. None of the patrol units had been able to find her. No one was going home tonight until we found her. That was how it was with a legitimate missing persons case. We worked around the clock until we found the missing person, either alive or dead. I was already tired.

"We should get out there and start searching with them. I want to trace her usual route again. Might see something. I don't know." I sighed. "I just need to do something."

"Understood." She stood up. "Let's go do something."

We left town. She drove a few miles up the road. Marissa told us which exit her sister would have taken and where she came from. We started there. Then we turned around and followed her route from the gas station, where she'd followed that man. There were no signs of a fender bender or a horrible accident. There were no cars or disturbed branches. There was nothing that indicated there had been an accident. My heart sank into my stomach. Made me nauseous. If Delilah wasn't in an accident, then someone had to have taken her. Unless she decided she didn't want to go to her cousin's baby shower and instead wanted to go for a long drive. Maybe she turned her phone off so they couldn't call her. Maybe she just needed to take a break.

I clung to that thought while we followed the route into town. Maybe she drove through town and went somewhere else. *Maybe. Maybe. Maybe.* A lot of maybes. I needed something definite. We circled back through town and met up with two patrol officers, Officer Lewis and Officer Robbins.

"Hey! You hear anything?"

Officer Robbins sighed. "Nope, been looking for her all day. She's not here. We scoured her route and nothing. Got calls into other stations but haven't heard back. We were thinking about doing a grid search along that highway into town and some of the more remote areas. The ones that people don't go through a lot. She might have gotten turned around or something. It's possible."

"Yeah, it is." I looked at Zelina. "I'd be up for doing a grid search." I glanced up at the sky. "Get to it before dark."

"I'll radio reinforcements."

We drove to the station and cleared it with Captain Williams.

"I just want her found. However you need to do it, do it. We got enough going on with Craster and his bullshit. Don't need any more eyes on the town. Bad enough being home to a serial killer."

"Okay."

"Might need to get some help with the search."

Zelina grinned at my words. "I know just the people." We drove out to the road, and cars were already parked in the middle of the road.

"A lot of people showed up," I remarked. It wasn't the whole town, but there were a lot of people. I recognized a few of the faces. One in particular. Logan Elwood. He wasn't dressed in his usual button-up and tie. He wore a white tank top and dark blue jeans. I saw a piece of the tattoo on his arm. He waved when he saw me.

"Hey," he said. "Zelina said you guys could use some help."

"Yeah. We're still searching for Delilah. Thanks for coming out."

Zelina rested her hand on the hood of the car and watched us. I ignored her, and it wasn't difficult to do so. It was hard to concentrate on anything outside of Logan. Underneath his shirts, ties and white coat was a layer of muscle I had not expected. He worked out. Not enough to be bulky, but lean.

A few more tattoos peeked out on his chest underneath his tank top. It made me so curious about him. "So what do we do?" He looked behind him at the group slowly forming in front of two officers.

"Let's go up here. The officers will explain everything," said Zelina. Logan walked ahead of us. I looked at Zelina, who was still grinning. I nudged her with my elbow. Another police van pulled up, and two officers and two dogs jumped out of the van.

"Listen up, people. This is called a grid search. We will divide you all into two groups. One on this side and one on the other. You'll stand a few inches apart and move through the area slowly. Make sure you are within sight of your teammates at all times. Keep your flashlights on."

"Logan, you're on our team." Zelina looped her arm around mine, and pulled me to the left. He followed behind me. We divided into groups and then started the search. Zelina stood on one side of me and Logan on the other. We stalked through the grass, slowly looking in every direction for a trace of anything. A headlight. A body. A shoe. Anything that might point us in the right direction.

"How long has she been missing?" asked Logan.

"Since last night. Her family was looking for her car, but they didn't find it."

"Damn. Maybe she didn't want to bother with them. Needed some alone time before going home. I would."

"My family lives here, so there is no alone time. I see them every day."

A smile pulled at his lips. "I get that. Remember, my brother lives here now. He's cooking up some experiments at the diner."

"He made the po-boys?"

Logan nodded.

"Yeah, those were incredible. I wanted another one when I was done."

"So did I."

"Any other family around?"

He shook his head. "Nope. If my mother comes and tries to move here, I'm moving."

I laughed. "Well, if you want family, mine is available."

"You renting them out?"

"Yes. Payment is an hour of peace and quiet."

"I might take you up on that." He laughed.

"Please do. My father will make you pastries."

A whistle sounded, and everyone stopped dead in their tracks. Logan's head jerked toward me.

"What does that mean?"

I took a deep breath. "Someone found something."

"Good or bad?"

"Don't know yet."

His brows furrowed, and he stared up ahead. Zelina's phone beeped. My head jerked in her direction. Her eyes narrowed at the screen as her smile disintegrated into a frown.

"It's not good. We need to get everyone to go home and send for the coroner," she said, her voice barely above a whisper.

"Anything I can do?" Logan offered. "I do have medical training."

She shook her head. "I think this might be beyond your skill set."

"Okay." He nodded slowly as he looked around the area. "I'll start telling people that it's time for everyone to head home. I won't get into specifics. I'll just tell them the police found something and want everyone to clear out, so we don't contaminate or trample evidence."

"Look at you, knowing the lingo," I said.

His lips turned into a slight smile. "*Law and Order.*"

He walked away and started talking to other volunteers in hushed whispers. Zelina showed me her phone, and we walked in the direction of the whistles. Officers Blaese, Rainwater, and Robbins were already putting up yellow tape to mark off the scene. The body was on the ground and had been for a while.

Her skin was bluish gray, her lips a bright blue. There was a bruise on her cheek. She looked clean. She didn't look like she had been tortured. I bent down and slipped a glove on my right hand. I pulled down the collar of her shirt. There was a line across her neck. She had been strangled with something. The ligature around her throat was pronounced. Flies swarmed around her.

"No cuts that I can see," said Zelina. "Who found her?"

"I did," said Officer Rainwater. "We were walking, and she was underneath some branches that I kicked with my feet. Scared the shit out of me. Really wasn't expecting it."

I stared at her face. She looked like Delilah. I searched her pockets, but there was nothing. No wallet or ID. Not even lint. Maybe it was her. I stared at her for a long time. Seemed like hours. This woman had been out in the sun for a long time, judging by flies. Delilah went missing last night.

If it wasn't her, then we should have been looking for another missing woman, and now it was too late.

CHAPTER SEVEN

Riley Quinn

"Y'ALL BETTER NOT BE FUSSING ALL OVER MY BODY," KEITH SAID as he approached the scene. He gave us a glare. He hated when cops hovered over where he was trying to work, or disturbed the body before it was properly documented and he had finished the initial examination.

I threw my hands up. "We know the drill. Just looking at her and the scene waiting on you."

"Alright." He shooed us away. "I'll tell you when to come back."

I didn't argue. I was eager to get the body down to the morgue as quickly as we could. I walked back toward the road and Zelina joined me a moment later. The scene before me was interesting. If we hadn't done a grid search, we would never have found her. It was far enough away from the road that someone just driving by wouldn't have seen her.

"This isn't a place many people go," Zelina pointed out. She turned around and stared at the wooded area where crime scene techs swarmed like bees looking for their hive. A dozen flashes seemed to go off at once.

"I know. Either the killer got lucky, or they knew she wouldn't be found for a while."

She nodded. If it was the latter, then the killer would have been familiar with the area and Pine Brooke. This was the real wilderness. There wasn't even any trash on the ground. Maybe that gave them a clue that no one came out here.

"You think it's Delilah?"

I shoved my hands in my pockets as I watched Keith bent over the body. "I'm not sure. She looked shorter than Delilah. Her sister said she was five foot seven. It does kind of resemble her, though."

"She looks like she's been dead longer than a night. But it could be the heat and humidity."

I opened my mouth to say something, to say that I'd noticed that and thought the same thing, but Keith met my eyes and waved us over.

"Did the family say anything about her having tattoos?"

I glanced at Z, and we both shook our heads. With a gloved hand, he turned the woman's hand so we could see her palm. A beautiful pink rose looked back at us.

"Doesn't mean it's not Delilah. She could have gotten a tattoo and not told anyone," said Zelina.

"True. But they would have noticed, I think," said Keith. "It's not exactly in a very hidden area."

"How old is it?" I asked.

He stared at his palm. "Well, it's healed and no longer peeling. It's not new. At least a few months old."

"I'll ask her family." I dreaded asking her sister the question because I knew how she would take it. If I asked her if Delilah had any tattoos, she would immediately start asking questions, the first one being *have you found her body*. And since we didn't know exactly who we had here, it was a question that I couldn't answer.

"Actually, maybe we wait until Keith has finished processing the scene," I said, turning back to Zelina. "I just feel like it's not her. It isn't adding up."

A question mark bloomed between her brows. "So... what, we just let it be for now?"

I shook my head. "No. I just think we're looking at things wrong. I don't want to jump to any conclusions before we have anything conclusive. The tattoo is one thing, but... Keith, how tall is she?"

He quickly measured. "Five-three," he reported.

"I thought so. That woman is not Delilah Preston."

"Then who is she?"

"I don't know. Let's go ask the captain."

⁓

The cool air of the station was a welcomed change from the hot and sticky night. My body was slick with sweat. I was so ready to go home and take a shower, but I couldn't rest until I got answers on what to do. Hell, even a direction to go in would have been helpful.

I gave Captain Williams the run-down of the scene out there and he groaned, pressing the bridge of his nose between his fingers.

"And you're positive the body isn't Delilah's?"

It was Zelina's turn to sigh. "We don't think so, sir. Keith is working on it now, but the physical characteristics don't line up. It's likely that this could be a completely separate case."

"Just great. So now we have a missing woman and a dead body, and no indication if they're connected?"

I nodded. "Seems to be the case, sir. I just don't know how to proceed. We could do another wide search for Delilah, but I don't know how much use it would be."

"Could she be one of Craster's?"

"I don't think so, sir. She wasn't buried; she was left there for us to find. And she was strangled, not stabbed, and I think she's too old for him, anyway."

He shuddered. "There's a thought that sickens me."

"I try not to think of it myself. While we're waiting to hear from Keith, we'll pull up the missing persons reports to see if we can get a match."

"Good idea, Quinn. That reminds me of something else I wanted to ask you about, though. Cynthia Harmon."

I cringed. I had wasted a lot of time chasing a lot of empty leads on that case. "What about her, sir?"

"Prosecutor's putting together the list to make the case. You still convinced that Craster didn't do it?"

I let out a loud exhale. "It just bothers me. He's confessed to all the other crimes, most of which we knew nothing about. So if he took Cynthia and buried her somewhere, why not confess to it, too? But he's adamant."

"While I understand that, we need to make the case here. Who else could have done it? It had to be him, and maybe he's not confessing because he knows how much you want to solve this one. It's bothering you, and maybe that's what he wants."

I chewed on my bottom lip. I didn't want to admit it, but he had a point. Tory Craster could be holding out because he knew how much it would bother me. It would get under my skin and I'd never be able to get rid of it. And yet, I still wasn't sure it was true. It was like there was some sort of illusion puzzle in front of me, and I needed to cross my eyes a certain way to see what was really going on.

But how could I focus on that when I needed to find a missing young woman and solve the death of another?

I took a breath. "I understand that, but—"

He held up a hand to stop me. "But you're still going to keep investigating anyway. Yeah, I figured as much. Just don't let it get in the way of any active cases."

I couldn't help the smile that bloomed on my face. "Yes, sir."

"Now get to work."

CHAPTER EIGHT

Jamie Washington

"*If you let him hurt her, I will never forgive you...*"

Jamie woke with a start, her sister's voice ringing in her ears. Sweat pooled between her breasts. The bed sheets underneath her were soaked. She kicked the blankets off. The cool air blasting from the air conditioner mingled with her sweat and made her shiver.

It took a moment to steady her breath. In the dream, her sister dangled from the windshield, half in and half out of the car. Blood-stained glass jutted out from the gash on her forehead. She could see it clear as day. Her face contorted in pain. Whispering: "*Don't let him hurt her.*"

Jamie would never let anyone hurt Dani, not even her father. She had to get her out of that house. She rolled over onto her right side and let the cool air wash over her. She usually didn't sweat so much in her sleep. Her night was filled with tossing and turning and vivid dreams. She felt like she hadn't gotten any sleep at all.

Jamie glanced at the clock and noted the time. It was almost nine. She needed to get up and get ready to look at houses for rent. Better yet, she should have been ready and waiting for her lawyer to call. She wanted to go over their strategy for dealing with Logan and his inability to see the truth. But instead of pulling herself out of bed, her eyes drifted closed, and she got the first solid sleep she had since she left Logan's home. She missed it there, being surrounded by all the laughter and warmth she never had as a child. She wasn't doing this because she hated Logan. She didn't like him, but she didn't hate him either. She felt nothing for him whatsoever.

He was a bug on the bottom of her shoe. It made no difference to her what happened to him. This was about Dani and only Dani. She wanted what was best for her, and Marie believed that living with Jamie was best.

Jamie woke with a dull ache on the side of her head. It was the kind of headache that told her she had been asleep for too long. It would go away in a couple of hours once she ate something.

She rolled over and stretched. A light caught her eye. Her phone lit up.

"Shit!" She tapped the screen. "Missed call?" She sighed. Jamie knew that her lawyer would call her when she fell asleep. She called the number back. "Hello? I'm so sorry I missed your call."

"I figured you were sleeping or something. Your husband said you had a long couple of nights."

"Very. Long days and long nights. I'm so ready to get out of this town, but I'm not leaving Dani behind."

"I understand. Now, your husband told me you told him that there was abuse in the home?"

"Yes," Jamie sat up and swung her legs off the bed. "Mostly emotional abuse. He's very negative when speaking to her. Putting her down and calling her names. I've seen him shaking her a few times and her crying. I would go to the police here, but he knows them. He's the town doctor, and they all know him. He's friends with one detective and eats with her at the local diner and takes care of her mother."

"I see, so you don't think you'll get any help from the local police. I understand that. I see it a lot with women who are divorcing their police husbands and are getting harassed by their coworkers. Cops are very protective of each other, so you might be right. Tell me more about what the home is like. Is it just him and Dani?"

"No. His brother, a known degenerate who is always getting into trouble and gambling, also lives there. I don't know how permanent it is, but he's there. There's also a nanny. She is pretty nice, but she won't stand up to Logan. She's too loyal to him. But Dani does like her. I just… I don't know what to do. I suspect the abuse was why he chose to move away from us. He didn't want us to witness how he was treating her. My mother has never been to see Dani, so she doesn't know about this."

"Right. Well, the next step since he won't consent to giving you custody is to get social services involved. They will do a home visit and see what the home is like."

"Will the social workers come from Pine Brooke? I'm sure some of his friends could pull some strings and get one that would say the home was great and there was no abuse going on."

"I see your point. I'll see what I can do about that. I know a social worker that I have worked with before. I'll let you know when the visit will be. Does he have a lawyer yet?"

"I don't know." Jamie wasn't sure what Logan's plans were. Part of her thought was that he would just ignore it, hoping it would go away. She prayed he did that. It would have made it easier for her, for sure. She could just take her home with her; that was all she wanted. Logan could visit during the summer when she didn't have school.

"Okay. He probably does have a lawyer now, after the letter I sent him. I was just reiterating what you had already said to him, how Dani would be better off living with someone who didn't work so much and could give her more attention. I know as a doctor, it can be difficult making time for your family. It's the same for lawyers, and that's why I don't have any children. But I did tell him this is about doing what's best for Dani."

"That's all I want, to do what's best for her. I just want her to be safe. That's all."

"Your concern is commendable. Usually, after a sibling dies, people don't really care about the children. Their nieces and nephews are of no consequence to them. And they just go on. It warms my heart to hear how much you love your niece and are willing to fight for her. And like I said before, I will do my best to make sure we win."

Jamie sighed in relief, relaxing her body. It was good to hear that someone was on her side. That was all she wanted. She wanted someone to listen to her. To understand where she was coming from. A smile pulled at her lips. "That's great to hear. It really is."

"Now, I will come see you in a few days, and we can go over our strategy."

"Great. Just let me know."

They said their goodbyes and hung up the phone. Jamie grinned. Things were finally moving forward. Her body vibrated with both relief and excitement. She laid back on the bed and chuckled. Jamie knew she could have gone through legal channels and spoken with social services to get her removed. Most likely, she would have been sent to foster care or a foster home before being placed in Jamie's care. She didn't want that for her.

Jamie herself had been placed in a home for troubled children when she was twelve. Group homes were horrible for children. No place to live, even for a night. She didn't wish that kind of life on anyone. She was released back into her mother's care eventually, but it took three years.

It was years later when she learned that her stay in the home was not involuntary. Her mother had told her she had to go to the home because a judge had said so, but that wasn't the case. Her mother had elected to leave Jamie there for some time so she could get her act together. She could have picked her up at any time if she wanted to. She could have gotten her the next day if she wanted to. But she left her there for three years just because they got into an argument and Jamie had told her what a horrible mother she was. And she was.

Everly didn't have a maternal bone in her body. She always cared more about herself than her children or anyone else. It was all about her. It had to be. If anything deviated from that, she would throw a tantrum. It was why their fathers left her, and why Jamie and Marie left her as soon as they were able.

The second Jamie could split, she did. Marie loved their mother, but she knew how bad she was at mothering and how she had neglected them on multiple occasions. Marie loved her, but she knew to stay away. It was something Jamie took a long time to learn how to do, but once she did, she stayed away.

She glanced at her phone, wanting to call someone and tell them her good news. Her plan was to move on to the next steps, but there was no one she could call other than her husband, and his voice wasn't one she felt like hearing. No one understood why she was fighting for Dani. Why did she want her so much? But they didn't need to understand it. She knew what she was doing, and Marie approved; that was all that mattered.

Before she could set her phone down, it started vibrating. She glanced at the screen. It was her husband.

"Hey."

"Hey honey, how's it going?"

His voice rubbed her nerves raw. She winced when he spoke. Jamie loved her husband as best she could. But sometimes, she loved him a little less. A lot less. Sometimes just hearing his voice made her want to slit his throat. She was like that with some people. She never liked anyone all the time, not even herself. Now was one of those times.

"I'm fine. How are you guys?"

"We miss you." Jamie paused for a moment, trying to remember what was expected of her. "I miss you all too." *There it was.* She was expected to miss her husband and her children. If she had told anyone that she didn't really care about what had happened to them, people would have thought she was crazy. But she wasn't.

Sometimes, her children had the same effect on her as her husband. Their tiny voices scraped against her nerves like sandpaper, rubbing them raw. She'd sit in the house with earplugs on just to block out the noise. They were always talking unless they were asleep. Well, Casey spoke in her sleep sometimes, so she always talked.

They were so young; what did they have to say twenty-four hours a day? Just thinking about it exhausted her. Her husband asked about her day, and she told him what the lawyer had said.

"I'm glad that things are finally moving along. I know a judge that might be able to help if you need him; just let me know."

She smiled a big toothy grin. Having a judge in her back pocket in case of emergencies could only help her cause. "I appreciate that. I'll let you know if I need it."

"I just want you to be happy, and I want Dani to be safe with us."

She smiled. Christopher would do anything for her. She lucked out in marrying him. He was now the only person who loved her despite all her faults, and she had many. He saw past them and focused on her as a person. She liked that about him. He always looked for the good in people, and he thought she had a lot of good in her. Some days, she wasn't so sure.

"Thank you for saying that. I really appreciate it."

"Always, Jamie. Always." He inhaled sharply, "Well, let me get back to work. Before I go, I put some more money into your account. And I think renting a house there would be a great idea. You might be there for a while as this all gets sorted out. And it would give the kids and me a place to stay when we come to visit."

Her stomach soured. "Yeah, that would be great." She didn't want them to come visit. She didn't want to see them. She didn't want to deal with them. Once she had Dani, she would leave. She might grab Dani and take her as far from Logan as possible. A place where no one would ever look for them.

Jamie had it all planned out in her mind. She had turned the plan over and over, marinating on the steps, rearranging them, removing the ones that didn't fit or wouldn't work. She had turned it over and over until she was left with something she was sure would work for her and Dani.

She'd have to take all of the money out of the account, so there was no paper trail. She'd have to get a job, which she hadn't had in a while. But that was fine. She'd have Mar… Dani, and that was all that mattered to her.

She didn't want to see her children or her husband ever again. Chris could raise them on his own; they liked him more anyway. Jamie laid back on the bed and tossed her phone near her pillow. She stared up at the popcorn ceiling, letting her eyes rest on the strange dust pattern on it.

"You're doing good. Thank you for trying to take care of Dani. Now you should find a lovely house that she'll like and want to stay in. Do that for me."

"I know, Marie. That's exactly what I'll do."

Jamie, under the guidance of her sister, spent the day searching for a house that was nice enough for her to live in and close enough to Dani's school. She wanted to keep an eye on her.

"I think you will like this one." Amy, the realtor, walked ahead of Jamie and opened the front door. Jamie was her first client in a while. She worked in three towns in the area and hadn't seen a lot of business lately. No one had wanted to live in a small town. It was something she understood; it could be quite boring. Amy was happy to see Jamie and was doing her best to show her houses she thought she would like, but so far, she hadn't liked any of them.

"Now, this house has four bedrooms, a beautiful backyard, and a gorgeous kitchen. Recently remodeled, and the appliances come with it."

"What about the furniture?" Jamie eyed the pieces that had been left in the house. It was all pretty neutral: grays, black, and white. It was exactly what she needed. It didn't matter how the kitchen looked; she didn't cook anyway. But it was nice with stainless steel appliances and a dishwasher.

The two women moved through the house quickly and mostly silent. Jamie glanced around at each room. It suited her needs. The primary bedroom and the ensuite weren't as nice as hers, but it would be nice in a pinch.

"I think I'll take it," said Jamie as they walked downstairs. "It's really nice."

"I knew you would like it. And the school is right across the street."

A ghost of a smile kissed her lips. She moved toward the front window and stared at the school, a smile slowly blooming on her lips. She could see Dani walking to school from her front window, day in and day out. She could even stop her and talk or walk her the rest of the way.

"This is perfect, Jamie. She's going to love it here. Thank you for keeping an eye on my Dani. Thank you for doing all you can."

"This will be perfect. Absolutely perfect. I can't wait for my daughter to see it. She's going to love her room here."

CHAPTER NINE

Logan Elwood

I TOOK A DEEP BREATH AS I LEANED BACK IN MY CHAIR AT THE OFFICE. Bert was coming to see Dani in a couple of days, and I didn't know why, but I was worried. More anxious than worried. I couldn't sit still, nor could I stop thinking about it. It plagued my mind every second of every day. I was more anxious about what Dani would say to him and what questions he was going to ask her. He wouldn't tell me, and I found that frustrating. I understood why he wasn't telling me anything. He didn't want me to coach her, not that I would. But it still made me nervous.

I sighed. It was so weird thinking about some stranger talking to my daughter, trying to figure out if I was abusing her or hurting her in any way. It irked me that my role as her parent could be questioned by someone who didn't even like her own kids. What the hell gave her the right to question my parenting?

"You okay?"

I opened my eyes and looked toward the doorway. Nicole stood there leaning against the door frame, her arms folded across her chest. She stared at me, those big brown eyes searching for something.

"I'm okay. Just thinking, which is something I should probably stop doing for a while. It's definitely not helping me in the slightest."

"Yeah, get out of your head for a little while, and let me talk to you for a moment."

My heart dropped into my stomach. I didn't like the sound of her voice when she said that. It was something serious she wanted to talk about. I shifted in my chair, my spine straightening. "Okay, hit me."

"You remember Gloria Raydor?"

I nodded slowly. She was one of my first patients. A nice older woman who didn't like to make trouble. I told her to go to the hospital, and she said she didn't want to make trouble for anyone so late at night. But I drove her to the hospital in Woodvine myself. And we were lucky I did, as she needed emergency surgery to remove a blood clot.

Mrs. Raydor was so sweet but tried to take up as little space as possible. I didn't understand it, yet I did. I had been trying to do the same thing since I moved to this town. Keep my head down and just get this shit done. I wasn't concerned with making friends; I just wanted a nice place for my daughter to live and grow up. I wanted a job that would let me slow down and spend more time with her, but I didn't want to be noticed.

Neither did Mrs. Raydor. "Is she okay?"

She smiled. "She's doing a lot better and has been cleared to resume her regular activities. So I was talking to her about what we had talked about. It took some convincing, but she's open to it."

I smiled. That was the first bit of good news I had heard in a while. I wanted Mrs. Raydor to work as a receptionist here at the clinic so I could keep an eye on her and her health, so she could get out of the house more and see people, and so Nicole could start taking more patients on her own, and we could share the workload. It was a win-win all around.

"That's great."

"She can start Monday."

I sighed. "That's great to hear. Where are you putting your office?"

She grinned. "And that is the second part of the conversation. I think I know where I'm putting my stuff." She pointed down the hallway and started walking like she wanted me to follow her. "I think this would be the perfect place. I'll have to clean it out over the weekend."

I peered inside the room. It was an old storage room. It housed so many things that I hadn't used or seen since I got here. "I think that would work. There's more than enough space for a desk and file cabinet. And right across from one of the exam rooms. I think this is perfect for you."

She grinned. "Yeah, I thought so too."

"When do you want to do this? I'll help you move everything out. Where do we put it?" The room was stacked with things covered with sheets.

"I don't know. Since I've worked here, we have never used anything in this room. It was always just for storage. Things we didn't need or weren't using."

"Yeah, we should get rid of all of this, probably. Maybe look through it and decide what we might be able to work with before we throw it away." I didn't want to just toss it all if there was something that might help our practice.

"Logan?"

The sound of her voice made my body tense up immediately. My heart dropped into my stomach as I slowly turned around. Jamie stood next to the receptionist's desk. She waved.

"Can we talk?"

There was a softness to her voice that I didn't like. I didn't trust it. She smiled at me, but that didn't look right. It was fake, for appearances only. If Nicole hadn't been there, her demeanor would have been different. Jamie was always good at playing for an audience. Making you think she was a good, sweet woman when, underneath the fake smiles and false flattery, she was plotting your downfall.

I eased down the hallway, my eyes locked on her. She wanted something, and that was the only reason she would have come to my office. I pointed to my door, and she walked past me and entered my office. I looked behind me at Nicole, her brows pulled together, a deep scowl etched into her face.

"I'll be here if you need me." She walked over to her desk and sat down. "Don't close the door all the way. I don't want her to throw you under the bus or something when she leaves. I'll be your witness."

I smiled and nodded. I was thankful for Nicole. Jamie was the kind of person to do that. I walked into my office and pulled the door closed halfway; that way, Nicole could still look in.

I sat at my desk, and she sat in the chair in front of me. We sat there for a while before I finally broke the dam. "What do you want to talk about?"

"I want to talk to you about Dani."

I opened my mouth to reply but she held up her hand. "Please let me finish."

How many ways could I say it? How many times did I have to tell her I was not giving her my daughter? I leaned back in my chair, my hands folded and resting on my stomach.

"I know you love her. I love her, too, and I want to do what's best for her. That's all this is. Doing what's best for Dani. I know that is important to you too. You have to see that your current arrangement is not good for her. You are barely home, and she's being raised by a nanny. Bonnie is great, but she's not part of the family. Wouldn't it be better if she lived with family, at least during the school year? Doesn't that make more sense? It would take some of the pressure off of you. And she gets to spend time with family. I think that is best. You must agree."

I took a deep breath, trying to squelch the fire roaring in my veins. *Who the hell does she think she is?* How could she know what was best for my daughter? She didn't even know her. I took my time talking. I didn't want to let my anger get the best of me, but I was on the edge.

"Jamie, I understand that you miss your sister. I miss her too. But trying to replace her with my daughter is not going to work. Dani is her own person; she's not Marie. I get that you care about her, and I appreciate that, but you can't take care of her better than I can. You don't take care of your own children. You don't want her because you love her, and you believe you can give her a good home. You want her because you are so used to having your claws in Marie that you can't let go. You want her to be a replacement for the sister you lost, and if that is the case, Dani will be miserable with you. And you know that."

Her eyes narrowed as she pressed her lips into a thin, firm line.

I continued. "Living with you is not what Marie would have wanted. She knew that you were not mentally put together and are still dealing with your abandonment issues caused by your mother. I'm sorry, but it's the truth. You would not be a good caregiver to my daughter. She would end up taking care of you just like Marie had to, and I will *not* let you suck the life out of her just because you can't get past your sister's death. I will not give you custody. I knew my wife, and she would never have given her permission for what you want to do. She wouldn't want this, and deep down, I think you know that."

I exhaled sharply, waiting for whatever retort she had. She stood up. "You don't know shit!" she roared tearfully. "Marie was my sister. No one knew her better than me, and I'm telling you, this is what she wanted. She wanted me to have her. If you believe differently, then you don't know her as well as you think. You're a horrible father to Dani. What kind of father doesn't make their child their first priority? You work late, and you're never home when she needs you. What kind of father is that?"

I jumped to my feet. "I work; I know that's not something you understand, having never held a job for longer than a couple of months. But I don't have anyone paying my bills, so I can lie around and do nothing. Someone has to pay the bills, and that person is me. She is well taken care of. She is loved and happy, and I will not let you destroy that like you destroy everything else in your life. If you want to visit, then visit. But she is my daughter. Mine. Not yours."

Her frown deepened. "You don't know what you're doing. She will be mine."

"She is not a prize to be won or fought over. She is a person. A human being. You can't own her like you did Marie."

"I didn't own Marie, she was my sister, and we were close. I wouldn't expect someone who abandoned his brother and his family to understand."

I clenched my fist in my pockets. I hadn't abandoned my family. I moved out on my own when I started college, and that was what I was supposed to do. At some point, I had to leave the nest, but she didn't understand. She never left the nest. Marie was the nest, and she clung to her like a life raft in the middle of the ocean. She had nothing else in her life for so long, that she didn't know how to live without Marie. She still clung to her, but she was using Dani as a replacement.

"I left the nest; I didn't abandon anyone," I said through clenched teeth. "You should try it sometime. Being independent and living life on your own. Stop clinging to the memory of your sister."

She took a step back. "I thought you would see reason, but I guess I was wrong."

"What you are saying is not reasonable! There is no reason you should have custody of Dani. It doesn't make sense to anyone but you."

She moved toward the door. "I'll see you in court!" She slammed the door behind her.

I slumped back into my chair. A few seconds later, Nicole burst through the door.

"That little heifer. What is wrong with her? Is she crazy?"

I shrugged. "I'm not sure. There might be something wrong with her mentally, but Marie never really talked about it. When Jamie did something strange, Marie always said it wasn't her fault; it's just how her brain works. But she never elaborated on that. I think there was something wrong with her that they just didn't talk about."

"They should have; at least then, you would know something about what's going on with her." Nicole glanced behind her, toward the front door. She folded her arms across her chest. "There's something not right about that woman. You need to watch her."

I nodded. "I know. I've already contacted a lawyer. I'm just ready to be done with this. I don't want her disturbing Dani in any way. She's settled in now and has friends. She likes this town, and I won't let Jamie ruin it for her like she ruins everything else in her life."

Nicole's arms dropped to her side. "I'm sorry this is happening. I feel so bad for you and Dani. Someone can just come in and mess up your happy lives, it isn't right."

"Yeah. I appreciate the concern." I exhaled slowly, trying to release the tension in my shoulder, but it wasn't going anywhere. Instead, it wove itself into my muscles, rippling down my back. It had started out as a good day. I was happy about what was to come, but now my mood had shifted. I was annoyed and angry and no longer in a rush to go home. It wasn't a good idea to go home this tense with Dani around.

She was a smart kid and empathetic. She read my emotions so easily sometimes it scared me. It reminded me of Marie. As soon as I walked through the door, she knew how my day had gone without my having to say a word. If I went home now upset, she'd know, and she'd wonder why. And right now, I didn't know what to tell her.

"Why is she doing this? I don't understand it."

Nicole stuck her hands in her pockets as she walked over and sat down. "Maybe she feels like having custody of Dani is her last chance to be with her sister. Her last chance to watch her grow up and be a part of it."

"To her, Dani *is* Marie, and there is no separation between them. To have Dani is to have Marie back, and that is all she cares about. Nothing else. No one else. It's all about what she wants. Marie used to say that until she got what she wanted, she couldn't focus on anything else. She could never let it go. I fear this is one of those situations, and I don't know how it will end."

As if my day couldn't get any worse, Isaac strolled through the door. Seeing him was nowhere near as bad as seeing Jamie, but I was still getting used to seeing him and not feeling uneasy or filled with rage or resentment. Looking at Isaac now, a calmness flowed through me. It caught me off guard, but I appreciated it.

"What are you doing? Need a physical?" I wiggled my eyebrows.

A smile bloomed on Isaac's lips. He pointed at Nicole. "She can do my physical." He pointed at me. "You are not touching me."

A laugh bubbled up Nicole's throat. "I'll add you to my schedule."

Isaac grinned.

"Stay away from my nurse," I said.

Isaac threw his hands up. "Okay. My bad. I just came to say hi to my favorite brother on my lunch break."

"I'm your only brother."

"It still counts."

"Like you have other options."

"Not liking you was always an option."

"Just feel the brotherly love in the air." Nicole's voice broke through our bickering. She smiled.

"And to talk to you about Mom," he said quietly. I collapsed back into my chair while Isaac sat on the edge of a table facing both of us. "I know, but... I think she's going to come anyway."

My head fell into my hands. "Why?"

"She thinks you need her. I tried talking her out of it. She called ten times the other night, but I was too tired to answer."

"Damn, that's too many."

"Yeah, well, no one else is talking to her, so she calls me. She thinks you need her to help you deal with Dani and Jamie and all the shit going on. I told her you don't, and you have enough going on, but she wouldn't give in. I told her I'd talk to you about it."

"You guys don't like your mother?" Nicole's eyes darted between us.

We both sighed heavily. Isaac spoke first. "It's... complicated. My relationship with her is okay, but with Log... I don't know."

"It's bad," I said glumly.

Isaac nodded. "Even now, and we're grown. She tries to pit us against each other so she can have control over us. If we aren't getting along with each other, she can control one or both of us. She wants people to think she's a good mother, which is the only reason she wants to come here."

"Wow!"

"What do you think, Sac? About her coming here."

Isaac took a deep breath. "I don't think it's a good idea. We've got enough going on. I don't really want her near Dani while we're still dealing with Jamie. It's not good—mentally. If she does come here, she can't stay at the house."

I took a deep breath. "Yeah, it's not good for me either. I think she sees that we are finally trying to fix our relationship, but she feels threatened. She doesn't want us to talk to each other without her, I guess."

Isaac shook his head. "I hadn't thought about that. I kept thinking, why now? Why did she want to make amends now?"

"She always has an agenda."

"Your childhood sounds so depressing," said Nicole.

Isaac looked at her, a hint of a smile softly curling his lips. "Yeah, it was."

"I'll think about it. I have to get with the lawyer. He wants to speak to you, Bonnie, and Dani. Make sure the home is good for her."

"Okay. Just let me know when, and I will make myself available." He stood up. "I'm taking your nurse to lunch. You can be without her for an hour."

Nicole stood up and grabbed her purse.

"Never turn down a free meal."

Isaac opened the door, and she walked past him. "Yeah, me either." he started to close the door behind him. "Respect the *Sailor Moon* tattoo."

When Nicole got back from her lunch break she was pretty quiet. I waited for her to say something about it but since she didn't, I didn't bring it up. At the end of the day she slipped a piece of paper into my hand. I knew what it was without having to open it. I slipped it into my pocket and shook my head.

I ordered a few pizzas when I got home giving Bonnie and Sac a night off from cooking. Isaac walked in a few minutes after the pizza arrived.

Dani jumped in his arms as soon as he closed the door behind him. "Hey, kiddo!"

"Uncle Sac, Papa got pizza."

"Oh, that's great."

"Yeah, I figured you wouldn't feel like cooking."

"I would have, but no, I don't feel like it."

Dani disappeared into the kitchen. I walked over to him and handed him the paper Nicole had given me.

"What is that?" He took it and put it in his pocket without looking.

"Nicole wanted me to give you her number."

Isaac grinned as he followed Dani into the kitchen.

CHAPTER TEN

Riley Quinn

"**D**ETECTIVE QUINN?"
I looked up. A patrol officer stood next to a man with a worried look on his face. It was difficult to say who looked more out of sorts. The officer was new and didn't have much experience dealing with victims. And the man looked like he was ready to ask for a supervisor. I'd have to tell Zelina my thoughts later.

"How can I help you?"

"Mr. Hernandez wants to report his daughter missing."

I blinked. Another missing daughter in another day. We'd put in a lot of long hours last night, and now we'd be stretched even thinner. "How old is she?"

"Thirteen." He held out his phone. I stared at the photo on the screen. "Mia was supposed to walk up to the gas station and come straight home."

"Okay." I nodded slowly. I found it worrying that he let her walk to the gas station by herself. But then again, when I was thirteen I walked all over town and my parents didn't seem to care. "How long has she been gone?"

"Two nights now. I tried calling all her friends and their parents. I thought maybe she went to someone's house. But they all said she's not there. We… got into an argument about her grades. I thought she just needed to cool off or something."

I glanced back at Zelina who was already taking notes. "Why don't you come with us to the conference room? We will take your statement there." He followed us quietly. There was a nervous energy to him. He fidgeted with his phone when he sat down at the table.

"Now, you said you two had a fight and you let her go?"

His eyebrows pulled together. "What are you implying?"

"I'm not implying anything. Just trying to get clarification on what led to her leaving the house."

"She's… well, she's going through a lot, I think. A lot of emotions," he said. "She's flunking math and not doing her homework. I ask her about it every day and she says it's done, and then I got a call from her teacher to find out that she's been lying to me. She's been skipping class, acting out in school… of course, I got on her about it."

I nodded. "Did it escalate?"

He sank back in his chair. "Oh, yeah. Screaming, crying… she said I wouldn't understand. I try to be there for her. I really do. But things have been difficult since the divorce. She views me as the bad guy. I try to give her space when she gets angry, but… I don't know how to deal with all this. I'm just worried something may have happened to her."

I wrote that down as well. I felt bad for the girl, and her father, but to be honest, it all sounded like a pretty typical story for a thirteen-year-old. I certainly did not miss being a thirteen-year-old girl.

"Does she go to her mother's house? Your ex-wife?" Zelina asked.

"Mia's mother has very limited custody," he explained. "She lives out of town, anyway. I don't think she'd be able to walk all that way. I called, but she's not answering me. Which isn't new."

I passed him a pad of paper and a pen. "Write down her number and the numbers of any of her friends. And then—" I paused. A thought flashed in my head. "You said she went missing two nights ago?"

The man seemed surprised. "Yes."

"Z, take the statement. I'll be back." I rushed out of the room. Zelina's voice trailed behind me but I was on a mission. I burst through the doors of the computer lab. "Hey, Jose, can you print out a screenshot of the man and the girl outside the gas station?"

Jose blinked. "Um... sure." He tapped away and the printer fired to life. We both went to retrieve it and I scrutinized it carefully.

"This is as good as I could get it. Not exactly super-HD quality—"

"That's good enough, thanks."

The man's face was turned away from the camera. It was side profile, and not a very good one. But the girl was clear. Or as clear as she could be. Still a little grainy, but it would do.

I jogged back into the conference room with the page in hand and presented it to Mr. Hernandez. "Is this your daughter?"

He gasped and snatched it out of my hand. "How did you find her so fast? Who is that she's talking to?" The words rushed out of his mouth as he stared at the picture. "Yes, that's her, and that's what she was wearing when she left. How—why do you have this?"

I took a deep breath and explained how we had it. I told him about the search for Delilah Preston, and how we'd seen her looking at his daughter. I told him about the car she got in and offered to show him the video. Maybe he could identify the man if he watched it.

At first, I thought maybe she knew the man. The way she talked to him, it seemed like it. But it was seeming more and more like that wasn't the case. My mind swirled with questions. Why did Mia get in the car with that man? And why did Delilah follow them? And who was the body we'd found? Somehow, I got a sinking feeling that all three mysteries were connected.

We showed Mr. Hernandez the video and he seemed crestfallen. "I don't know him. He doesn't look familiar at all. No one she knows."

I closed my laptop. There was a question nagging at me but I wasn't sure how to phrase it that didn't make it seem like I was judging him and his parenting skills. But I had to ask. The video was taken late at night. Even if she had stormed out angrily after a fight at home, what was she doing out that late?

"I'm sorry, but I have to ask—why did you let her leave that late at night?"

"It wasn't night when she left. It was five, maybe. She... she hates me a lot of the time, I'm the bad guy, and I thought she needed a break. So I let her leave. She's done it before, she'll leave for a couple hours to clear her head. I figured she was with her friends. But when it got dark and she still wasn't home, I got worried. I'm just... I'm doing the best I can. And I walked all over Pine Brooke when I was her age. I didn't see it as a big deal."

"Okay. Well, I think you should go home and wait for her. We'll send an officer with you just in case someone calls."

"Like for ransom?" His jaw dropped and his posture changed. "You think someone took her for money?" His voice cracked.

"That's not what I'm saying. It's just a precaution. Better to be safe than sorry. We'll conduct a search, and if we find anything on our end we'll let you know." I stood up and guided the man out of the room. He was visibly shaken as I found an officer to escort him home.

Zelina and I then went to fill in Captain Williams.

"You think Delilah might have witnessed a kidnapping, tried to follow them, and then got herself caught too?" His brows furrowed the more he thought about it, and his lips pressed into a thin line. "I don't know." He stared at the screen as we replayed the video yet again. "The girl doesn't look like she's in distress at all. It's like she knows him. Maybe Delilah recognized them."

"That might be possible. But right now, it's our only lead for either of these cases, and that can't be a coincidence. This has got to be connected somehow," I said.

He leaned back in his large leather chair and drummed his fingers against the desk. "It's like there's something more to the story that we're not hearing. Talk to the ex-wife. I'll get officers searching for Mia and get pictures of her circulating. While you're at it, talk to her friends. If she left at five, I want to know where this girl went before she found herself at the gas station at midnight."

"On it."

Mia had probably been hanging out with a friend and stopped by the gas station on her way home. That's what made the most sense to me; it's what I would have done if I was trying to avoid being home at her age. But I wouldn't have gotten in the car with a man I didn't know when I was her age. He must have been familiar to her.

Our first stop was Mia's best friend, Lani Bricks. The small brick house was quiet when I rang the doorbell. It was in a nice part of town, not too far from the school. A woman in a thin gray robe answered the door.

"Loretta Bricks?"

"Yes?" Her eyes went wide when I held up my badge. "Can I help you?"

"Detectives Riley Quinn and Zelina Carter. We're actually looking to speak with your daughter, Lani. Is she home?"

She frowned and crossed her arms. "What's this about, Detectives?"

"We're looking for Mia Hernandez. Her father has been looking for her and can't find her. He's reported her missing."

Loretta looked surprised, but opened the door wide enough for us to enter her home. "I thought it was strange that Rafael called me today," she said. "Mia never went home?"

"I'm afraid not, ma'am."

She gestured for us to sit down on the couch, while she sat across from us on an armchair. "She was here the day before yesterday. To tell the truth, I don't like Lani hanging out with that girl. She's trouble. But Lani sees the good in everyone."

"Did she mention any difficulties at home?" Zelina asked.

Loretta shook her head. "You'd have to talk to Lani. She was only out in the house for two minutes before heading back to Lani's room. Those two stay shut up in there for hours. I don't know what exactly they get up to, but they're thirteen. I try to give them their privacy."

"Is there any way you could bring Lani down here? We'd like to see if she knows anything."

Loretta turned her head and yelled up the stairs for her daughter.

"Oh my god, Mom, I'm right here," came an irritated voice from up the stairs. A skinny girl with light brown hair and big brown eyes huffed and puffed down the stairs. "What do you want?"

"Detectives Quinn and Carter would like to speak with you," Loretta said. "And they're guests in our home, so treat them with respect."

Lani rolled her eyes but sat on the floor in front of us.

"Hi, Lani," I tried with an encouraging smile. She didn't seem impressed, though. "We're looking for Mia. Do you know where she is?"

"What, is she in trouble or something?"

"Maybe. But not from us. She never made it home after she was here. Have you heard from her at all?"

Lani looked up sharply, worry darkening her features. "No, I haven't heard from her all day."

"Why don't you take us though what you guys talked about when she was here," Zelina said.

"Just stuff. School. Boys. Dumb drama," Lani said. "She said her dad was mad at her. He usually is. She stayed until it was time for dinner and then my *mom* said she had to go home."

Loretta cleared her throat, but didn't reply.

"You haven't talked to her since?" asked Zelina.

Lani shook her head. "I tried calling her before bed but she didn't answer." She took in a breath and some of her mask crumbled, and her eyes went wet with emotion. "Do you... do you think she's okay?"

I hesitated. "We don't know. Did she give you any indication of where she was going when she left that night?"

The girl shrugged. "I just thought she was going home."

"What about your other friends? Would she go to their houses?" I showed her the list of names and numbers her father had provided us, but she scoffed.

"He's so behind. He doesn't know anything about Mia. We don't even hang out with them anymore." There was a strong trace of annoyance in her voice. "We stopped hanging out with those girls a while ago."

"Why did you stop hanging out?"

Lani took a deep breath. She glanced at her mother, who pinned her in place with her eyes. "You tell them what they want to know. Now."

"They were mean to Mia."

Loretta angled her body toward her daughter. "In what way? You never told me that."

"You would have agreed with them and their parents and I didn't feel like hearing the whole 'Mia's a bad influence' speech again. She's not. She's really not. She's just going through a lot right now and none of the *adults* are listening to her. And that's frustrating."

My heart broke for Mia, but I couldn't dwell too long on this side of things. I needed a lead, something tangible for us to follow. But it seemed the only way to get one was to keep following this road as far as it went.

"We're listening now, so tell us," I said.

Lani inhaled sharply, and then a word tornado was unleashed on us. She spoke so fast without taking a breath that I wasn't sure I caught everything.

Mrs. Bricks clamped a hand on her shoulder. "Take a breath so they can understand you, *hija*."

Only then did Lani pause and reset herself. "Sorry. But like I was saying. Because of all the stuff going on with her parents, kids at school think there's something wrong with her. Like her mother is a drunk and that means something's wrong with her. They started treating her differently and saying mean things. And I get how that feels, you know. When my dad died they were mean to me too."

"Is that why you're still her friend?" Zelina asked.

"Yeah. She was there for me and now I want to be there for her."

"Okay. Do you have any idea of where she would go?"

She thought about it for a long moment. "The park, maybe, but really that's it."

I turned back to Loretta. "How bad was the divorce?"

She made a face. "Bad. Horrible. And it's always harder on the kids than the adults. Marli wanted custody, and she got it, at first. But then she got so drunk one day, she picked Mia up from school and drove into a tree. They were lucky to get out with just some scrapes and bruises. I didn't know how bad her drinking was until then. Her drinking really fell off the deep end after the divorce was finalized. Rafael tries, but it's not easy to raise a thirteen-year-old by yourself. I would know. And I think Mia resents him because of what her mother puts in her head.

"Mia is mad at both of them," Lani said. "She can't wait to get out of this town."

"Has she ever talked about running away?" I asked, reminding myself it was a possibility. It wouldn't be totally out of character for a troubled young teenager to run away with no plan or money.

Lani shook her head. "No. She knows there's nowhere she can really go."

"Okay. I have one last thing." I took out my phone and called up the screenshot of the security footage with the mysterious guy outside the gas station. "Does this man look familiar to either of you?"

Loretta looked closely and then shook her head. Lani stared at and held the phone so tight she nearly crushed it in her hand.

"Did that guy take her?" she asked sharply. Her walls were crumbling now and tears were spilling out even as she said it. "Did he take her?"

"He's just a person of interest," Zelina said quickly. "We're just following a few leads."

"*Hija*, it's okay," Loretta said, trying to soothe her daughter. "It's going to be okay."

Lani collapsed into tears and Loretta held her tight for a long moment before looking back up at us. "I'm sorry, Detectives. I don't know if there's anything we can do to help."

"I'm sorry, too. I promise, we'll do what we can. If anything comes to mind, just give us a call."

"I will. Thank you. And please, find her."

CHAPTER ELEVEN

Riley Quinn

The last thing I was looking forward to was tracking down and talking to Mia's mother, Marli Hernandez. And after a grid search in the area where she and Delilah had both gone, I wasn't sure that returning to the scene would help us at all. But after such a long night and a whirlwind of a morning, I needed a minute to put my thoughts in order.

I sent Zelina back to the station, while I stepped into my parents' bakery and slunk into a chair with a heavy sigh.

"Hey, kid," my dad said, sliding a croissant over to me. "Hot or iced today?"

"Iced. With oat milk. And two... no, three sugars."

He laughed. "Wow. You must be really going through it today."

I took a couple nibbles of my croissant. "It's like every teenage girl in Pine Brooke decided to go missing lately." I explained the complex web of cases we had, skimping out on some of the more gruesome details. "It reminds me of the Cynthia Harmon case, too. I still can't find any evidence there. It's all just so frustrating."

His face darkened. "You think it could be another killer?"

"I hope not. I would hate if a copycat or successor or something came to our town."

"Well, you'll solve it, Detective. You always do." He smiled proudly and got up to make my latte.

"Hold on," I said. "What's with you?"

"What's with what?"

"You're being like…" I gestured vaguely. "Normal."

"Well, I feel a lot better. I've been doing some new treatment options and medications for my blood pressure. It's all thanks to Doctor Elwood."

"Doctor Elwood? I know that guy," called out a voice from the door. We turned around to see Logan himself waving and heading our way.

Dad laughed. "Thanks again, Doc. Today's coffee is on the house."

"You realize it's all that coffee that's gotten you in trouble, right?" he asked.

Dad waved him off. "Yeah, yeah. But is life really worth living without coffee?" He bustled back to make our drinks.

"He's in a good mood," Logan said as he slipped into the chair across from me.

"I know, it's weird," I said. "But he's grateful to you."

"Just doing my job."

We sat there for a minute in silence, but it wasn't awkward. "How have you been?"

"Not great, to be honest. Got a meeting with a lawyer about the whole Jamie situation."

I shook my head. "I can't believe that woman is still after your daughter."

"Believe me, me either. But hopefully we can find a way to get her out of our hair for a while. What about you?"

"I've got two missing young women—one of them a thirteen-year-old girl—and a dead body that's as of yet unidentified, all possibly part of the same case."

"Oof."

"Yeah. Honestly, I can only stay for a minute. I just needed a boost. I'm headed out to Elk Crossing to interview the girl's mother today. We're hoping she just left her dad's house and walked there."

"But that's like twenty miles away. That would take… a while to walk."

I nodded slowly. "I know. But at this point I don't know what other options we have. She disappeared in the same region we just did the grid search on. I'm hoping that she's with her mother."

"Well, good luck."

"Thanks." I grabbed my coffee from my father, gave him a wave, and headed out.

"What has Rafael said I've done now?"

I stared at Marli Hernandez, who glared at us suspiciously. She stood in the door of the apartment complex on the edge of Elk Crossing.

"I haven't done anything. I haven't gone to his house. What, did he call the cops on me?"

"We're looking for your daughter, ma'am."

She blinked. Her body immediately straightened. "What do you mean?"

"Mia has been missing for two days," I told her. "She isn't at home, her father hasn't heard from her, none of her friends have seen her."

"Oh my god," she said, her hand flying to her mouth. "Is she okay?"

"We hope so, ma'am," I replied.

"Come on in, come on in." She waved us into her apartment and gestured for us to sit down. "Can I make you a drink? Tea?"

Zelina and I entered the apartment. It was clean. Almost fanatically clean. I almost didn't even believe someone lived there. There was not a single speck of dust to be found, and nothing was out of place. It was almost like it was a show apartment for potential renters, not where she actually lived.

"Thank you, but no. We really can't stay long if she's not here."

She was wringing her hands as she returned to the living room with a tray of steaming tea cups anyway. "Oh, that man must have done something to set her off. I knew he wasn't right for her. I knew it."

"Do you mean her father?" Zelina asked.

Marli dabbed a tear from her eye and nodded. "Mia has told me that they don't get along. He's so harsh on her. Always yelling and screaming at her for no reason. It's no wonder she ran away."

I nodded slowly. I never said she ran away. Marli took a sip of her tea and gestured again for us to take some, but both Z and I shook our heads. The whole thing was odd to me. I couldn't put my finger on it.

We searched the whole apartment, but Mia wasn't there. Marli was hovering behind us, wringing her hands again in the hallway as we picked through the house. Not that there was much to find.

"Does Mia come and stay with you?" I asked, already knowing the answer.

Marli took a sip of her tea that she had taken with her into the hallway. "No. I'm still working with the court on that. They… they took away my baby. But they're going to give her back. We're working on it. That man should not be allowed to raise my daughter. This is all his fault."

I kind of doubted that. But she was being helpful, so I didn't want to blow her up on the spot. We returned to the living room and before even sitting down, Marli quickly fixed herself another cup of tea, her third one since bringing us in. I glanced at Zelina.

"She really likes tea," I whispered.

"I don't think that's just tea. Smell her breath," Zelina replied.

When she came back in, the stench of alcohol immediately wafted over me. I remembered what Loretta Bricks had said about her drinking. I didn't want to agitate her, though, so I didn't bring it up.

"There's one last thing we need to ask you, ma'am."

I showed her the picture of the man at the gas station. She didn't recognize him, but when I explained that Mia had been seen getting in a car with him, she gasped and downed her cup of tea.

"I can't believe Rafael would allow her to just get in the car with a stranger," she said. Tears burst from her eyes. "Oh, my baby! My poor baby!"

She collapsed into tears—no doubt exaggerated by the amount she'd been drinking. But we couldn't get much more out of her, so we got up to leave.

"Detectives, I hope you put my ex-husband in jail for what he's done," she said. "Promise me that."

That was odd. She seemed to care more about getting back at him than she did about us finding her daughter. I thought back to what Loretta Bricks said about their divorce. I had a comment on the edge of my tongue, but I kept it to myself.

"We'll do our best to find her, Mrs. Hernandez."

We left before she could collapse into any more tears. I shook my head on the way back to the car.

"That was so weird," I said. "Why would she care more about us arresting the husband than finding her daughter?"

"Mrs. Bricks did say the divorce was pretty nasty. And she must have drank at least four or five shots in the thirty minutes we were there."

"Do you think she's involved somehow?"

"Well, Mia's not here … so I guess not," Zelina said.

I shook my head. Yet another dead end. We returned to the station with no leads and nowhere to go.

"Please tell me we have something," I said out loud as I strode back into the station.

"We got a hit on the guy in the footage," said Officer Williamson, bustling over to me the second I sat down at my desk. He handed me a file. "Jimmy Louis."

I glanced down at the mugshot and compared it to the screenshot. It was a close resemblance.

"He's got a pretty long rap sheet," Williamson went on. "Mostly possession, but one for battery. He beat up his girlfriend while high on meth."

Zelina sighed. "And Mia's with that guy? Poor girl."

"Let's just hope she's okay," I said. "You have an address for Jimmy?"

Officer Blaese was already on it, typing it into the search. "Looks like he lives in the trailer park out by the gas station."

"Well I'm sure that's not a coincidence. Come on. Let's roll out."

Zelina and I took the lead, but we brought along Blaese, Rainwater, and Williamson for backup. We were not going to take any chances in case this scumbag took Mia. We arrived as quickly as we could, but with our lights and sirens off and as silently as possible. We didn't want to spook Jimmy and send him running.

"You three, surround the back. Make sure there's no way he can jump out a window or something," I said. "Z and I will take the front."

The officers did as ordered and spread out, taking up strategic positions on the outside of the trailer. They drew their guns and waited for my signal.

Zelina took the lead to knock on the door while I stood back, pointing my weapon at it. She banged her fist hard against the door; it was so loud it echoed. No response. She knocked again. There was no movement inside the trailer. No TV playing. No music. I looked around at the officers, warning them with my eyes to be on alert, as an uneasy feeling curled into me.

"Mia? You in there?"

Zelina tried the doorknob. It wasn't locked. She opened the door and I rushed in, gun drawn. But the room was empty. Well, not empty. Not completely.

There was a body stretched out on the floor. Eyes stared up at the ceiling lifelessly. A needle stuck out of his left arm.

"Well, there's Jimmy," Zelina muttered.

"Mia?" I called out. There was no answer. I signaled for the officers outside to stand down and we searched the trailer carefully, sidestepping the body and roping off the scene. It was a mess in there. Trash everywhere. Spoiled food on the counter, with flies and gnats floating around. Drug paraphernalia strewn around. Fast-food wrappers tossed on the floor, piled up trash bags in the corner that hadn't been taken out in I don't even want to know how long.

And of course, Mia was nowhere to be found.

"Dammit! Call for the coroner," I grumbled as I stepped outside to protect myself from the smell.

By now, there was a commotion outside. The neighbors were gathering to gawk at the proceedings. When they saw me approaching, though, most of them slunk back away to their trailers. I got the feeling that they didn't trust the police, which was fine. I wasn't interested in whatever they had going on in their homes. Just if they'd seen something.

"Is he dead?" asked a woman as I walked over. Her eyes flicked back to the trailer. "I bet he's dead."

I sighed. "He is."

"Figures. All that poison he kept shooting up his arm, I'm surprised he wasn't dead long before now."

"And you are...?"

"Traci Harrison. I live three lots over that way," she pointed.

"Has anyone been to see him lately?"

"I ain't his keeper," she said. "He's always got shifty-looking people coming in and out of there. Definitely a dealer of some sort."

"Yeah, I figured as much," I said. At the mention of that, a few more people in the crowd backed away. "But I don't really care about that right now. We're trying to find a couple missing people that were last seen with him."

"Well," said the man who stood next to her, "there was a woman a couple days ago that stopped by and she didn't look so sketchy. She looked... I wouldn't say respectable, but she wasn't the kind of woman you typically see around these parts, if you know what I mean."

"Sure," I said. "Can you describe her?"

"She looked... clean. Like she took care of herself. Long brown hair, a bit shorter than you. She went in with a brown paper bag, probably liquor. I don't know when she left but when I woke up the next morning her car was gone."

"What kind of car?"

"A silver Hyundai. I remember because the front bumper was all crashed up."

I turned my phone toward them and called up a picture of Delilah. "This her?"

They both squinted, but shook their heads. "I don't think so. She was a bit older," said the man.

That took the wind out of my sails. If it was too old to be Delilah, it was certainly too old to be Mia. But I showed them the picture of Mia anyway, and they confirmed it wasn't her.

"And you're sure?"

"Sorry, Detective," said Traci. "I'd definitely remember if there was a little girl like that around Jimmy. I don't care what poison he puts in himself, or in his customers, but a little girl? No, I wouldn't stand for that."

"Kind of looks like her, though," said the man. "Very similar. Could be like, her older sister. Or her mom."

My eyes went wide. "Just a second," I said, digging through my phone for a photo of Marli Hernandez before I showed it to them.

"That's her. I'd never seen her before, which was why she stood out. That, and I thought what kind of woman would mess around with a guy like Jimmy?"

"Thank you both for your time." I hurried back to the car and beckoned for Zel to meet me there. "The couple over there says that Mia's mom was here a few days ago."

"That can't be a coincidence."

"Guess we're headed back to Elk Crossing."

CHAPTER TWELVE

Logan Elwood

Bert looked nothing like I'd imagined. He was tall with short, curly black hair, hazel eyes, and broad shoulders. His silver-rimmed glasses sat low on his nose as he peered at Dani.

"Nice to meet you, Dani. I'm Bert."

Dani smiled and shook his hand timidly.

"Where can we talk?"

"Um, the living room?" I suggested.

Bert cut his eyes at me. Guess that wasn't a good suggestion. "How about her room?"

His eyes softened. "That would work better. Dani, can you show me your room?"

She shrugged. "Sure." Dani bounced up the stairs, and Bert followed.

I looked at Bonnie when they left. Her brows pinched together, her arms folded across her chest. She didn't like this any more than I did.

We walked into the living room and waited. I tried to busy myself with my phone, but it was of no use. I had nothing to hide, and yet I still wondered what questions he was asking her.

After thirty minutes, Bonnie was next. They went outside and walked around the neighborhood. Dani collapsed onto the couch and started watching TV. I wanted to ask what they talked about, but I had a feeling I wasn't supposed to. She seemed fine. Calm. Her usual self.

After another thirty minutes, it was my turn to talk to Bert. We went into my office, and I closed the door behind me.

"How did your talk go?"

Bert smiled as he took off his glasses and slid them into the breast pocket of his suit jacket. "Dani is a very bright girl. She's sweet and seems well-adjusted. Bonnie is lovely. You can tell she really loves you all and is overjoyed to take care of Dani. That being said, I still need to talk to your brother."

I sighed. "I figured you would have to."

"Not happy about it?"

I shrugged. "Isaac is a good guy. I don't know if you think he would be a good person to have around Dani. He's getting his life together, and she loves spending time with him. She loves her uncle, and he loves her. I think she is the main reason he decided to stay. He usually moves around a lot."

"Okay. Still need to talk to him, though, but even without that conversation, I still want to take your case. The girl is thriving here. She has a good family unit, friends at school, and people that love her. To take her away from that would be cruel. I don't see any reason why she should be moved."

I exhaled slowly. "Thank you for saying that. I really appreciate it."

"Well, don't thank me yet. We still need to understand why Jamie is doing this." He sat down, and I followed suit.

"I don't know. She had little contact with Dani after she was born. Neither she nor her mother came around a lot, especially after Marie died. And then, all of a sudden, one day, she came to visit and never left. She got it into her head that she was a better parent than me, and Dani needed her."

He took a notepad out of his bag along with a pen. "What kind of person is she? Is she responsible?"

A chuckle bubbled up my throat. "No, she's not. I think this is about Marie. That's it. Dani looks like Marie and Jamie had an unhealthy attachment to her sister. I think she believes that caring for Dani would, in a way, be like having her sister back."

"I see. How unhealthy was this attachment?"

I explained most of what Marie used to tell me about her sister and her mother.

"For a time, they were all they had, so they were very close. But while Marie grew up and was able to form bonds with other people, Jamie couldn't get the hang of it. She had few friends and fewer people who loved her or even wanted to be around her. Until she met her husband, and his money garnered her favor from some people. But her personality left a lot to be desired. She was not a nice person unless she wanted something from you, and then she was sweeter than honey.

"She was obsessed with Marie. Fixated. She'd always be hanging around, always the third wheel whenever we'd do anything. Even after her own kids were born, that didn't matter. Her entire life revolved around Marie."

"I see." Bert finished writing in his notebook. "Sounds like she needs help."

"I always thought that. But Marie loved her sister. She loved her with all her heart, and she was a little more forgiving than others. A lot more forgiving. But she knew how Jamie was. She knew what kind of person she was, but she always had a hard time saying no to her. Always. I could never understand why. I think she felt like Jamie still needed her, and I think Jamie knew that and used it to her advantage."

"Okay, so she's manipulative."

"With a capital M. And she's good at it. I don't know or understand how or why she's so good at it, but she could teach a class on it."

Bert chuckled, and then he sighed. "This might be a little tricky if she's good at manipulating others, then she might be able to get the judge on her side. I think we should try mediation."

I slumped back in my chair. *Mediation?*

"I know it's not something that you want to do, but it might help. Before she goes down this road of getting the courts involved, this might be the best option. The only reason social services hasn't been looped in yet is because she hasn't filed an official complaint. She and her lawyer want you to concede before they get the law involved. If you do, it will be less work for them."

"I understand that. Or maybe they know there's no evidence of abuse, so they are trying to scare me into giving her Dani."

Bert cocked his head to the side. "That is a possibility, but... just the mention of child abuse as a doctor will ruin your career. Even if you are not guilty, people will still believe that there had to be some truth to it. They will judge on that and that alone."

I took a deep breath. He was right. And that was what she wanted. If I wanted to keep my career and not have abuse claims hanging over my head, then it would be better to give her Dani. Once the claims went public, it would sow the seed of doubt in the minds of people in town, and that would ruin everything. No one wants to get medical advice from an alleged child abuser.

"Mediation, huh?"

A smile pulled at the corner of his lips. "I know you don't like it and don't want to talk to her. I get that. But it might be our best and only option. It would also give us a chance to see what evidence they have and where they plan on taking this."

"Yeah, it's a good idea. I just don't think she will agree with it. She wants what she wants, and any deviation from that makes her angry. She'll never give in. But we can try it if you think it will be best."

"I do. I've been able to help a few people see reason through mediation. Sometimes it works, but sometimes it doesn't, so we should be prepared for the worst-case scenario."

"Understood." Best case scenario she would see how foolish this was and give up. She'd go home to her children and her family and leave us alone. I didn't have a problem with Jamie spending time with Dani. I would have encouraged it even though I didn't like it. I wouldn't get in between my daughter having a relationship with her aunt, which was one of the last links she has to her mother.

But trying to take her from me... Jamie proved she couldn't be trusted. Even now, if it worked and Jamie agreed to back off if she was allowed visitation, I'm not sure if I would have trusted Jamie to be alone with Dani. I'd be too afraid that Jamie would take her and run.

"Now that I know I'm taking the case, I'm going to get one of my assistants to look into Jamie."

My eyebrow shot up. "Look into?"

He exhaled sharply. "From what you've told me, I think there is more to her than meets the eye. She has to have something in her past that can explain her sudden behavior. You say she's obsessed with her sister... I wonder if she's ever been obsessed with anyone before."

I frowned. That was a scary thought. "Marie never mentioned it."

"I wonder if she knew about it. Was Jamie ever away from her?"

I nodded. "I'm not sure where she went, though, and then there was college. When they were younger, Marie said that her mother had sent Jamie away. I don't know the particulars. It seemed like Marie never wanted to talk about it, and I didn't want to push her, you know. I have shit from my childhood that I don't want to dredge up. But wherever it was, she was there for a couple of years."

"I see. Yeah, I want to know more about that."

Now I do, too.

"Are you close or friendly with her mother?"

I shrugged. "I would say now we are a little friendly. She never really liked me. She was never the most present person even when Marie and I were dating. Always had something else going on."

"But you talk?"

"Occasionally. Not long conversations. She asks me about Dani, but she never comes to visit."

He regarded my comment thoughtfully, tilting his head to the side. "That's interesting. I wonder if she knows what her daughter is doing."

"I don't think they talk either. Marie tried to stay in contact with her mother. She loved her and had forgiven her for all the bad shit she had done. Jamie is a lot less forgiving. I don't think she talks to her unless she has to. When Marie was alive, it was a little more because she was there as a buffer."

"Without the buffer, they lost contact. Happens a lot."

"Yeah, I know."

Bert stood up. "Well, that's it for now. Where does your brother work?"

"At the diner on Main street. He's a cook there."

Bert nodded as he walked toward the door. "That works; I'm hungry. I'll call you if I hear anything about the mediation. Until then, get out more. Meet people. You'll want them to root for you."

He walked out of the room before I could utter another word. I had met people. Maybe not enough to satisfy him, but it was still something. Dani poked her head in the doorway.

"Everything okay?"

"Yeah, honey. Everything is fine. Just working some stuff out. Are you okay?"

She nodded as she entered the room. "He was nice. His sons like anime, too. He asked me a lot of questions, though."

"Yeah, honey, that was his job. He has to make sure that we are taking care of you and that you're okay."

She smiled. "I'm great!"

I chuckled. "Good to hear that."

Dani stared behind her into the living room. "Have they found that girl yet?"

"That girl?"

She pointed to the living room. I moved beside her. The TV was on, and the news was just starting.

"Her name is Mia. They think she's with that other lady too. Everyone is looking for them."

"Yeah, I know. I don't think they've found her yet, but they will." I swallowed the next few words that bubbled up. *They will be alright.* The police would find them, but by this point, both of them would probably be dead. I wanted to hold out hope, but I was too much of a realist to do that. They had been gone for too long. I knew Riley was pulling out all the stops to find both of them, but I doubted she'd find either Mia or Delilah alive.

But Dani didn't need to hear that. She stared at the screen hopefully, and I wanted her to hang on to that hope. I glanced at Bonnie, who looked at me with an eyebrow raised. When Dani moved closer to the TV, I shrugged.

"Let's find you something else to watch." Bonnie held up the remote and pointed it at the TV. Dani's shoulders dropped. I didn't want her learning that kind of stuff on the news. I left them in the living room and went back to my office. I needed time, more so peace and quiet, to think for a little while.

I thought about the mediation and what would happen. I doubted it would go as planned. Jamie wouldn't let it go. Once she got it in her mind that she was owed something or wanted something, she was like a dog with a bone. She had to have it. She had to have Dani.

I wasn't sure about it, but I would give it a try for Dani's sake. She would hate the idea of us fighting over her.

CHAPTER THIRTEEN

Riley Quinn

I wasn't surprised that Marli wasn't at her home when we returned to her apartment complex. We already had an APB out on her silver Hyundai, but nobody had reported seeing it yet. I rushed into the lobby to see if anybody had seen her.

"Detectives, you're back!" said the receptionist, somewhere between confused, embarrassed, and afraid. She had been the one to point us in the right direction when we'd arrived that morning. It felt like a lifetime ago.

"Did Marli Hernandez leave after we did earlier?" I asked.

She nodded. "Yes, she left shortly after you arrived. She looked like she was going out of town."

Zel and I traded glances. "What makes you say that?"

"She had two suitcases with her. I helped her with one down the stairs. I asked her where she was going and she said she just needed a break. Is something wrong? Should I not have let her go?"

"You had no way to stop her," I replied. "Did she give you any indication of where she was going?"

"No, sorry. I thought something was strange, but... I didn't know what to do." The woman chewed her lip and glanced at the TV in the corner of the lobby. "Her daughter's missing. I saw it on the news just a bit ago. Why would she leave when her daughter's missing?"

"I don't think Mia is missing at all," I said. "I think Marli knows exactly where she is. That's why we have to find her."

"I'm sorry. I should have said something. I should have called you."

"Really, don't worry about it," I said. "You've been a great help."

We rushed back out to the car. Zelina already had the station on the phone. "Please tell me you've got eyes on this Hyundai," she demanded.

I couldn't hear the squawking voice on the other end of the line as I sped back to Pine Brooke. I slammed the pedal to the metal and put on the sirens so people would get out of my way. I didn't know where I was going yet, but it didn't matter. They needed to get out of my way anyway.

"The Star Motel!" Z reported. I didn't even need to ask her where it was. I skidded to a quick turn as soon as I could off the highway and beelined in that direction.

We both knew the Star Motel. It was the cheapest place in town. It didn't require ID to check in and didn't ask questions. Of course she would have gone there. Was that where she was keeping Mia?

My mind whirled as we approached the motel. "She must have paid Jimmy to kidnap Mia. Bring her to the Star Motel. She tried to lie low for a while, put on the face of the perfect mother hoping her kid would come home. That was why she was acting so strange when we interviewed her."

"Exactly. She was more concerned about getting back at Rafael than finding Mia. Because she knew exactly where Mia was. And then the first minute she could, she'd grab Mia and get out of town."

I nodded. That was the only thing that made sense. I still couldn't figure out how Delilah fit into the story, or the body we'd found, but for right now all I cared about was getting to Mia before something happened to her.

We rushed into the lobby. The clerk sat behind a sheet of bulletproof glass flipping through a magazine.

"How many beds," he grunted, without even looking up at us.

I held up my badge. "Did a Marli Hernandez check in today?"

That got him to look up, but only so he could give us a dirty look. "I dunno."

Anger flared in my nostrils. "There's a thirteen-year-old girl who could be in serious danger and we think she's been held here at your hotel."

"Not my problem."

"We can *make* it your problem if you don't help us," I snapped.

As usual, Zelina kept a cooler head. She showed the clerk a picture of Marli. "This woman. Did you see her?"

He grumbled. "They don't pay me enough for this shit. Yeah, she checked in. I remember her because she had nice…" he cupped his hands suggestively near his chest and chuckled grossly at his own joke. "You know."

I barreled forward and knocked hard on the glass. "Tell me what room she's in or I'll arrest you right now," I demanded.

He recoiled and put his hands up. "All right, jeez." He flipped through the sign-in book and pointed at a name. "Room 276."

I didn't even bother to thank him. Guns drawn, we ran out and up the stairs in single file. Zelina followed close behind me. I inched toward the door and pressed an ear to it.

"The TV's on," I whispered back to Zelina. I listened hard for a few minutes, trying to hear voices beneath the loud noises of whatever was on the TV.

"Turn that down," Marli snapped. "I can barely hear myself think in here."

"Well, what else am I supposed to do?" replied another voice. "You won't let me go home. You took away my phone. You won't even let me call Dad."

My veins froze. That was definitely Mia.

"You don't need to call your father, sweetie. You don't need him. You know how bad he is for you."

"At least he's not always drunk like you! You're always drunk!"

"I'm not drunk," Marli relented. "I've just had a long day. I needed to take the edge off."

I'd heard enough. "Call for backup, just in case," I whispered to Zelina. She took a few steps back out into the breezeway and began calling it in, but I stood back up and didn't take my eyes off the door.

I lifted a fist and knocked hard. "Marli Hernandez?" I called out.

"Shit!" I heard from behind the door.

"Mom, what's going on?"

"Open the door, Marli."

It took a minute or two, and I heard a lot of shuffling—most likely Marli trying to hide her daughter in the bathroom or under the bed or something—but that was fine. It gave us more time to prepare, and besides, there was nowhere she could escape out the back from. Z returned and told me they were on their way before the lock finally slid open. Marli opened the door but kept the chain lock on, so I couldn't force my way inside.

"It's over, Marli. Where's Mia?"

"She's not here!" Marli stammered. The stench of alcohol on her breath was rough. Even through the tiny gap in the door it wafted over me.

"I heard her through the door just now. I know you have her back here. She needs to be with her father."

Marli's eyes were frantic. "You don't understand. She needs me. I'm her mother. He can't take her. He has no right."

"Legally, he does," Zelina said. "That was solved a long time ago."

"You can't just take my baby away from me!"

"You need to take it up with the court," I replied. "Now we need to take you in."

"No!" she yelled, and tried to slam the door, but before she could, I shoved my leg into the small crack that was left by the chain. The wooden door slammed hard against my ankle. I winced and bright flashes popped in my vision. That would be a heck of a bruise in the morning.

"Mia! Are you hurt?" I yelled out.

"What's going on?" she called back. She was pushing her way out of the closet that had been blocked shut. "Mom, what's happening?"

Marli turned back. "Don't worry about it, sweetie. I'll take care of this, and then we can go away, okay?"

"Don't listen to her, Mia! She's dangerous!" I yelled out. Marli tried to shut the door on my ankle again. I let out a grunt of pain but tried to keep my focus. "We're going to get you out of here—"

I didn't get to finish my sentence, because before I knew it, Marli swung the door open wide. I wasn't expecting it, and my momentum carried me forward and I stumbled into the room. Then she cracked me over the head with a glass bottle and I pitched forward, falling to the ground, stars exploding in my vision.

"Mia, run!"

I wasn't sure who said that. It could have been Marli, trying to grab her daughter and escape. Or it could have been me, trying to get her out of this situation.

I rolled over and struggled to my feet. My ankle was still hurting really bad, and my head was still a little dizzy too. I stumbled to the door frame to see Marli dragging her daughter harshly by the hand down the stairs and out into the parking lot, with Zelina hot on their heels. I tried to run after them, but my legs wouldn't cooperate.

I dragged along slowly, not really able to put weight on my right foot. I was just making my way down the stairs when sirens and lights turned the corner and bore down on the street. The cavalry was coming. We just needed to keep her here a minute longer.

"Freeze, Marli!" Zelina barked. "I will shoot you!"

Marli paid her no attention. She yanked her daughter's arm and shoved her against the passenger side of the Hyundai. "Get in the car, Mia. We're going."

Mia pulled away. "I'm scared, Mom."

"I said *get in the car!*"

I watched as the terrified girl shook her head and pulled back. Her mother screeched and grabbed at her anyway, then opened the door roughly. Mia scrambled and opened the car door, but she couldn't force herself out of her mother's grasp and get out of the car at the same time. She managed to writhe around and kick the door open, but her legs dangled out the side; Marli still held onto her arms. Marli slammed on the accelerator even as her daughter was dangling halfway out the door.

"Stop!" I screamed. By now, I'd made it down the stairs, and I watched, my heart hammering in my chest as the police cruisers sped into the parking lot at the exact same time that the Hyundai was trying to exit.

I heard it before I saw it. Tires screeching to a halt. Metal slamming into metal. A scream.

My own scream.

"Mia!"

The girl had been thrown from the car and was lying in a heap. I stumbled over while Zelina ran. The pain was lessening in my ankle now, and I could at least sort of walk on it, but I knew I shouldn't. The officers quickly leaped out of their car and immediately began rendering aid.

My heart dropped through my stomach as I made my way to the scene. Zelina was already on her knees, performing CPR on the girl. Her leg was twisted at an odd angle, and she was pretty scraped and bruised up.

"Come on, Mia, come on..." Zelina grunted. She pumped her heart a few times, then took a deep breath and breathed into her mouth. She did it again, and again. "Come on!"

After the longest two minutes of my life, Mia coughed and her eyes fluttered open. Relief flooded all of us like a tidal wave.

"She's going to be okay," said the EMT as he loaded her up onto the ambulance a few minutes later. "How's your ankle?"

"Hurts," I said. "But don't worry about me. I'll get it looked at. You focus on her."

I gave him a wave as they carted her off to the hospital in Woodvine, then stared glumly at the scene as the crime scene techs picked at it.

Marli wasn't so lucky. Her head rested, lifeless, against the airbag that had opened too late. Blood dripped from where it had hit the windshield. Glass was shattered everywhere. Her eyes were blank and unblinking, turning to where her daughter lay.

It was over. But even as I sat on the curb, watching the lights fade into the distance, I wondered:

Where was Delilah Preston?

CHAPTER FOURTEEN

Logan Elwood

MY PHONE RANG AS I WAS PUTTING DANI TO BED. I WANTED TO click to ignore it, but when I saw the name Riley Quinn on the screen, I paused.

"Who is that, Papa?" Dani asked sleepily.

"It's one of Papa's friends. You remember the nice police lady Riley?"

She lit up. "Yeah, she's really pretty!"

I chose not to respond to that and kissed her on the forehead. "Sorry, kiddo. I've gotta take this. Why don't you read a little bit before bed? I'll come back and tuck you in."

"Kay. Love you, Papa."

I pressed answer just before the call failed. "I love you," I called out as I quickly exited the room.

"Um. You what?" came the voice on the other line.

"What? Oh. Sorry," I said quickly. "I was putting Dani to bed."

"Ohhh. That makes sense. I thought you were just answering the phone that way."

I chuckled. "You think I just answer the phone by saying 'I love you'?"

"I don't know, man. You're weird."

"What can I do for you, Detective?"

"I'm actually calling to ask a pretty big favor. I know it's late, but I got my ankle hurt pretty bad on a case this evening. I was wondering if you could take a look at it tonight."

I frowned. "What happened?"

"Long story. I can explain it at the clinic, if you want."

I hesitated. On one hand, I was home, enjoying a nice evening with my daughter. But on the other hand, everyone kept telling me to get out and meet people. Get myself into the community. And Dani was right… Riley was really pretty.

"Okay. I'll meet you at the clinic."

We hung up, and I went back to tuck Dani in and tell her goodnight before I left. Riley was already waiting for me in a chair outside the clinic when I pulled up.

"You got here fast," I called out as I parked.

"Oh yeah, they dropped me off here from the station. They said I couldn't come back in until I got it looked at. Stupid," she grumbled.

"Well, let's get you inside." I unlocked the door and held it open for her, but she didn't get up. "Riley?"

"Um. Yeah, just give me a minute." She started to get up by leaning against her left leg, barely keeping her balance, wincing and groaning in pain. I rushed up to help her.

"Wow, you weren't kidding," I said as I put her arm over my shoulder and guided her into the clinic. "You can't put any weight on it at all?"

"I mean, sort of. It's not as bad as it was," she said.

"It seems pretty bad," I said.

I got her into an exam room and laid her out on a table, where I quickly removed her shoe and sock and rolled up her pant leg. "What got you?"

"I got a door slammed on it," she said. "One of those hotel doors with the chain lock."

She told me the whole story of the mother who faked a kidnapping and the teenage girl who felt so alone and so scared.

"But Mia's okay?" I asked.

"Yeah. Her father is so relieved. They took her to the hospital in Woodvine."

"And they didn't take you?" I asked pointedly.

"I thought I was doing better. But it's been a couple hours now and I still can't really walk on it very well."

I took a look. The ankle was swollen and pretty purple with bruising. I did a quick examination, squeezing this way and that, and Riley exhaled harshly in pain.

"Right there."

"Well, good news is, it's not totally broken. Probably just a hairline fracture, maybe a sprain. I want you to keep ice on it and stay off it as much as possible for at least the next couple weeks. You'll need painkillers, too."

I got up and rifled through the cabinet for the medicines she would need.

"I really don't want a cast, Logan," she groaned. "Or one of those stupid boots."

"You don't have to wear a stupid boot," I told her. "But you will need to keep it bandaged, and I'm going to send you with a crutch for the next couple of days. No more high-intensity chases, got it?"

She rolled her eyes. "Got it."

"I'm serious," I told her. "You're going to have to let Zelina do all the superhero moves for a couple weeks."

"Don't tell her that. It'll go to her head. Oh, she got my head too. With a bottle."

I felt around her head. It was a little soft, but nothing too alarming. The painkillers would help with that, too.

"Well, this is about all I can do for you tonight. I want you to come back in a couple days to see how the healing's coming."

I filled out her prescription and brought out the crutch from the back storage area.

"I don't know what I would do if someone took Dani like that," I said as I bandaged her ankle and wrapped everything up. "I would lose my mind and stop at nothing to get her back."

Neither of us needed to say what we were obviously both thinking: that situation was eerily similar to what I'd been going through with Jamie.

"She's not going to take her away from you," Riley finally said. "You're a good father. You're the one she needs."

"Thanks," I said. I just wish I felt more confident in that. The conversation with Bert was still fresh in my mind, and I could only hope that soon we could have this over and done with.

"I mean it, you know. I owe you big time, especially after all this. If anything happens, call me right away. Or even if you just need support."

"Thanks," I repeated. "That means a lot."

I caught myself smiling stupidly for a while at her. Despite the obvious pain she was dealing with, she smiled right back, those bright blue eyes drilling deep into my soul. I cleared my throat and looked away. "So, uh, what's next for you?"

She sighed. "Well, we solved Mia's case, but that seems to just open more questions. I'm not sure how any of the other missing young women fit into this at all. And we still can't find Delilah. It's like every time we solve a case, three more open."

"You'll figure it out eventually," I said.

She blew out a laugh and tested her weight on the crutch. "You're awfully confident in my abilities. You barely know me."

"I know enough, I think. Enough to know you're pretty good at your job."

She got to her feet with the crutch. "Well, thanks for the compliment. Let's hope I'm good enough to solve all these open cases."

I got up and gathered all her things as well as the medications I was sending her home with. "But ice and elevation first," I insisted as we headed back out the front door.

"You're not my mom," she grumbled.

"No, but I am your doctor. Oh, speaking of your mom, have her give me a call. I have test results for her. Nothing bad, I promise. Just a couple of routine things for a woman her age."

Riley threw back her head and laughed—and then groaned from the pain in her head. "Don't *ever* let her hear you say that," she said. "As far as you're concerned, my mother is a ripe thirty-nine."

"What are you talking about? She doesn't look a day over thirty-five," I replied. We laughed a little more as I turned around and locked up.

"Thanks again, Log. You can head home now. I'll call Z to come pick me up."

"Absolutely not. It's so late, and you can't walk. Let me take you home," I insisted.

"You don't have to do that. I'll be fine."

"I want to do it," I said. "I just, uh…" *want to kiss you?* I shook the random thought out of my head before it could escape my mouth. "Want to take care of my patients."

She finally relented. "You know, you've gotten a lot better at your bedside manner lately."

"Yeah, well, you were right. I just needed to get the stick out of my rear end."

She laughed again and we got in the car. I dropped her off at her house and again reminded her to keep her ankle iced and to actually use the crutch. I waited until she made it inside before I finally pulled out of the driveway and returned home.

When I got back, Isaac was on the couch watching the news. "There he is!" he said as I got in the door. "Bonnie said you just rushed out the second you put Dani to bed."

"I had to take care of a patient," I said.

"This late at night?" he said. He started ribbing me a bit, but I tuned it out. The news reporter on the TV was summarizing the case I'd just heard from Riley, complete with the dramatic rescue of Mia Hernandez.

"Detective Riley Quinn of the Pine Brooke Police Department had this to say earlier tonight..."

And then there was Riley, a little scuffed up but otherwise fine, giving a quick statement to cameras. Somehow her eyes shone even brighter through the TV.

Isaac turned back and saw the way I was gawking. "Holy shit. You were with Riley?"

"It's not like that," I stammered. "She got hurt in the case. I just needed to patch her up."

He rubbed his hands together and snickered. "Oh, this is just perfect. I need every single detail."

"There are no details because it wasn't like that, Sac," I groused. I was so tired. It had been an extremely long day, and I was absolutely not in the mood for any of my brother's shenanigans. "I'm going to bed. Turn that down so you don't wake up Dani."

"Sheesh. Don't bite my head off."

I groaned and headed to bed.

CHAPTER FIFTEEN

Riley Quinn

AFTER SUCH AN EXHAUSTING COUPLE OF DAYS, I SLEPT IN THE next morning. Not that I could have gone in to work, anyway. My ankle was still killing me, and Captain Williams had ordered me to take the day off, anyway.

I argued with him about it, but he wouldn't listen. Even though Delilah Preston was somewhere out there and we needed all hands on deck, he would hear nothing of it.

"I've got other officers following up every lead we have for Delilah. We're doing another search and you'll only slow us down with that ankle of yours. Heal up at home, and then you can come back. I don't have time to listen to your arguments."

And that was that. So I sat there on my couch with my foot up, randomly flipping through channels, while Luna curled up next to me. I couldn't relax, though. I couldn't stop thinking of all our open cases. So

I got up and hobbled my way over to my laptop and brought it over to my station on the couch. Maybe I couldn't officially do any work, but they couldn't stop my brain from working.

So many things swam through my head. So many open cases. Cynthia Harmon, Noah Jameson, Delilah Preston. While I ate, I did a search on my computer looking for Noah's case. He and his wife had been found in their bedroom murdered the same day I went to speak with him about Larry Cole, who Noah represented. Larry was in prison for the rest of his life for killing two families. Many people believed he was framed.

"Still nothing." The case was cold; they had no leads, no evidence, and no suspects. Nothing. "How is that possible?" I was on the scene, and there was so much blood everywhere. All of it could not have been theirs. I searched through the folder and found no crime scene folders. No autopsy photos, nothing. "How is this even possible?" I remembered being at the scene. There was someone taking pictures of the scene, the placement of the bodies, and the blood spatter. Where were those pictures? Why weren't they in the file?

I clicked over to Cynthia's case too, remembering my walk through of their house only a few days ago. It bothered me that Tory hadn't claimed her, and that there were no other leads. It was like she was just going to be forgotten.

But I wouldn't forget her.

"What are you looking up?"

I looked up and blinked in confusion. Zelina was standing there in my entryway, holding a bag of food and a coffee for me. I was so lost in thought that I didn't even hear her come in.

I shook my head. "When did you get here?"

"Seriously? Did you not hear me calling? And knocking?"

I looked over at my phone to see several missed calls and texts from her. "I guess I didn't notice."

"Whatever you're looking at must be crazy if you didn't notice all that."

"Yeah, I guess so."

"I let myself in with that key inside that obviously fake rock. We need to talk about that later," she said, as she handed me my box of food and sat next to me to eat her own. "You'll be glad to know that Mia's going to be okay. Her leg is broken, but otherwise she just has a few scrapes and bruises."

"Oh, that's good."

"Yeah. And we're still following up on Delilah, but I figured I'd stop in and check on you for a little bit. Make sure you weren't working."

"Yeah, about that..."

I told her about Noah's case file and what wasn't in it. She stared at me for a long moment, even ignoring Luna's curious sniffing.

"Sounds like a cover-up that's out of our jurisdiction. You shouldn't even be looking at the file," she whispered as she finally stooped to pet the girl. She was right, I shouldn't have looked at it. But my curiosity got the best of me. It always did.

I closed out the file and took a bite of my breakfast sandwich. "I know. I know. I just found it odd. They didn't even try to make it look like they were investigating his murder. And their captain let it slide. Our captain would never have signed off on that. Never in a million years."

"I mean, maybe the Oceanway cops just haven't sent it to our database yet."

"Maybe," I said. "Between that and the Cynthia Harmon case, I just can't help but feel like I'm missing some huge thing here."

"What about Cynthia is bothering you?" she asked as she plopped down next to me.

I told her all about my conversations with Cynthia's mother and what happened when I went to the house. She frowned.

"Yeah, that does seem a little off. What is your first thought? What is your gut telling you?"

After reviewing the information in my head all morning, I could only draw one conclusion. Her mother left the house, but she didn't move everything out. She took her stuff and some of Cynthia's, but not her husband's. He had killed himself, and perhaps she felt betrayed by this action. I would have. But maybe there was another reason.

"Honestly, I think the father killed Cynthia, and her mother found out. Maybe he killed himself, or maybe he didn't. But I think we need to dig up their backyard."

Zelina nodded. "Maybe that's why she still has the house. She wants to sell. She wants to know, or maybe she has a feeling, but she doesn't want to be the one that finds her. We can call and see if she will consent. I'll look up reports."

I raised an eyebrow. "I thought you said I shouldn't work today."

"I never said that. The Captain did," she replied. "Now come on. I really only have a little bit of time before I have to get to work."

I dialed Mrs. Harmon, put the phone on speaker, and took a deep breath as I listened to the ringtone. It rang longer than usual.

"Yes, Detective?"

"I know this may sound strange, but—"

"You want to dig up the backyard."

My eyes darted around the room, looking for cameras or a recorder. How did she know we were just talking about that? "Do you have this place bugged or something? We were just talking about that." There was a smile on the edge of my voice that was not returned.

"I thought you might ask one day. I've been preparing myself for the day you find something there."

I had so many questions to ask her, but I held them back. "So, do we have your permission?"

"Yes," she said, before abruptly hanging up the phone.

"Whoa. That was sudden," Zelina said. "What do you think?"

I regarded the question for a minute before I answered. I had several ideas about what happened, but I didn't know where to go with them yet.

"I think she knows more than she's telling," I said. "She knows or suspects that her husband might have done something to her daughter, and she just doesn't want to admit it to herself."

"I get why she wouldn't want to admit that to herself. Hard to think of someone you loved being a monster."

I nodded. I wanted to stay on task and focus on Delilah's case, but something about this one kept nagging in my mind. Like a fly buzzing around my head. "I need to look at her husband's crime scene photos."

"It was a suicide. There are probably photos of the scene, but that's probably it."

I did a search on my computer, and she was mostly correct. It was ruled a suicide, and the case was closed, but the pictures of the scene were still in our database. Mr. Harmon's body was found near the closet, a rope still around his neck. The ceiling fan with part of the rope around the base a few feet away.

I stared at the pictures, focusing on all the little details. Something felt off. The longer I stared, the more it felt like something was missing.

"I don't think this angle is right." I turned my screen so she could take a look.

She cocked her head to the side. "Should he be there? If he tried to hang himself and the ceiling fan broke, would he have fallen there?"

"'See, that's what's wrong... if the ceiling fan broke, then how did he die?"

Zelina looked back at her screen. "Yeah, I think they missed something."

I flipped through the pictures until I found the report from the first officer on the scene.

Camille Harmon discovered the body of her husband in the room of their missing daughter. He was dead when I arrived. First impression of the scene: Mr. Harmon tried to hang himself using the ceiling fan, but it broke before it could be finished. He then wrapped the rope around the bar in the closet and sat down until he passed out and then died. Mrs. Harmon found the body and cut him down, thinking she could administer CPR and save his life. Her attempts failed.

Interesting. So he did kill himself in the closet, and she cut the rope and pulled him so she could give him CPR. That might explain the angle of the body. But something still didn't sit right with me. I told Zelina what the report said. She stared at me for a long moment.

"Judging by the look on your face, you don't believe that's what happened."

I shrugged. "Part of me feels like I should let it go. It doesn't matter now. But not knowing the truth is nagging at me. I know I'm missing something, but I just wish I knew what it was."

She tapped her fingers on the side of the couch. "Hmmm, can't think what it is."

I scanned through the file until I got to the autopsy pictures. "Huh." The pictures showed his body through the different stages of the autopsy. Before the coroner started, he took pictures of the body. "When you give someone CPR, isn't their chest bruised?"

Zelina nodded. "Oh yeah. When you do it, you have to press down pretty hard. I nearly cracked one of Mia's ribs last night. Why?"

"Give me a minute." I scoured through the notes on the autopsy. "In the officer's report, he said that Mrs. Harmon performed CPR, but the coroner doesn't mention it. At all."

Zelina blinked. "Should they mention it?"

I tapped my forefinger on my chin. "We need to call Keith."

I got out my phone, but Z stopped me. "I'll call him. You're technically off work, remember?"

"Hi Keith, it's Z," she said cheerily. She didn't tell him I was there, or that he was on speaker. I made sure to stay as quiet as possible.

"I'm still working on that prelim for you. Should have it for you by tomorrow."

"No—though that's good to know—but that's not why I'm calling. When someone is given CPR, the coroner can tell, right? Like if there's a cracked rib?"

"Usually it's just some bruising on the sternum. Why?"

"Do you put that in your report?"

"Any coroner worth their salt knows that any bruising on the body before an incision is made goes in the report. Why? Did I miss something?"

"No, you didn't do this autopsy. But the officer on the scene says that a woman did CPR on the victim, but the autopsy photos show no evidence of it, so I was curious."

"Huh, who was the coroner?"

Z checked the file. "A Madeline Brunner."

"Oh, okay. Yeah, if there was any evidence on the body that indicated CPR was done, she would have added it to the report. She was meticulous about her notes. I mean, she wrote everything down and took several pictures. She was amazing. I wish she'd come back."

"Why did she leave?"

"I'm not sure. I think she just needed a break. She had been at this for a long, long time. Sometimes it gets to you, you know. Sometimes, before you start to crack, you need to take a step back."

Z gave me a pointed look, but I said nothing. "Thanks, Keith," she said.

Not even a second after she hung up, I burst out with, "Why would Camille lie about doing CPR?"

"Maybe she wanted people to believe that you tried to save his life because it would look bad if she didn't at least try."

I shrugged. "I guess that's a point. I keep feeling like he didn't kill himself, and she knows more than she's saying."

"You think she did it?"

I nodded slowly. "I think Mrs. Harmon realized her husband killed their daughter, and she killed her husband and then staged it to look like a suicide."

"It's what I would have done."

Sometimes, Zelina surprised me with the stuff that came out of her mouth. She was a cop, but she said very un-cop-like things. I shook my head. "I don't think a cop should say those things."

She shrugged. "Maybe, but it's true. Anyway, I gotta get to work, babes. Stay off that ankle and stay out of work!"

"You know I can't!" I called after her as she got up.

"Fine. I'm taking your laptop, then." She snatched it before I had a chance to argue.

"Hey!"

But Zelina was already out the door. "You can pick it up tomorrow."

I groaned and turned back to the TV, but I still couldn't focus on anything. My mind was still churning, trying to find these missing women.

CHAPTER SIXTEEN

Logan Elwood

"So I went over things with that lawyer last night." Isaac sat back on the sofa with a loud sigh. "This is really happening, huh?"

I nodded. It was really happening. It was my turn to let out an equally loud sigh. I didn't want to believe it. I wanted to just look the other way, and then maybe everything would just go away. I hoped for that. Prayed for it even. I hoped Jamie would come to her senses; maybe a friend would talk her out of it. But that didn't happen, and now the lawyers are involved.

"I can't believe her, man. How could she be so selfish?"

I wanted to point out that it was in her nature. It was who she was. She hadn't changed a bit; we just all hoped she would. And now we knew. I swallowed the words. I didn't really want to talk about it anymore, but I wanted to let him know he might be more involved with this potential case than he wanted.

"I'm here for you whenever you need me. You know that, man. I think you got a good lawyer, too. He was nice, a little weird. And intense. He has the most intense eyes I think I have ever seen, as if he were staring a hole through me. Made me a little uncomfortable."

A chuckle bubbled up my throat. The first time I had laughed all day. "I'm glad you two talked. As far as I know, he's still taking the case, so you didn't say anything to discourage him."

"I was on my best behavior."

"Good. Keep that up."

Isaac laughed. "I'll do my best."

We sat in silence for a long moment. I never knew what to say to Isaac or what to keep to myself. He was such a mystery to me. I never knew what to say to him or what to ask him. Our mother ensured that we didn't have the best relationship. She was always pitting us against each other. I was never sure why; maybe it was for her own enjoyment. Or maybe she just wanted to see what we would do.

I didn't realize it until I went away to college, but by then, it was too late. Our brotherly relationship had been fractured. Damaged beyond repair, or so I thought. The fact that he was here made it seem like we could repair it. There was hope. The silence wasn't uncomfortable. It was familiar.

I decided to start with something small and easy to answer. "How's the diner?"

He smiled. "Pretty good. They let me add something new to the menu today."

"Look at you. What was it? 'Cause that po-boy was amazing."

He beamed. It was a nice thing to see him so happy and proud of his work. "Grilled hot dog with mango salsa."

I raised my eyebrow. I had never heard of anything like that. "Hot dogs and mango?"

"When the dog is charred a little, it brings out the saltiness and then the sweetness of the mango and the bite of the cilantro... it's good. A few people ordered it today, and they really liked it."

"I'll have to try it with Nicole the next time we go to lunch. Speaking of which..."

Isaac shook his head. "You ask me about her, and then I get to ask you about that pretty detective with those bright blues."

"Fair enough, forget I asked." I threw my hands up and sat back. There was nothing to tell, really, but I still didn't want to talk to him about it. Especially after he teased me so much about it last night..

"You like her," said Isaac out of nowhere.

I looked up; his grin turned my stomach. "I don't *like* her, like her."

"You've talked. I've seen you having lunch together. And you ran out last night to her rescue the second she called."

I rolled my eyes. "Shut up. It wasn't like it was a deep conversation. Mostly talked about her work."

Except for the parts that we didn't. But I didn't need to give him any ammo.

Isaac held up his hands. "I'm not saying you should start dating her or anything. I know you aren't ready, but you could use a friend. Someone you don't live or work with. No harm in making a friend."

I exhaled slowly. He was right, and I knew he was right. He was saying the same thing everyone else was telling me. That being said, I didn't think I was ready for it. Having a friend. I had been so focused on rebuilding my life after Marie died and taking care of Dani that I lost touch with everyone. At first, it wasn't intentional, but then I thought they'd be better off without me.

No one wanted to hang out with a new father grieving over his wife's death. That wasn't fun. "I know," I said quietly.

"I'll be your friend until you make another one."

I felt my eyebrow lift slightly. "Only until I make another one."

He shrugged. "Or as long as you need me to."

"Good save."

He looked at his watch.

"Good night," I said before he could say anything.

He sighed. "Yeah, got to go in early to start making the bread and stuff. I'm going to tell them we could do more if we buy the bread from the bakery. You know, outsource it. We spend so much time baking that it would take some stuff off our plates."

A smile pulled at my lips. "Look at you."

"Shut up." He stood up. "I think sometimes."

"And I am very proud to see it."

He laughed on his way up the stairs. The house was quiet. I stared at my phone for a long moment. Before even realizing what I was doing, I started dialing.

"Hello?"

"Uh… I probably shouldn't have called you. I forgot you were probably on a case."

Riley laughed. "Stuck at home today. Boss's orders. Could use a distraction."

"How's your ankle?"

"How do you think? It hurts," she griped. "Why aren't you in bed? Shouldn't doctors get at least eight hours of sleep?"

"Not just doctors. Everyone should get at least seven to eight hours of sleep."

"Huh, some nights I'm lucky to get three."

I tried to fight the urge to lecture her about missing that much sleep, but the words tumbled out of my mouth before I could catch them. "What? Why?"

"Missing persons case. No one sleeps until we find her."

"That's a hazard. Can't you all sleep in shifts or something?" My voice was slightly higher than I planned. She laughed.

"Appreciate the concern. And we do. I just can't sleep until I know something either way."

I sighed. "I get that. But still, you have to take care of yourself. In order to keep your mind sharp so you don't miss something... you need rest. And cut out all those energy drinks."

There was a slight pause, and then I heard something hit something hard.

"How'd you know?"

"It was a lucky guess. Those aren't good for your heart. Don't drink too many." There was another pause, so I added, "Don't drink more."

"Okay, now that I can try to do... after I finish this one."

I sighed. Her laugh vibrated through the phone.

"Don't worry, Doctor Elwood. I will endeavor to follow your caffeine restrictions and pass them on to my partner. I lost count of how many she's had. Now tell me about you and what you've been up to today. Any updates on your deal?"

I didn't know what to say for a few minutes. "Well..." I told her about the possibility of mediation.

"That just sounds like a nightmare."

"She hasn't filed an official complaint, but once she does, social services gets involved. I think she was hoping I would just hand Dani over, but I'm not."

"You want me to beat her up—well, not me. I'll outsource the job to Zelina; she likes to fight. She could handle it for you."

I laughed. "I appreciate the offer, although as a member of law enforcement, I don't think it's something you should be offering. I'd rather not bring violence into this."

"Yet... I understand."

"I don't think that's what I said."

"Heavily implied. Does Dani like it here?"

"Umm… yeah, I think she does. She's made a lot of friends. And she likes her school. So that's good."

"Well, that's good. If anyone asks her what she wants, she'll probably say she wants to stay with you. Some judges ask that and take it into consideration."

"That's good to know. What have you been up to all day since you're at home? I know you haven't just been relaxing."

She took a deep breath before recounting the Cynthia Harmon case. She told me all about the missing girls and the bodies found on Tory Craster's land. What he did with his wife and how that affected his son.

I had met Tory once. He came to the office because he had a deep gash on his arm. I told Riley, and she inhaled sharply.

"On his arm?"

"Yeah, he said he was fixing his truck and wasn't paying attention under the hood. When he stood up, his arm caught on something. I never looked under the hood of an eighteen-wheeler, so I didn't know if it was true or not. But it was deep, like something dug in and tried to take a piece of his arm."

"Huh, when was this?"

"Not long after I moved here. He was like my fifth patient, I think. He seemed so nice and welcoming."

"It was probably one of the girls that he kidnapped. She might have tried to fight back."

"Damn... I never would have thought that of him, but I guess people are full of surprises."

"They really are."

"I saw you on the news last night," I said after a beat of silence. "They played your statement after you rescued that girl."

"Oh, god," she groaned. "I probably looked like a mess."

"You looked fine. Honestly a lot better than you did a couple hours later. You've been taking your painkillers, right?"

I heard the rattle of a pill bottle in the background and a swallow. "Yes, I'm taking my painkillers."

I chuckled. "I can't call you to remind you every time, you know."

"I'm taking them!" she protested. "I need to get this thing healed as fast as possible. I'm going back in tomorrow to help find Delilah. But…"

"She probably won't be alive. I thought that earlier. The longer it takes, the more likely you'll be looking for a dead body."

"Exactly. We're just trying to brace ourselves for that. And I'm looking into a few other leads. I worry that I may have used up all our good luck in rescuing Mia."

"Don't think of it like that," I said. "You rescued her. That was a good thing. And you'll try your best to find all these other people."

"Again with the vote of confidence in my abilities. But, thank you."

"Right, well, I won't keep you. Just wanted to say hi."

"I appreciate the distraction."

"Yeah, me too."

I hung up the phone and tossed it over on the cushion next to me. There was something about Riley. In some ways, she reminded me of Marie; she was sweet and helpful. I saw it when she dealt with the old man in the decrepit house. He was ornery and didn't want us there, and she didn't like me too much, but she still asked me to join her on that excursion. She wanted to make sure he was okay even though no one seemed to care about him.

Marie was like that, too. Always wanted to take care of people. Always there to lend a helping hand. But where Marie tried to keep the peace, which usually meant she kept her thoughts and opinions to herself, Riley seemed to do the opposite. She was filled with snarky remarks and had no problem telling someone off. A quality I wished Marie had when it came to her sister.

When Jamie came around, it was made clear to me, especially after we were married, that I was not wanted around them. I would leave and go to a friend's house for a few hours. When I came back, she was usually gone. Marie never told me what they talked about, even though I asked. She never talked about her sister when she wasn't around. Their relationship was truly strange. At first, I thought I couldn't understand it because of my strained relationship with my mother and Isaac at the time.

"Nope, it's weird," my friend Reggie had told me. He was one of the few people I knew who had an older sibling who knew both Jamie and Marie. "Yeah, their relationship is hella awkward. I mean, Marie is married now; you would think that Jamie would have loosened the reins a little. She still seems to think that her sister is all hers."

The conversation had started when I first told him Marie was pregnant. We hadn't announced it yet, but I was so excited that I couldn't hold it in. He grinned, but his smile had faltered for a moment. A dark cloud had passed over his face.

"What?"

"I just... I wonder how Jamie's going to take it. Once Marie has that baby, Jamie won't be in the picture anymore."

"Well, she's still her sister. She can come over."

Reggie had shrugged. "When has that ever been enough for her? She wants all of Marie's attention, but you can't get that with a newborn. She's going to realize she's not number one in Marie's life anymore."

He was right. When we finally announced it, Marie was twelve weeks along. We gathered our friends and Jamie together and told them the good news. Shouts of "Congratulations!" scattered around the room, but stopped at Jamie. She glared at Marie like she had betrayed her. Like Marie had done something wrong, and she was going to get her for it. Later that night, I heard them talking in hushed voices in the kitchen.

"You said you would never have a child. You didn't want to end up like Mom!"

"I never said that. You did. I'll be a better mother than ours, don't you think? Don't sour this, Jamie. Be happy for me."

"I am. I just think you are making a mistake. A baby will just tie you to him more than you already are. You don't want that."

"My life is perfect right now, and I'm happy. Be happy for me, please."

Jamie wasn't. All throughout the pregnancy, Jamie was cold toward Marie every time she mentioned the baby. That conversation was why Jamie's actions now confused me. She never wanted Marie to have Dani. She even told her one night over dinner it wasn't too late to have an abortion. Marie said she was joking, but I never thought she was.

Why would she want her now?

CHAPTER SEVENTEEN

Riley Quinn

The next morning, I hobbled into the station on my crutch. I felt a lot better, but still not a hundred percent.

"Any developments while I was away?" I asked as I slowly settled into my desk.

"Not really," she said. "Keith said he's almost done with the body we found. I've been checking missing persons reports from all over the state, and I have four contenders so far." She turned her screen so I could see it. Four pictures of women who resembled each other were on the screen. They all looked like Delilah.

"All of these women have gone missing in the last four years. Rory Fowler is the most recent. She went missing from Fresno two months ago, I believe."

"That's pretty far away. She does look like the victim, though. That might be the one." I stared at the screen for a long moment. "Any tattoos or marks?"

"It says she has a tattoo on the palm of her hand."

"That's her. We just need Keith to confirm it."

As if on cue, her phone rang.

"Keith has it for us. He wants us to come down so he can go through it with us."

The morgue was so cold I felt like I needed a jacket just to stand in the room. I had to admit, it made my ankle feel better, though.

Keith smiled at us when we walked in. "How are you doing, Riley?"

"Been worse," I said. "What have you got for us?"

"I was able to run her fingerprints and there was a hit in the system. Her name is Rory Fowler and she's been missing for a couple of months."

"Yeah, we were just looking through missing person reports and saw her."

"Oh, well, good. This is her, and she's been in the field for a while. I suspect she's been there since the night she disappeared, judging by levels of decomp and bug infestations. That being said, her manner of death at first was difficult to find because the tissue around her neck had started turning to mush. After studying the layer beneath her skin, I can confidently say she was strangled. Now, with what, I don't know. A rope or a scarf."

"Was she sexually assaulted?" asked Zelina.

He shrugged. "That I can't say for sure. She might have been but any evidence of it is all gone. From the waist down, I mean, it is pretty much gone. Other than that, she doesn't look like she was beaten or anything."

My head tilted to the side. "So there was no evidence of bruises or a beating or her being dragged to that area?"

"Nope. I think she was killed there. There were no signs of a struggle or anything. Someone strangled her and left her there. Which is odd for a variety of reasons."

I found it strange too. How did she even get out there? Did she drive? If she did, then where was her car? Did someone drive her out there, kill her, and dump her?

"And we found nothing with the body, on or around. The area was clear, and there was no evidence of the body. I believe that the killer has done this before. There's no hair, no blood, no DNA under her fingernails because someone clipped them," he said.

I blinked. "Really? The killer knew enough to do that. Yeah, he's probably done this before."

"I looked everywhere. Searched what was left of her body for foreign DNA and hairs. I even looked in her mouth. There's no sign of the killer. He was careful, which is scary."

"Yeah," said Zelina.

"I wish I had more to give you, but this was all we found."

"That's more than we had when we got here, so thank you." I walked out of the room and headed back to the car. The sunny day was blistering compared to the cold of the morgue. I leaned against the car. Now there was another family that we needed to notify.

A patrol unit passed by. Everyone was still looking for Delilah. We wouldn't rest until we found her. But now we needed to find Rory's next of kin and figure out what she was doing in town. The station was quieter than normal. Most of the patrol units were out searching for Delilah, looking in ditches, abandoned buildings, and other places where someone could hide a body.

When we got back to the station, I dialed the number on the missing person report. It rang three times before someone picked up.

"Hello?"

"Hello, I'm Detective Quinn, with the Pine Brooke PD. Is Rachel—"

"Have you found my daughter?" she asked sharply, her voice laced with panic and alertness. "Have you?"

I took a deep breath. "We believe so, ma'am. We've found Rory."

"I see." She paused for a long moment. "She's not alive, is she?"

"I'm so sorry, but no she's not. We'll… we'll need you to come down to the morgue to identify the body."

"How did she die? Was she murdered?"

"We believe so. We are still investigating, so we don't know exactly what happened yet. Can I ask you a few questions?"

She swallowed hard. "If it will help." Her voice was small and thin. I heard the tears behind it. I needed to make this quick before she broke down on the phone.

"Thanks. I know this is hard. Do you know why Rory was in Pine Brooke? Was she moving here or meeting someone?"

"Rory liked going places on her own. She loves… loved the outdoors. Camping, hiking, fishing. That sort of thing. I couldn't go with her because my arthritis had started acting up."

"When did you last hear from her?"

"We texted a little while she was down there. She sent me pictures of the fish she caught, stuff like that. But then she went quiet for a while. I figured at first it was the reception, you know. Sometimes it'll be a few days. But she will always let me know when she's on her way back. She was supposed to come back that Sunday and I still hadn't heard from her. I waited for her, but she never showed up. I called and called. I left so many messages, but her mailbox is full. She never called me back."

"Is that like her?"

"No. She might not have called me right back or answered my every call, but she did call back. She would have come home, I don't care what anyone says."

"Why do you say that?"

"Rory had gotten into a little trouble when she was younger. You know, people, sometimes they have a hard time letting things go. She had some run-ins with our local sheriff in the past. But she's been clean for a long time. And he didn't believe that she hadn't just run away."

"I see. Did she have something to come back to?"

"She just got a good job that she was really excited about. That's why she was on her way back Sunday, they called her and asked her to start that Monday. But she never came home. She was so happy about it, she would have come home. She would have come home to me or at least let me know she was okay."

"I understand. We haven't been able to find her cell phone or her purse, or her car for that matter. What kind of car did she drive? I can't find a car registered in her name."

"Oh, the car was mine. It was registered in my name. It was a white Volkswagen Passat. There's a Hello Kitty charm hanging from the rearview mirror. If that helps."

"It does. Do you know your license plate number?"

"Yes."

I wrote down the number and told her that I would call her and let her know if and when we learned anything. She thanked me, a sob on the edge of her voice before she hung up. I hated talking to the loved ones of our victims. Absolutely hated it. It was the hardest thing I had to do as a detective. Telling them that someone they loved was murdered and listening to them cry and then having to ask them questions before they had time to sit with their grief, never seemed right to me. But it was the best time to ask questions while the last time they saw the person was fresh in their mind.

I told Zelina everything Rory's mother had said while I was putting a BOLO out on her car. "You know what? I'll tell some patrol units to check local tow yards. Maybe someone towed the car from the side of the road since she's been gone for so long."

"That's a good idea. Hopefully someone will find it."

"Yeah, hopefully." After I put out the alert, I looked over my notes from my conversation. "There has to be a link between her and Delilah. Their disappearances are almost identical. Both women were driving and then nothing. No one's heard from them."

"So we're ruling out the connection to Mia?"

"I hate to say it, but that must have been a coincidence. We found Jimmy, we found Marli. I don't know if Delilah's involved in that case at all."

"Which puts us right back at square one."

Zelina started looking through missing person reports searching for women who resembled both Rory and Delilah. It was clear that Rory was not his first murder, and she wouldn't be his last.

It only took a few minutes before my phone rang.

"Yes? Okay. We're on our way."

I shoved the phone back in my front pocket. "They found Rory's car in the tow yard. Along with Delilah's."

CHAPTER EIGHTEEN

Riley Quinn

WE DROVE TO THE TOW YARD FOLLOWING THREE PATROL CARS. A sinking feeling came over me. We still couldn't find Delilah. Part of me wanted to find her, but part of me hoped we wouldn't find her in the trunk of her car. It had been so hot lately; if her body had been in the trunk, it would have been unrecognizable. Turned bone stewing in liquid fat, skin, and other liquids.

I didn't want to see that. And I didn't want her family to hear about it. We followed the officers until they stopped in front of a white car. I moved toward the trunk and looked at the license plate. It was a match for the car Rory was driving the night she went missing.

"Well, this is the car." I slipped on a pair of gloves and opened the car door. "Interesting." On her passenger seat rested her car registration. But everything else was missing. No purse, no phone, nothing. "That's so strange."

Zelina checked the backseat. There was nothing back there either. An officer popped the trunk.

"It looks like it's been cleaned out." Officer Rainwater ran a gloved hand along the trunk. "There's no hair, no fibers. Nothing. Who cleans their trunk out like this?" He looked at me, his brows furrowed.

"I know I don't."

I looked in the trunk. It was like someone took a vacuum cleaner and vacuumed out the trunk, then shampooed the carpet. I couldn't think of anyone that would do that. Unless there was sand in the trunk or something.

"He knows what he's doing," I said, mostly to myself. It looked like the killer wasn't sure what fibers he left behind, so he cleaned everything. The car smelled of some kind of lavender-scented cleaner with a hint of bleach. There was no trace of Rory or the person that abducted her.

"Riley!"

I looked up. Zelina waved me over and I ambled over with the crutch. "Take a look at Delilah's car. Looks like it's been cleaned."

"So does Rory's. Wiped down with bleach on the inside and vacuumed out. The killer knows their business."

"Probably watches a lot of *CSI* and true crime shows."

She had a point. They might have learned something from TV. But it was too meticulous. Usually, killers left something behind. They didn't intend to, of course, but they got caught up in the moment and left hair or saliva or something.

This person went through both cars with a fine-toothed comb. There weren't even hairs from the victims. I walked over to Delilah's car. "Did you find her registration?"

"No," said Zelina.

"I searched Rory's car; all through the glove box, there was nothing there, except the registration on the front seat."

Zelina opened the passenger side door and searched through the glove box. "Same here. Also, no purses, IDs, or her bags. She was coming for a few days; she had to pack some stuff. But it is all gone."

"He's trying to make it harder to identify them. You keep everything in your purse and your phone. If we don't have that, it might take us a while to figure out who they were. Or he wants to keep a souvenir."

"That's possible. He could go through their stuff, find something he likes, and throw the rest away," said Zelina.

"Okay, I know it looks like the killer left nothing behind, but I still want both cars searched and printed. There has to be something in one of them."

While the techs got busy, Zelina and I spoke with the owner of the truck yard. "Hey, Nicky!"

I waved. Nicky Wilkes was the owner of the tow yard. She was one of three people that worked there. "Hey, ladies! I'll help any way I can, but I don't know anything."

"Well, we need to know where you picked up the cars."

"Oh... yeah. I can get that for you. Just let me check the logs." She turned around and walked into her office. She came back with a clipboard. "Alright. I know the second car I found on Jerry Rodgers's property. He said it had been there for a while, and he was tired of looking at it. It happens sometimes and he really hates people being on his land."

I remembered Mr. Rodgers. He had lived on that property for years. His family always lived there. Just on the edge of town. "Okay. That's good. What about the white Passat?"

She lifted one sheet of paper, then another one. "Here. You know what, I found that car on the same property. He called that one in, too. Let me see... yeah, when he went to bed that night, it wasn't there. But when he woke up the next morning, it was there. And no one ever came back for it."

"Yeah, she was already dead."

"The body you all found?"

I nodded.

"Her poor family."

"Thank you." I turned to walk away, but a thought stopped me dead in my tracks. "Could you do us a favor and check your records for any other cars you found on that property? And then get back to us?"

She shrugged. "Sure. If you think it will help. I'll make the list and send it to you."

"Thanks."

I followed Zelina back to the car. "If Mr. Rodgers's property is where he drops off their cars, I wonder how many he's left there."

"Yeah, I wonder why he feels so comfortable doing that."

"No one goes there."

Mr. Rodgers lived alone after his wife left him. She was tired of his drinking, so she left him and took the kids with her, and none of them ever looked back. He lived alone on the property ever since. He didn't like anyone on his land. There was a rocking chair on his front porch where he sat and watched people drive by. Daring them to stop near his fence.

No one liked him. He was not a nice man. Always looking for a fight and a drink. Pretty much the opposite of nice old Mr. Gill.

~

I held up my badge as I neared the front porch of Mr. Rodgers' property. The morning had already turned to afternoon. A search party was put together to search remote areas to look for Delilah. We were stuck talking to him.

"What do you want?" the man asked. "Break your leg or something?"

I didn't take the bait. "We wanted to speak with you about the cars found on your land in the last few weeks."

"You here to tell them to scram?"

"We hope to be able to."

"Bout time the cops did something useful around here."

I smiled. "Of course." I considered rescuing a kidnapped teenage girl something useful, but for the sake of this conversation, I tried to be as reassuring as possible. "Did you see who left them?"

"Nope. I went to bed and woke up, and there they were. No one was in them, and the doors were locked… I called the tow trucks to take them."

"Did you do that in the morning when you found them?"

"Nah, I waited a little while. At first, I thought someone had run out of gas, because that I can understand. So I waited for them some time to get back to their car, but no one ever came. Before or after they were towed."

"So they just left their cars here and walked away. Have you noticed anything strange around your property other than the cars?"

He shrugged. "Same ole shit, different day. No one comes through here. That's why seeing the cars was so weird. Like, where the hell were they going?"

"That's a good point. If you think of anything that might help, please give me a call." I handed him my card.

"Will do. If it happens again, I'll call you before the tow truck."

"That would be great."

We left him on the porch and headed to where the search party was supposed to meet up. "Whoever left the car is from the area. They knew that no one came through here because of Mr. Rodgers. So they knew that they could leave it there and it would be a while before someone found it. Or it would get dragged to the tow yard and sit."

"Okay. So someone from town. Shame Tory is in jail."

"He would have been the perfect person to blame this on." My phone vibrated in my pocket. "Yes? Okay, we are on our way."

"Techs want us to go to Cynthia's house. They found something."

Before heading to the place where the search party was supposed to meet up, we went to the house. I followed techs to the backyard, which had been dug up. Still on the ground were skeletal remains. "Cynthia," I breathed.

"Probably," said the tech. "The hyoid bone in the neck is broken. We also found this in her hands, and we think you might want to take it with you." Another tech handed a plastic evidence bag that contained a single piece of paper. It was covered in dirt, but still seemed intact. "Once we dig her up and take her back to the morgue, we will be able to give you more information."

"Okay, thanks." I had thought she was buried at the house, somewhere on the property. At first, I thought maybe it was in a wall or something. But no, he put her in the backyard. There was no proof that her father killed her, but who else could bury her in the backyard without anyone noticing? It had to be him.

"What is that?" Zelina asked.

"It's like a note or something. The handwriting looks like it could be Cynthia's."

Once we were back in the police lab, I carefully smoothed out the crumpled-up page, brushed dirt away from it, and everything became clear. I looked up. "I think I know why he killed her and why her mother killed him."

Jason, he's my boyfriend. I think he is. We kiss a lot and he tells me how much he loves me. I believe him but sometimes I find it hard to believe that anyone could love me. He wants to do more, but I'm not ready for that. Sometimes, when he touches me, it makes my skin crawl. I try not to let it show because I know it would upset him if I pulled away, but I want to. The thought of another person touching me, being inside me, is more than I can handle. Dad would be mad. I'm only supposed to love him; he made me promise.

My stomach soured. Zelina shook her head "Well, that answers all of my questions. What are we going to do with it?"

I looked at the side of her face. "What do you mean?"

"That note is Camille Harmon's motive for killing her husband. Are we going to turn her in and question the validity of the coroner's report, or are we going to walk away? I looked into that coroner that Keith spoke so highly of, and she was the best of the best. But... while she was working in the morgue, her daughter was raped, and then she hung herself. That was why she had to step away. Mr. Harmon was her last case."

"You think she knew something?"

"She and Camille knew each other. They had grown up together. Small town, they are probably still friends."

"She fixed her report to corroborate what Camille said." My fingers drummed against the desk. That would make sense. Was this enough to satiate my curiosity? I didn't know. I had an idea of what happened, but until Camille told me the truth, that was all it was—an idea.

The only thing I could do was call Camille. "I need to meet with you. You aren't in trouble, but there's something I want to talk to you about."

We agreed to meet at a coffee shop in the morning and hung up.

"Okay, that takes care of that. What was Delilah's car doing there?" I asked, and my brain switched cases automatically. "It's miles away from where she was last seen and where she was headed. What was she doing there?"

"Maybe she wasn't. Maybe the killer just dropped her car off there because it was convenient."

"Possible."

The Preston family came back to the station after another unsuccessful search. Marissa stared at me for a long moment before she walked over.

"Did you identify the body?"

"We did. It wasn't your sister. It was a woman named Rory."

Her face fell, her anger melting away. "I heard you found her car."

"We did. If she was coming for the baby shower, what would she have brought with her? We found nothing in the car."

Marissa looked startled. "That's not like her. She always brought a lot more than she needed. Clothes, books, extra decorations in case we needed them. There should have been several bags in the car. What about her purse? She never went anywhere without it and her phone."

"Not in the car."

"Maybe she took it with her. Maybe the car broke down, she had to walk and got turned around."

"That is possible…" *Possible, but also very unlikely.* Someone would have seen her in the last few days. If she had been wandering around with constant patrols looking for her, she would have been found. But if she passed out due to the heat, it might have been a lot more difficult to see her. "Her car was completely intact. No broken windows or dented doors. I don't know, it could have broken down, but it didn't seem that way."

Marissa frowned. "Either she walked away from it, or she got out to help someone, and they got her away from her car."

"Now that is possible. I didn't think about that until you said it. She could have pulled over thinking she was helping someone with a flat, and she was walking into a trap."

"And then they took her car and drove to a place they knew no one would look for it or that it would be towed," Zelina finished.

We answered a few more of Marissa's questions and then she went back to do more searching with the patrol officers. But she didn't seem very hopeful.

Now we just needed to find her body. That would give us something to go on. The killer couldn't have been that careful with every kill. He'd have to slip up sometime. Maybe in his early kills, he might have left something behind. That would explain why he was so careful now. He didn't want anyone to be able to link the cases together.

"Where is she?" asked Zelina. "She didn't just vanish. That was impossible. Maybe someone is keeping her."

Tory immediately popped into my mind, along with the young woman he kept in his back room. If someone was keeping Delilah for an extended time, then that might explain why we hadn't found her. Keith said Rory was probably killed the same night she went missing.

"I know what you are thinking. But Keith said he couldn't say for certain. She might have been killed a day or two after she went missing."

I leaned back in my chair. It was possible. Maybe he kept his victims for a couple of days before killing them and dumping them. "Did Tory trigger something in this town?"

Zelina shrugged. "There's bad people everywhere. He had nothing to do with this, and it isn't happening because of him. This person has been at this for a long time."

CHAPTER NINETEEN

Riley Quinn

I started calling more of Rory's friends. I needed to know everything about her life; maybe there was a link to Delilah that we may have missed or hadn't explored yet.

"Yes?"

I explained who I was and why I was calling. The woman on the other line gasped. "I knew something had happened to her. She wouldn't have just disappeared like that. But I hoped it wasn't like this."

"I need to know more about her personal life. Maybe some things that her mother didn't know. Was she dating anyone?"

"No, not recently. She broke up with her boyfriend a year ago. I don't think there has been anyone since him."

"How did he take it?"

She sighed. "He was upset. More so than her. He stalked her for a little while. I told her she should get a restraining order or something, but she didn't want to do that. She said he'd get over it."

"Why did they break up?"

"He wanted to get married, and she wasn't ready. He had this dream in his head of a wife and five kids. Rory was twenty-five, and she'd finally gotten off the drugs that she did when she was younger. Her life was just getting started. She didn't want to rush into that."

"That's understandable. So—" The words caught in my throat. What she said sounded very familiar. *Where had I heard that before?* "What was his name?"

"Tyler Rosales."

"I see. Was there anything going on in her life?"

"Nope. She was just trying to get back on her feet, you know. She got laid off and was looking for a job. She had just got one before she disappeared. It isn't fair."

"I know it's not. Thank you for speaking with me. If you think of anything else, please call." By the time I hung up, Zelina had returned to her desk with four energy drinks. She slid two over, but I only took one.

"Pace yourself," I said. "Doctor Elwood says these are bad for your heart."

She rolled her eyes as she popped the top.

"Guess what?" I asked as she took a long, slow sip.

She set the can back on the desk. "Seriously? Stop making me wait."

"Rory and Delilah dated the same guy. Tyler Rosales."

Zelina straightened in her chair. "Are you serious?"

I nodded. "We need to talk to him again. This can't be a coincidence. And she broke up with him for the same reason Delilah did. He wanted to get married and have children."

"Can't be a coincidence."

I picked up the phone and put it to my ear. A thought popped into my head, and the phone slipped from my ear. "Better yet, I'll get patrol units to pick him up."

"That's a better idea. What are you going to do?"

"Oh, I need to go follow up with the doctor," I said with a wink. She nodded knowingly at me as I slipped out of the station and headed out of the town.

By the time I found the coffee shop, I was five minutes late.

I recognized Camille Harmon in the back booth from her driver's license photo. She looked the same but different. Tired. Like she hadn't gotten a good night's sleep in years. I quietly slid into the booth. She looked up. Her eyes bloodshot, her bottom lip shaking. She craned her neck to look outside when I joined her at the booth.

"You came alone."

"Like I said. You aren't in any trouble. I just want to know what happened. I mean, I have an idea, but it's just an idea. I want to know the truth."

Her shoulders relaxed a little. "Did you find her?"

"Yes, ma'am, I believe so. We found a body buried in the backyard. We still need to confirm her identity, but I believe that it is her."

"This whole time, she was already home. All that looking for her and for nothing. She was dead before I even knew she was missing." A single tear rolled down her cheek. She dabbed her eye with a napkin.

"Tell me what happened."

Mrs. Harmon took a long, slow sip of her coffee. She reached into her bag and produced a small pink notebook, a teenage girl's diary. "I read her journal. Not while she was alive but after she had been missing for a couple of days. It was in her room, and I thought it might help me figure out where she might have gone. People kept telling me she ran away. Said I was too hard on her. It was possible, but I didn't want to believe it. So I read it. I got to a passage—" more tears streaked her face.

"Take your time, ma'am." I passed her a tissue, which she took gratefully.

"My husband was... he was raping her. I didn't know. I swear I didn't know." She choked down a sob. "I swear. I couldn't believe it. How could he? I didn't tell anyone. At first, I wasn't sure. I thought maybe she just slipped that in there in case I read it to catch me or something. I just couldn't picture him hurting her. He loved her. He was the main one looking for her; in every search, he was there even if he had to take off from work. But then I started watching him. I mean, really watching him. Paying attention to his every movement. He spent a lot of time in the backyard. He would sit by the flowerbeds near the back window. Rocking in the rocking chair, staring at the flowers."

A chill ran down through my spine.

"I thought maybe he missed her so much that he needed to be by himself. Sit still or something like that. I did. I'd sit in my room in the dark and just cry. Sometimes, I'd pray. The more I watched him, the more I realized something didn't feel right. He seemed paranoid every time the police came to the house. He'd jump to his feet and talk to them in the doorway. He'd talk fast to get them away from the house. And when they were inside, he kept looking behind him and toward the backyard. I thought it was weird, and one night, I confronted him with the journal. I earmarked all the pages where she talked about him. There were so many instances, and it didn't just start. She never said how long, but it seemed like it was a long time. He looked at it and stammered over his words so many times he wasn't making sense. Finally, he said that she seduced him. If it wasn't for her, it never would have happened. Apparently, she and her outfits were *enticing* to him. His own daughter!"

My heart broke for her and Cynthia. "I'm so sorry."

"He broke down crying, and that's when he told me what happened." She took another sip of coffee and swallowed hard. "She had a boyfriend, and she really liked him. But she couldn't let him touch her. He kept asking her why, and in her journal, she wrote that she was going to tell him. She trusted him. He read it, and he knew he was running out of time. And he was scared. They got into an argument that day. He tried to talk her out of it. He told her that if she told, it would ruin the family. It would ruin everything. That's what he told me. He didn't do it because he knew how upset I would be if I found out. What would the people in *town* think?"

I leaned back. It was exactly what I thought it was.

"I didn't care what people thought. He was just trying to save his own ass. He would have lost his job and gone to jail. He tried to make her be quiet and even told her he would stop. He'd never do it again. But she wouldn't listen. She wanted to finally say something. She wanted to tell on him so he could go to jail. And he got really angry, and he killed her. Choked the life out of her, but he raped her first."

I shook my head. I knew he killed her, and her hyoid bone was broken. So she was telling the truth about that.

"I got so angry. I killed him. Tried to make it look like a suicide, but the medical examiner saw right through it. She came to me, she was an old friend. I told her everything, and she said she would make it go away."

"Why did you take the page out of her journal and bury it with her?"

"I didn't... I didn't want that to be the story people told about my girl," she said tearfully. "If she was just missing, maybe she ran away. Maybe she had gone to live a whole new life. Even if they eventually figured she was dead, none of that happened to her. But if people knew the truth, that would be all that was left of her memory. The horrible story of what happened to her. It was the least I could do to preserve her memory. So I buried the pages with her in the backyard." She leaned back in her seat. "And there it is. That's what happened. Are you going to arrest me now?"

I sat there for a long time, trying to figure it out. "I don't think so," I said. "I'm so sorry. If I had known… well, if I had known, I wouldn't have needed to try to find out the truth."

"I knew you would. As soon as you came snooping around, I could tell that you were going to find out the truth eventually. I can't blame you for that. You were doing it for Cynthia. I can never blame you for that."

I took a sip of my coffee. "It's a shame that Tory Craster killed her," I said. "I'll make sure the evidence puts him away for a long time."

She looked up at me and slowly nodded, understanding in her eyes.

I slid back out of the booth. "Thank you for meeting with me. Goodbye, Mrs. Harmon." I walked out of the coffee shop and headed back to my car, rage and sorrow filling me.

Of course I wasn't going to arrest her. I had never planned on doing it. I just needed to know what happened, and now that I did, I could move on. Cynthia got justice, in a way. It wasn't a way that I would have liked to solve things. But it was the way it was.

I drove back to the station in a hurry, trying to get back before the officers returned with Tyler. When I walked in, Zelina sat at her desk. She looked up as soon as I walked in. She threw her hands up.

"I know." I looked up just as Captain Williams exited his office. "I'll tell you about it later."

She gave a small nod before Williams walked over to us.

"Anything?"

I told him about Rory and Delilah having had the same boyfriend and that we were waiting for officers to come back with him. He nodded as he listened.

"And no signs of Delilah?"

"No. I'm starting to think the killer might keep his victims for a little while before he kills them."

"It would make sense," added Zelina. "Coroner can't say for sure how long she was out there because of the heat and where her body was found."

"Okay, so she might still be alive. Squeeze the boyfriend. There's got to be more to this story than this."

"Yes, sir."

The officers arrived with Tyler, but he did not look pleased to see us. He stared at me as he was led to the front desk. I moved toward him.

"Well, Hello, Mr. Rosales." I leaned on the front desk. "Nice to finally meet you."

"You're the detective that called me about Delilah." He looked around the room. "If you wanted to talk to me again, you could have just called me." He grinned.

"I could have, but I wanted to talk to you about Rory in person."

His smile evaporated instantly. His eyes darted to the door.

"Yeah, we have a lot to talk about. Take him to an interrogation room."

The officers dragged him back down the hall..

"You think he did something to them?" Zelina asked.

I shrugged. "I wasn't sure, but I wouldn't put it past him."

She sighed. "Okay, let's get this over with."

Tyler sat at the table with his hands clasped, and I sat down across from him while Zelina closed the door behind her.

"I didn't do anything to Rory or Delilah."

"Except date both of them at the same time," I said. "Did they know about that?"

He faltered. "Well, no, but—"

"So this whole thing about wanting to settle down and have kids was, what—was that some sick joke? Just stringing them along like that? No wonder they left you," I growled. I was sick of his crap.

"Look, I don't know what Rory is saying about me, but that's not true."

"Rory's dead."

He blinked and leaned back. He looked genuinely startled by the revelation, but that could have been an act. He had time to practice.

"I didn't kill her. I swear."

"Okay. But two women connected to you turn out to be missing and then found dead. I don't believe in coincidences. So what do you think happened?"

"How the hell should I know? They left me. I wasn't keeping tabs on them."

"Really?" Zelina walked around the room with her hands in her pockets. "See, the way I heard it, you stalked Rory after she left you. You couldn't let go."

"You seem to have a habit of choosing women who do not want to be with you. Why is that, you think?"

His eyes narrowed at me. "I didn't do anything to either of them. They didn't want to be with me, and I let it go. I have an alibi."

"Okay. For which one?"

He snarled. "I don't know when Rory was killed. I hadn't heard about it until now."

"Oh, right. Let's fix that. She was probably killed two months ago."

"I was on a business trip in New York around that time. I was there for a week trying to fix a deal that fell through. Delilah's been missing for a couple of days now. I was in LA for a few days. Hanging out with friends. I checked into the hotel at about two o'clock."

I slid my pad across the table with a pen. "Write down the name of the hotel and your friend's numbers so we can check your alibi. Also where you stayed in New York."

"Done."

He scribbled down the information and slid it back. "Check that, and then let me go." He folded his arms across his chest. I rolled my eyes.

Maybe he didn't do anything, but he knew something. Zelina and I went back to our desk and called both hotels and his friends to check his alibis.

"I guess he didn't do it," I said when I set the phone down. Tyler was right; he had been nowhere near Pine Brooke for weeks. I went back into the room. "I guess you were telling the truth." I sat down.

"Can I go now?"

"Tell me more about Delilah. Did she have problems with anyone?"

He shrugged. "She was a pretty easygoing person. Maybe her boss."

"Why would she have problems with her boss?" I leaned back in my chair as I listened.

"She was suing him for sexual harassment. There was a class action suit or something. He groped her and propositioned her. She wasn't the only one either. There were other women. I don't really know if the process got started or whatever. It was around when we broke up."

"Her sister never mentioned it."

"I don't think they know. Her family would have been more than upset about it. They would have tried to make her come home. And she didn't want to."

"Why not?"

"She wanted to be on her own two feet or whatever. I don't know. It's been a while since I talked to any of them, but I got the feeling that Delilah didn't want to confront them on it if it was bad news. She didn't want them to worry."

"Okay. Thank you for coming in. You can go now."

He jumped up. "Good. I told you I didn't do it." he walked out of the room while I sat there tapping my fingers on the table.

Could her boss have had something to do with it? Then what about Rory? What did she have to do with this? "Curiouser and curiouser."

CHAPTER TWENTY

Jamie Washington

JAMIE PEERED OUT THE WINDOW EVERY MORNING SINCE SHE HAD moved into her new rented home. It wasn't as big as she would have liked, but it served its purpose. She stood in front of the window, coffee cup in hand, watching the children walking by.

Her heart stammered in her chest when she saw her. Dani looked every bit like her mother. Dark curly hair, sparkling hazel eyes. She even walked like her. She was Marie reincarnate. Her chance to make things right. To fix what she had done. She just wanted the chance to make it all better, and she would as soon as Dani came home with her.

Dani bounced down the sidewalk with Bonnie in tow. She had once walked to school by herself, but not anymore. Jamie noted the change and knew it was because of her. They were afraid she'd try to talk to her niece or perhaps take her away. A ghost of a smile kissed her lips. She had them nervous. Worried even. That was good. They might be more amenable to her demands if they were scared she would go to the police about the abuse.

"Don't let him keep her. Do whatever you have to do. I'm putting all my trust in you, Jamie."

It was never clear when Jamie's mind cracked, shattered into a thousand pieces she could never put together quite right. Something was always missing. It might have been in her childhood, or it could have been when her sister died. She didn't know. In truth, she didn't care, but she was curious about it. Something always felt off with her.

She never did the things children normally did. She hadn't liked playing with others, and when she did, she had to be in charge. She didn't want a dog or any kind of animal; they were pointless. Just another mouth to feed. Another thing to give attention to. When her mother's boyfriend of the week bought the girls a puppy, Jamie despised it. She never asked for a puppy, and yet there it was, something she had to take care of. But Marie loved it, and it loved her like everything else in this world. It curled up in Marie's lap every day and slept in her bed. When she left the house, it was clear who its favorites were.

She hated it for a variety of reasons, the main one being that it took Marie's attention away from her. Jamie slept in Marie's bed when she couldn't sleep, but now her spot was taken by the dog whose name she could never remember. She sat next to Marie on the sofa and sometimes fell asleep in her lap.

The dog was taking too much from her, so when it ran away, she was delighted. Marie cried, though. She sat outside for weeks, yelling for it to come home. Jamie was glad when she finally gave up.

"I know Marie. I know. I will do whatever I have to do to bring your daughter home. Don't you worry."

"I know you will."

She watched as Bonnie stayed on the sidewalk and Dani ran up to the front door of the school on her own; turning around to wave at her before entering. The nanny stood there for a long moment before turning around and walking back across the street. Jamie was curious as to how long this would last. How long would they keep such a close eye on her? It couldn't last forever. They would get complacent, having gone so long without seeing Jamie. Eventually, they'd forget they were supposed to be on guard, and then Dani would be left alone. Just long enough for Jamie to get her hands on her.

She had been staying in the house since she moved in. She wanted to go out, but there was nothing in Pine Brooke worth exploring. She had seen all she needed to see. And going to the diner was out of the question. She hadn't been since she had a run-in with Isaac, who had left the kitchen specifically to speak with her.

"You've got some nerve."

She shrugged. "A girl's got to eat."

"Don't they have places for you to eat elsewhere?"

"None as good as this shit hole. Figures you'd be working here. Probably all you'll ever be good for." She gave him her best smile. Warm and kind. A smile she practiced over the years until she got it just right.

He grimaced. "Well, since you're here, you do not want to eat the food anyone brings you. Can't speak to what's in it." It was his turn to smile. He walked away and left her staring at the menu. She closed it and slid out of the booth. She would never eat there again. It was the third time he had said that to her; there wouldn't be another.

But the town had limited food options. She ended up going to the grocery store and picking up a few things that she could make easily, including lots of wine. She stuck a pan of biscuits and pre-cooked sausages into the oven. Packaged food repulsed her, but she had to eat something. She couldn't keep surviving off of wine and bottled water. The biscuits were buttery, and the sausage was... well, it did its job. Now that her hunger had been satiated, Jamie started searching on her computer. She made a list of things she needed to know if this plan were to go without a hitch.

When she received custody of Dani, she was not going back home. She didn't want her own children to taint Dani's innocence or her goodness. They were horribly selfish children, and she didn't want Dani to pick up on their bad habits.

Marie had never been selfish. She was the most giving person Jamie had ever met. She didn't have an uncaring bone in her body. She wanted Dani to be the same, just like Marie. She smiled at the thought of having her sister back in her life. In the flesh, someone she could hug.

Where was she going to take her? Where would they go? Jamie hadn't settled on that yet. There were so many places she could have taken her, and yet, as she did her research, none of them felt right. She wanted somewhere they would both love but would make it difficult to find them. Difficulty was important to her. Logan would come looking for her, and he would never stop. She needed a place where they could live in obscurity for the rest of their lives. A big city would do that, but so would a small town. A very small town. Jamie didn't think she could survive in a small town without her creature comforts. She'd be miserable, but she would have Dani. That would have made it worth it. A city might be better, she thought. But where? Somewhere out of the country was ideal, but getting Dani a passport since she didn't already have one would be tricky. New York was a place where you could disappear. Change her name and her hair. Let her dye it any funky color she wanted to.

LA was too close to both Logan and her husband. That was the first place they'd look. "Maybe Portland?" Portland was a nice city, but it also had a small-town feel. And there were so many things for them to do they would never get bored. Her fingers drummed against the coffee table as she stared at her computer screen. Portland looked interesting enough. She could have lived there even without Dani. It was their chance for a new start. A second chance for both of them.

"I think that it's a good idea. It would do nicely."

Jamie grinned at Marie's approval. "Portland it is, then." She took notes on the city. She wanted to know everything, and writing things down helped her think. Portland was somewhere Dani was going to love. All of the walking trails, festivals, beautiful trees and parks. She'd make friends in no time.

Jamie also made sure to check the neighborhoods to find one she'd like to live in and then the local schools. Portland's schools were good. Not the boarding schools her children attended, but for a public school, they were more than adequate.

Okay. Now, she needed to rent a car and figure out how she was going to take Dani away.

"Don't get ahead of yourself. Make sure you have all your ducks in a row before you make a move."

Marie was always telling her that. Since she was a kid. Jamie was quite impulsive. She never thought things through in their entirety before she started doing something she wanted to do. She never saw the full picture, just the parts she wanted to see. And the parts she wanted to see were the ones that worked out in her favor. Marie would remind her to stop and take a good look at what was going on. Look at all the possibilities and then plan accordingly. It was still something she had difficulty doing. She tried, but then she got bored of seeing the bigger picture.

"I know. I know. I'm just so excited. But you are right; I need to take a step back and look at everything. My lawyer is handling things on her end, and if all goes well, I might not need to take her."

"Exactly. It will all work out how it needs to."

Jamie smiled. "It will all work out how it needs to." She repeated those words over and over again. She believed her sister. She always believed her sister, and if she said she was meant to have her, then she was.

Her phone rang, and her pulse quickened as she reached for it. Hoping to see it was her lawyer calling. It wasn't.

"Yes, Mother?" She kept her voice emotionless, which wasn't that difficult. She had no emotions toward her mother. She didn't hate her or like her, nor did she love her. She was simply the woman who gave birth to her, and that was all. She didn't do anything else for her.

"I can't believe you are going through with this. What is wrong with you?"

"Nothing, Mother. Nothing is wrong with me. What is wrong with you?" Her tone was even and firm.

"Why can't you just leave that girl alone? She doesn't belong to you!"

"Dani is mine. Marie promised me," she spat. She caught herself and calmed down. She took the spite out of her voice. "Mar—Dani would be better off with me, and Logan knows it. Everyone knows it, even you. I'm doing what I have to do to make sure she's okay."

"That is not what you're doing. She is okay with her father. You are just her aunt. You have no claim to her!"

"I have every right to her. More right, even. More than him. She is mine, and I will not let you ruin this for me." She hung up the phone. It was a smartphone, so hanging up and slamming it down was not as satisfying as it could have been. She leaned back on the sofa. Jamie was in a good mood, but her mother ruined it just like she had ruined everything else. She could never let Jamie be happy. Whenever she was, her mother came along with that disappointed look on her face she always had and chucked her dreams in the trash. She shouldn't have answered the phone. She knew what was going to happen, and it was the same thing that always happened.

She looked back at the window. It would be a few hours before Dani walked home; she had time for a nap.

When she woke, It was almost time for Dani to walk home. She had a few minutes to spare. By the time she got dressed, she found a hat and pulled it low. Dani emerged from the front doors of the school.

Bonnie waited for her across the street while Jamie peered from behind a tree near her front door. Dani bounced up to Bonnie and grinned. The two had an exchange, and instead of going back the way they came, the pair went right. Jamie was perplexed by this change in routine. The two of them did the same thing every day. Well, almost the same thing. Somedays, they walked to the store to pick up food for dinner. But that was also in the direction of the house.

"Where are you going?" she whispered to herself. She followed them. Staying just out of sight as they rounded corners and crossed streets, only to end up at a park where two other young girls were waiting for her. She placed her backpack on the bench and ran over to them excitedly.

The three girls ran around and played, all while Jamie stood and sat on a bus bench across the street and slightly out of the way.

A smile bloomed on her lips. It reminded her of Marie and how the two of them used to play when they were younger. Most days after school, neither girl was ready to go home. More often than not, there was nothing waiting for them at home. Not food or their mother. There was never any point in going. So they went to the park, and they played. Sometimes, all they had was each other, and other times, children from their school would join them with their nannies.

Sometimes, the nannies felt sorry for the girls and shared snacks with them. Usually, when that happened, it was their last meal for the day.

Jamie watched as the girls chased each other all over the park. Dani liked being *'it'*. When they were out of breath, they sat down on the swings and talked in hushed voices. She smiled as she watched them. She saw so much of Marie in her, it was uncanny. She seemed so carefree and happy.

That was all that Jamie wanted for her. Happiness.

"And you are the best person to give her a happy life."

"I know Marie. I know."

She would be just as happy with her as she was with Logan. Happier even. Jamie could show her the world. She had more money than Logan and was, therefore, in a better position to provide for her. Jamie had been tucking money aside since she met her husband. Everything he gave her, including her allowance, she took half and squirreled it away into a secret savings account.

It was more than enough to run away with Dani and live a great life where no one would ever find them.

"Be careful. Don't let her see you."

Marie's voice startled Jamie. She jumped to her feet just as she saw Bonnie stand up. She waved at Dani to come over and pointed at her watch. It was time for them to go home.

And time for Jamie to start putting her plan into action.

CHAPTER TWENTY-ONE

Riley Quinn

"I THOUGHT YOU ALL COULD USE SOME COFFEE AND SOMETHING that didn't come out of a vending machine."

"These chips are quite good," I said. "Not even stale."

My mother rolled her eyes as she set a box full of piping hot coffees with sugar and creamer in a separate bag on my desk. Then she set a box of pastries on Zelina's.

"Thank you," we said in unison.

"Well, I figured it would be a while before you all went home and got some sleep or something good to eat. It's the least I could do."

"Thanks, Mom. Oh, Doctor Elwood said for you to call him."

She gave me a look. "Spending a lot of time with the good doctor, aren't you?"

"Well, we… he helped my ankle," I stammered.

She looked like she wanted to say something, but thankfully didn't. "I gotta get back. Can't leave your sister working the counter for too long." She waved and then walked away.

My sister wasn't really a people person. She was smart, though, and she remembered everything a customer told her. She always got the orders correct. She just couldn't deal with the customers without an attitude or a snide remark.

I sipped the coffee slowly, my conversation with Logan replaying in my mind. My lips curled into a small smile as I set it down and drank from my bottled water. I did, however, take a strawberry Danish from the box. Zelina and I moved the box to the front desk and made an announcement that the coffee and pastries were for everyone.

I sat back at my desk and stared at my screen. We did a search and found the lawsuit Delilah was involved in. Her boss was being sued in a class action lawsuit for sexual harassment. Zelina scrolled through to find how many complainants there were as part of the suit. My jaw twitched when I saw it. Over thirty women were suing him.

I wondered how far back his behavior went. If it was that many women, it wasn't recent. He had to have been at it for a long period of time. I picked up the phone.

"What are you doing?"

I looked at my screen for a minute and then started dialing the number. "I'm curious about something."

"Well, that is never good."

"Hello? This is Detective Riley Quinn, Pine Brooke PD. I'm calling to speak with Mr. Emmet Ryan. Is he in?"

The woman on the other end stammered over her words before finally saying that she would check. A moment later, the line clicked over, and a man with a husky voice started talking.

"What have I been accused of doing now?" He sounded annoyed already.

"Well, I want to talk to you about Delilah—"

"Listen, whatever that woman says I did, I didn't do it. She's lying just like all the others, and I don't have to talk to you without my lawyer."

"I'm calling because she's missing."

There was a sharp intake of breath and then a slow exhale. "What do you mean missing? She was just here the other day."

"She still works there? Even with the lawsuit?"

"Yes, and if I tried to fire her, it would only make me look worse, so my lawyer tells me."

"Understood."

"She's a good worker. Competent, even though she could never take a joke. I had nothing to do with this before you even asked. She just put in her two weeks' notice a few days before she left for some time off."

"Okay. Can you tell me the name of her lawyer?"

"Alex Ryan."

My brow instantly shot up. "Ryan?"

He sighed. "She's my ex-wife."

"Ahh, I'm guessing the split wasn't amicable."

"It was on my end. Can I go now? I've got work to do."

"Thank you for speaking with me."

"Yeah, whatever." He hung up the phone.

I chuckled as I sat back in my chair. "His ex-wife was working on the class action suit."

Zelina laughed. "I bet she's getting a nice chunk of whatever the settlement is."

"You think they'll settle?"

"It's a global tech company. The lawsuit is bad for business and makes the entire company look bad to foreign investors."

"So he either has to settle so it will go away, or he has to step down. I don't think he's stepping down."

I found Alex Ryan's number and called her.

"I'm sorry, but I can't disclose that information. I don't think my clients would approve. "

"I just need to ask you a few questions about Delilah Preston. Did I mention she's missing?"

"You did. I just can't believe it." Her tone softened. "What do you need from me? I don't know anything about her personal life. Not really."

"Tell me about the lawsuit. Have there been any threats to silence the complainants?"

She laughed. "Maybe a few weeks ago, but not now. The company is settling. It hasn't been made public yet because we are still working out the kinks."

"How much does each plaintiff get?"

She paused for a moment. "Each plaintiff gets about 1.6 million after taxes."

My jaw dropped. That was a lot of money, and some people would kill for it. "Who gets the money if she does not claim it? Would it go to her family?"

"Yes, it would legally be awarded to their estate. Whoever she had in her will would get the money next. If she doesn't have a will, well… it would probably be distributed to her family."

I considered it. I had thought for a minute that the money might go back into the pot so other plaintiffs could claim it. But according to the lawyer, that wasn't how it worked. I couldn't tell if the lawsuit had anything to do with her disappearance. Not many people knew about it in her life. She kept it secret from them, and her family probably didn't even know about it. I finished speaking with Alex and then recounted everything she said to Zelina.

"That's a lot of money, but... enough to kill for?"

"I don't know. And it's not like they could have stolen it. It would have had to be someone in her will to get the money. Someone in her family."

Zelina's eyes narrowed. "I mean, I guess that could have happened."

It just didn't ring true. If the family had done it, then why report her missing at all? Just as I was thinking it, the words came out of Zelina's mouth.

"Because she can't be declared dead if no one ever finds her. In order to get the settlement, she has to be declared dead, and that doesn't happen if she's just missing. Not unless she's been missing for over seven years. No one wants to wait that long."

I nodded. "I still don't like the family for this, though. Something about it doesn't seem right to me."

"Yeah, I know." said Zelina.

I leaned back in my chair with my hands behind my head. Something about it wasn't right. I yawned so deeply that tears slipped out of the sides of my eyes. "Oh, wow. I don't know why I'm so tired."

"Because you've been at it for twelve hours today."

"So have you."

She rattled her empty energy drink can. "I've been keeping myself caffeinated. And you're still recovering from a major injury."

"It's not that bad," I replied. I adjusted in my seat but my wince of pain gave me away.

"Go take a nap."

It wasn't a question, barely a statement. It was an order that I had to follow. It felt like there was sand behind my eyelids. I had yawned four times in the last ten minutes. I was incredibly tired, so I did what she said and hobbled over to lie down. The back of the station housed a bunker room filled with bunkbeds and a few cots. I crawled into one of the bunkbeds and curled up.

I woke with a start to Zelina shaking my leg.

"You were dead to the world. I called your name several times. I even called your cell, which is right by your head, and now I've been shaking you for several minutes."

"What's so important?" I sat up and grabbed my phone.

"Something I saw that I thought you'd want to see."

She handed over her tablet. There was a news story on the screen.

Well-known family killer Larry Cole dead. Found in his cell with two slit wrists and his throat slit as well. Police believe suicide.

"How is that a suicide?"

Zelina shrugged. "I mean, slit wrist, sure, but who slits their throat as well?"

I handed her the tablet. "That's crazy." He was killed. I knew it, she knew it, and the police knew it. There was no way he killed himself by slitting his own throat. I had tried to visit Larry Cole on several different occasions since we arrested Tory Craster. I was turned down every time. Not by him—I never got that far—but by the correction officers.

The last time I went and was sent away, and when I walked back outside, there was a detective standing by my car. His hands in his pockets, a slimy grin on his face.

"Can I help you?"

"Yeah, I heard you wanted to speak to Larry Cole. You keep coming here even though no one will let you through. I must say I admire your tenacity, but now I'm curious: why the sudden interest?"

"I'm curious too. I keep hearing he was framed, and I wanted to get his side of the story."

His eyes narrowed. "Larry Cole is a murderer, and he's not worth your time or effort. Trust me, people like him are not worth saving. You should let it go."

"What if I don't want to?" I inched toward my car. "What happens then?"

"I can't speak to that. Maybe nothing. Maybe someone comes to your house and tries to make the point a little clearer." He smiled in a sinister way.

"Well, do you want to write down my address? Better yet, I'm sure you know how to find it, so we'll do this. Tell *someone* that if they want to stop by, they better be armed because I always am. And I don't miss."

I unlocked the car and slid into the driver's seat. He walked away when I started the car. When I got back to the station, I was called into the Captain's office and told I needed to leave the Larry Cole case alone.

"Leave everyone involved with the case alone. I mean it, Quinn. Don't ruin your career over this. You'll end up helping no one."

Part of me still resented him for that comment. It was our job to help people. It was our job to get to the truth; if we weren't willing to stick our necks out for the truth, what were we doing here?

He was just looking out for me, but I wished he had joined me in my search for truth. Stuck his neck out for me. But there we were.

Remembering this exchange, I stood up slowly. "How many hours did I get?"

"Two and a half."

"Well, that's something." I stalked back to my desk and collapsed into my chair. "Anything new while I was sleeping?"

"Nope." Zelina sat down. "Nothing came in, though I do think I found something interesting." She turned her screen so I could see.

"Are those similar cases?" I rested my elbows on the desk and leaned forward.

"Yup." She flipped through the pages, case after case. "So far, there are six."

I leaned back. "How could there be six cases? Why haven't we heard of this?" Before I could get an answer, my phone vibrated on my desk. "Yes?"

"Found a body. Might be the girl we're looking for," said Officer Blaese.

"We'll be right there. Text me the address." I jumped to my feet. "They think they found Delilah."

Zelina sighed. "Dammit!"

I had the same reaction internally. We knew deep down she was dead. Or at least I knew. I felt it deep down in my bones this would be a recovery. But hearing it was hard. It would be even harder to tell her family.

Zelina and I gathered our things and headed out to the scene. I left behind my crutch in the car as we approached. I was mostly okay on my ankle, but I wasn't about to start running or anything. Officer Blaese and Officer Rainwater had already taped off the perimeter and were waiting for CSU to arrive.

"We haven't touched anything, you know how Keith gets. He's on his way, but we thought you might want to see her."

I did. I did want to see her. I walked over to the body. It was a woman. She did resemble Delilah. Same dark hair. Ligature mark around her neck. She looked like she had been in a fight or a tussle. Her hair was a mess. Her shirt was cut up, but not by a razor or a knife. She was also dirty. Maybe she was running through the woods trying to get away from her attacker.

"Look at her feet."

Zelina moved toward her legs. "The bottoms of her feet are dirty. She wasn't wearing shoes. You think they came off in the struggle?"

"I'm thinking she was running from her attacker, and her shoes came off. She kept running. Her feet are caked with mud."

"There's a little bit of blood on her feet too. She might have run over some rocks or something. Scraped her feet on something," Zelina stood up. "You think it's her?"

I studied the woman's face. Even took out my phone and held it up to her face. The picture her sister had sent me on the screen. The resemblance was strong. "I don't know. I want to say yes, but I need it confirmed first. She does look like her though. She really does."

I stood up just as the coroner van pulled up. I glanced down at my watch. It was about time. Maybe if her face was free from mud and dirt, I'd be able to see her features better.

"I know you're not touching the body."

I stepped back with my hands in the air. "No, just looking. I can't tell if it's Delilah or not."

He walked over and bent over the body. "I'd have to get her on the table and clean her up a little. Looks like she's been down there a while." With a gloved hand, he pulled down the collar of her shirt. "The same ligature marks as the other body, though. Looks to be the same width. I can't say this is Delilah definitively, but I would say her killer is the same as Rory's."

"Yeah, that's what I was thinking."

"Okay!" he called out to his team. "Let's get pictures of the scene, and then we can take our Jane Doe back to the morgue."

"Could you search her pockets?"

Keith bent down and reached into both front pockets. "Nothing. I can't get to the back until we move her. Can't move her until we document the scene."

"Got it."

"I'll work on her tonight, and I'll get back to you as soon as I know something."

"Thank you." I followed Zelina over to the officers that found the body. "So, what were you guys doing out here?"

"Searching," said Blaese. "We didn't think anyone had looked over here yet because it was so far from where she was supposed to be. Figured it was worth a try with the dogs, too. Billie and Watson took the other side of the road. They didn't find anything. So they drove off looking for something else. We were moving a little slower over here."

"Okay. Did you see anything around the body? Anyone in the area?"

Blaese looked at Rainwater and shrugged. "I didn't see anything. Did you?"

Rainwater shook his head. "I didn't see anything. Hell, I didn't see her either. The dog smelled her."

"Is it her?" asked Blaese.

"We aren't sure. The coroner says he'll know more once he gets her on the table."

"Looks like her, though," said Rainwater.

"Hate to say it, but I hope it is. I don't know where else to look." Officer Blaese looked back at the body. "Feel sorry for the family still waiting for news."

"Yeah, me too." I left them there and went back to the car. Zelina followed close behind. I sighed as I slid into the car. I knew this was going to happen, but it was still difficult to see. Her poor family. Even if she wasn't Delilah, her family must be worried about her.

"I want to look into those cases that are similar to hers. Even if this is Delilah, I want to know what else this killer has been up to."

CHAPTER TWENTY-TWO

Logan Elwood

"I UNDERSTAND WHAT YOU'RE SAYING, BUT IT IS MY MEDICAL OPINion that you need to change your diet." I stared at the man in front of me, wanting to sigh. I had been having this same conversation with him for the last twenty minutes.

"I think you should be able to just give me some medication so I don't have to change anything about my diet," he whined.

I sat back on the stool. "I get that you don't want to change your diet. I get that completely. No one wants to change their diet. You like eating what you like to eat, and I don't want to take that from you, but..." I showed him his test results. Held the tablet up so he could see. "You are prediabetic. If you keep eating sugar the way you are, you'll have full-blown diabetes, and if you don't take your insulin, it will kill you. More to the point, you are on the verge of having a heart attack. You have to be mindful of your cholesterol. You don't have to eat bacon every day.

Or fried food. You need to move around more. Your heart depends on it." I took a deep breath. His eyes narrowed at me. "I know no one wants to hear this, but if you don't start making some changes and taking your medication, I'll be signing your death certificate."

I tried not to sound harsh, but he didn't get it, or he didn't care. He was one of those patients who felt like they didn't have to make any changes to get better. They had been eating what they liked all of their lives, and they were so set in their ways that they refused to give it up. His eyes narrowed.

"I think I need a new doctor." He struggled to get down from the exam table. After a few tries, his feet hit the floor, and he rocked back on his feet.

"I think you do, too, if you're not going to listen to my advice. You have to make a change, and I can't stress this enough, or you will die. Or you might lose a limb; diabetes can do that, you know."

His shoulders deflated. Was he more worried about losing a leg than dying? In a way, I understood it. When you were dead, that was it. But without an arm or your legs, it made you a burden on those around, especially if your health was failing. All because you couldn't let go of the sweets.

He sighed. "I know," he said quietly.

"You have to take the medicine and get serious about moving around. You don't have to go on a hike fresh out the gate, but move around more than you do now. Walk around your house. Walk around your yard. Start small and then work your way up. But you have to start."

Tears filled his eyes. "I know. I keep thinking if I ignore it, it will go away."

"Yeah, that's not how this works. It doesn't go away until you start making some changes." I wrote down the name of a cardiologist who was taking new patients. "She's nice, but she doesn't pull any punches. I'm going to make you an appointment for Friday. She'll tell you what you need to do and how you need to change your diet."

He took the piece of paper and stared at it. "Okay, I'll go." He wobbled toward the door. "Thanks, doc." His voice was so quiet I almost missed it. I thought I got through to him, finally, after months of trying. Now, we just needed to wait and see if he would follow through. I had high hopes for him.

Nicole strolled in.

"You made that man cry."

"Good. He needs to get on the right track soon, or I don't like his chances of survival."

Nicole frowned. "Speaking of survival, you know Mr. Carson passed. His wife called this morning."

I slumped back on the stool. I had known it was coming. He was in end-stage heart failure, and he was tired of fighting. He just wanted to die with dignity. He was tired of his wife taking care of him and wanted her to start living her life again. I understood it, but I couldn't help him end his life. Not the way he wanted me to. I felt bad for his wife, though. I wonder if he ever told her that he wanted to die.

She was so eager to take care of him. She didn't mind his attitude or how he blew up at her, unwarranted. She didn't mind having to put her life on hold so she could take care of him. She just wanted him to be okay.

"I figured that was going to happen soon."

"She said she came home from the store, and he was still in bed. He looked like he was sleeping, so she left him alone and went to start making lunch. When she came back upstairs and saw that he was asleep, she tried to wake him, but he was cold."

"At least he died peacefully in his sleep."

"Yeah, that's something. She was real broken up about it. I wanted to hug her through the phone."

I frowned.

"Oh, and Gloria Raydor is starting next week. Monday. She sounds excited."

"Have you arranged your office yet?"

She grinned. "Yeah, Sac helped me. Once you and I moved all that trash out, I got him to help move my desk in there and then everything else. I even had a plant. Artificial… but still."

She was so excited about her new office now that she didn't have to be the receptionist anymore. I pretended not to notice that she called my brother Sac, not Isaac. I guessed they were getting friendly, and it was none of my business, but I was going to mess with him later.

"Good. Now that all of that's situated, I guess we're good to go."

Nicole glanced at her watch. "Your next patient should be here in twenty minutes. Mrs. Falcon."

"Right, I need to go over her test results before she comes in." I sat at my desk and searched for her file. It was under my calendar. *"Mrs. Falcon."* Her results were good, and her A1C was down. She was managing her diabetes well, even though it took her a while to get the hang of it. She didn't like giving herself a shot every day. She hated needles, as did most people. But with the monitor on her arm, she had started keeping track of what she ate and when she was doing really well. Her cholesterol was still a little high, but better than it was six months ago. I was proud of her.

Twenty minutes later—Mrs. Falcon was always on time—she walked into my office.

"Hi, Doctor Elwood."

"Hello, Mrs. Falcon. How are you feeling?" I gestured for her to have a seat, which she did while I walked over to the door and closed it.

"Well, I will say I've had more energy, and I'm not tired all the time. So that's a good thing. Still miss some of my favorite foods, though."

"Like what?"

"Macaroni and cheese."

I nodded. "Well, you could still make it with wheat protein pasta, using pureed nonfat cottage cheese and some nonfat cheddar. It's a healthier option, but don't go crazy with it because carbs are something you need to watch out for."

Her eyes lit up. "You can puree cottage cheese? I never thought of that."

"Me either, but I saw a video on Instagram. It doesn't really have a taste to it, so you can add your own seasonings. Just be mindful of your salt intake."

"I'm making that tonight. I've really missed it the last few months." Her smile was wide and filled with teeth. She was so happy about finally getting to eat her favorite food, and it made me smile. "Have you gotten my results?"

"Yes. Your A1C is way down. As you know, it was 8.4, and now it is 5.6. This means you are doing a great job managing your diabetes. Your cholesterol is down, too. It was 206, and now it is 169, so it's coming down. Keep doing what you're doing. Have you been exercising?"

"I go for a walk every morning. I've worked my way up to a mile and a half a day."

"That's great. Walking is the perfect way to lower your blood pressure and manage your diabetes." I flipped through her file. "Right now, I'm not seeing anything that looks troublesome. You are on the right track, and I want to see you again in six months. Do you have any questions for me?"

She looked up at the ceiling. "Is it possible to get off of the medication that I'm on now?"

"Yes, it is possible. Type 2 diabetes can go into remission; basically, what that means is that your blood sugar is at a normal range and can be managed without medication. Now, bear in mind this is not permanent. You can slip back into it if you don't stay on top of your blood sugar.

Your cholesterol can also be managed, and if it gets low enough and you can keep it within that range, then I will feel comfortable taking you off that medication."

She sighed with relief. She was another patient who didn't want to take the medication but committed to it, so she was no longer at risk of developing heart disease. Her fervent work at both lowering her A1C and her cholesterol was all because she didn't want to take the medication. However, I didn't want her to lose motivation, so I didn't tell her that while the insulin may be discontinued, it may be replaced with a daily pill before fully eliminating medication.

"I understand. So if I want to go off the medication, I will have to work on this for the rest of my life."

I nodded. "What's important is that you make these changes a habit. When it becomes a habit, you will do it without thinking. Then eating right and exercising and knowing your limits won't bother you anymore because it is who you are now."

She nodded as she stood up. "I get that. I don't like it, but I get it." She walked toward the door. "Thanks, doctor."

"I'll go ahead and order another refill of your medication."

"Thanks."

I had one more patient after her, and then I was done for the day. I was ready to go home. Not because I was tired but because I wanted to keep an eye on Dani. Nicole and I locked up for the evening; she went her way, and I went mine. I was just getting to the diner when another car pulled into the parking lot before me. Riley got out and went inside—without her crutch.

Curious, or perhaps just drawn to her, I locked my car and followed her inside. She sat down at one of the booths in the back with her head down, staring at her tablet. I slid into the seat across from her.

"Penny for your thoughts?"

Her bright eyes looked up at me as a smirk bloomed on her lips. "My thoughts cost more than that."

"How much?"

"A thousand, maybe."

I patted my pockets. "Yeah, I don't think I have that on me."

"I do offer payment plans if you're strapped for cash."

A chuckle bubbled up my throat. She laughed.

"Why aren't you home, Mr. Elwood?"

I shrugged. "Noticed you were off your crutch."

"I feel a lot better."

"Don't push it, though. I saw you walking in. You looked determined."

She smiled. "Just flipping through a case I should not be looking at." Her eyebrow raised, "Would you like to be my accomplice?"

"What if I get arrested?"

"I won't tell anyone you were here if you don't."

She piqued my interest. *Why wasn't she allowed to look at the file?* I shrugged. "I'm not doing anything else right now." She slid the file over. I should have braced myself before I looked. Should have figured there would have been a dead body in the file.

"Sorry, should have warned you about the photos."

"Particularly gruesome." I studied the photos. A young black man sat on the floor of an empty room and leaned against a cot. His arms splayed at his sides, his legs outstretched. "Suicide?"

"That's what they're saying."

I stared at the pictures. I wasn't a coroner, but something didn't look right to me. "Hmm... give me a minute." The longer I looked, the less the picture made sense. "Now, I'm not a medical examiner, but even I can see that's bullshit." I turned the picture back to her. "If he killed himself by making those cuts, his heart would have still been beating. There'd be a lot more blood." In the picture, the young man had a little blood on his orange pants and a little around him on the ground next to his arms. "If he had slit his throat while he was still alive, the entire front of his shirt and pants would have been soaked."

"So he was dead when someone made those cuts?"

"That's what it looks like to me." In fact I was totally convinced.

"So why do this? Why go through all the trouble of cutting him like this? They could have just made it look like he hanged himself." Riley's question was on point.

"Yeah, but unless they were standing over him, the angle of the marks wouldn't be right. On top of that, if they strangled him, there would have been two ligature marks instead of the one."

She turned the folder back toward me so I could finish looking at it. "Although if they did this, knowing it wouldn't be challenged..."

"But the family might have had a hard time believing it and might have raised a stink about it."

"Why would he have two ligature marks? Could he hang himself twice?"

"Exactly. If they strangled him, but then made it look like a hanging, they'd never match up the hanging ligature with the strangulation marks."

We ordered two sodas and kept studying the pictures. And then I saw it.

"They might have tried." I handed her the last picture in the file. "Look at the post of the bed."

"Sheets wrapped around it like he was going to choke himself out." She sighed. "There's nothing else in that room to hang yourself from."

"Maybe they were going for it, but the logistics didn't make sense. He's already strangled. What can they do now?"

"Slit his wrist and make it look like a suicide. But then, why cut his throat?"

I pondered her question for a moment. *Why would they slit his throat?* I stared at the picture for a long moment before it came to me.

"Depending on what they strangled him with, there would have been a mark. A rope, a cord, or something like that. They could have been trying to hide it."

Riley stared at me, a smile slowly changing into a grin. "Are you sure you're not a coroner?"

I laughed. "Very sure. I thought about it early on in medical school. My mother was against it. Who wants to deal with dead bodies every day?"

Riley pointed at herself.

"Present company excluded. And they're not always dead, are they?"

"No, sometimes we find them alive, and that is a good day."

I looked at her soda. "Have you gotten any sleep?"

"A few hours. We found a body," she whispered. "Still waiting to hear back."

My shoulders dropped. I knew it would end this way; I just had a sliver of hope she was alive in a ditch somewhere, waiting to be rescued.

"Don't tell anyone," she added.

"Tell anyone what?" Our eyes locked as I closed the folder and slid it back across the table.

CHAPTER TWENTY-THREE

Riley Quinn

I got a call from the morgue just as Logan was leaving to go home to his daughter. He had some good insights about Larry's death. I appreciated talking to another person who thought his death was not a suicide. Zelina believed me, but she was my partner. I didn't think she would lie to me, but it was nice hearing someone with no involvement think the same thing I did.

I stopped by the station and picked up Zelina before heading to the morgue. Keith stood next to the covered-up body, shaking his head. He looked up as soon as he heard the doors open. "She's in better condition than Rory so I have more to go on."

"That's good."

"First things first. After cleaning up all the mud and leaves from her face," he pulled down the sheet to show her face only, "I can definitively say this is Delilah Preston. Still want to get the family in to confirm, though."

Cleaned up, she looked just like she looked in her picture, except she was missing that bright smile.

"I believe she got away from her killer. I can't say how, but judging by her feet, she ran through a wooded area to get away. She has scrapes and cuts on the bottoms of her feet, along with leaves and pieces of branches. The cuts on her arms and face also came from tree branches; I found dirt and remnants of broken leaves in them." He took a deep breath. "She was strangled like Rory. There are no signs of sexual assault."

"So he just strangled her?" It was a weird thing to ask, but it was also a strange thing to happen. "Usually, a killer wants something from the victim. Their money, jewelry, rape them, something. But all this killer wanted was to strangle her.

"Apparently. When I was done with her body, I did a search to find any others that matched the way she was killed, and I got two hits. Well, there are four, but those cases were solved, and the killer either left behind a mountain of evidence or confessed, but these two are still open, and they match your victim."

He handed over the folders, and I gave one to Zelina. I opened the file and looked at a woman who looked just like Delilah, with the same features and almost the same smile. She had been strangled and was found away from her car. "The resemblance is uncanny."

"That's what I thought, and they were all found away from their cars and without their licenses."

"Maybe he keeps them as a souvenir. Something to remember them by or to keep count." I closed the folder. "Did you find anything else on the body?"

He shook his head. "No hairs, no bodily fluids, nothing. He strangled her and then dumped her."

"Okay. We'll go inform the family and then bring them down here for an ID."

"I'll make sure she's presentable."

It was a long drive to her family's home. Not because it had to be but because we drove as slow as we could, neither of us wanting to be the one to inform them of Delilah's murder. It was always a difficult thing and something you never got used to. I walked up to the door and knocked.

It was late, almost midnight, and yet a light was still on downstairs. We waited for a few minutes, and then the door opened. Marissa stood in the doorway, her eyes welling with tears.

"I'm so sorry. We—"

She crumpled into my arms. I didn't even get a chance to tell her about her sister. She knew. Maybe she saw it in my eyes. Or maybe it was because we were there so late at night, and Delilah wasn't with us. Maybe she had always known. I patted her back as gently as I could while she cried against my chest.

"Come in, let's get you back inside." Zelina helped me lift her to her feet and then guide her back inside. I sat her down on the sofa while Zelina went into the kitchen and got her a glass of water. She took small sips.

"Are you sure it's her?" she whispered.

"We need someone to come down to the morgue and confirm, but we are pretty sure it is her," I said. A sob rippled through the room. A light turned on at the top of the stairs. Footsteps pounded down the wooden stairs.

"What is going on?" A man rounded the corner and entered the living room. He looked just like Delilah, too. It must have been her brother. He looked down at Marissa, ran to her, and wrapped his arms around her.

Marissa sobbed into his shoulder, and he looked up at us. "I take it you found her." He tried to keep his voice steady, but it wavered near the end of his sentence. I nodded.

"Okay. You need one of us to ID the body?"

I nodded again.

"I'll do it. Can I come down in the morning?"

"Yes. That would be a good idea." I looked down at Marissa; she was in no condition to identify her sister. "We are so sorry for your loss."

We exited the house and walked back to the car. Marissa's sobbing could still be heard from the edge of the porch. We could have gone home and fallen asleep. We were no longer looking for a missing person, so time wasn't of the essence. We could have said we were done for the day, but Zelina drove back to the station. We didn't even speak to each other, and yet we both agreed we needed to sort this shit out so we could relax.

We walked in. Silence rippled through the station. *I guess everyone knows that we found the body.* I slumped at my desk. I wasn't tired anymore. I guess all those energy drinks finally kicked in. The captain walked over to our desks.

"I heard a body was found."

"Yeah, her brother is coming down to the morgue in the morning to make an ID. But Keith says he's pretty sure that it's her."

His shoulders dropped slowly. "Any leads?"

"Not at the moment," said Zelina. "We just got back from informing the family."

"But we did find two more cases almost identical to Delilah's and Rory's."

"Okay, that's something."

Zelina pulled it up on her computer. The resemblance between the women was uncanny. They looked just like her. I looked down at my desk and noticed a folder, pink with bright red writing.

Sorry it took so long. I went through my files and found two more women whose cars were found on the same property.

I opened the file. Not only did Nicky put together the list, but she also handed over an inventory list of each car. I placed the lists side by side. "Interesting."

"What?"

"Those two women also had their cars towed from the same yard as Rory and Delilah. I have an inventory list of their cars. Both the women's purses and phones were missing. Along with their licenses and registrations."

"Maybe he wants to keep souvenirs. Something to remember them by," said Captain Williams.

"Yeah, that's what we figured," said Zelina.

My fingers drummed against my desk. *What am I missing?* The beat grew sporadic when something popped into my head. I turned the thought over and over and over again. Played with it until it felt right. Until it felt promising.

"If you are stopped by a cop and told to pull over. What's the first thing you do?" I asked.

"Pull out my license and registration," they both said.

I leaned back in my chair. "Yeah, that's what I thought. "

"Come into my office, you two."

I followed him to his office and sat down. A second later, Zelina joined us and closed the door behind her. "What's wrong?"

"Are you thinking that a cop did this?" he whispered.

"I think that's possible. Now, don't get me wrong, I hate to accuse a fellow officer of this, but what other conclusions can we draw?"

He moved around his desk and sat down. "There has to be another reason."

I turned to face him. "Okay. But think about it. The victim's license and registrations were gone. That's the first thing you hand to a cop when you're stopped; otherwise, why have it out? Look at the bodies, where they were found, and the evidence left behind."

"There was no evidence left behind," added Zelina.

"Exactly. Who knows how to clean up a crime scene better than a cop? There was nothing left behind. No hairs or fluids. Nothing."

The captain frowned darkly. "We need more evidence before I feel comfortable accusing a cop."

"Okay. We'll start looking for that." I stood up.

"Not tonight. I need you both to go home and get some sleep. Actual rest this time. I want you fresh and clear-eyed. I want you to overturn every rock, every *pebble*. If one of our own is responsible for this, I want you to exhaust every possible avenue. We don't want to point fingers at one of Pine Brooke's finest—but we also don't want a killer on the force. Tread carefully. No word of this leaves my office, you understand?"

I nodded. "Yes, sir."

"Now go rest up. Come back in the morning."

I looked at Zelina.

"That's an order. Go home."

I sighed and walked out. I didn't want to go home; I wanted to keep working. We could have broken the case by morning. I grabbed the case file off my desk and walked to the door with Zelina following. We didn't say anything to each other on our way out. We just went our separate ways, and the moment I got home, I collapsed on the couch.

I woke before seven. Six hours of sleep was more than I had been getting lately. Doctor Elwood would be so proud. The thought made my lips curl into a smile. I took out my phone and shot him a text, proud of my six hours. Before I could put the phone down, it dinged, saying I had a message.

Logan: *Lay back down and get two more hours.*
Me: *Gotta work.*

I jumped up and headed to my room. I needed to take a shower, wash my hair, and change my clothes. I was still a little tired, but I felt better as soon as the hot water beat down against my shoulders. The tension in my body melted away instantly. After lingering in the shower until my fingers looked like prunes, I got out and tied my hair up in a towel.

I got dressed, dried my hair, grabbed all my stuff, and headed back out the front door. I didn't have time to make coffee or get something to eat. Zelina was probably already at the station. I was right. I pulled up just as she was walking into the station. I followed her a few minutes later.

"You sleep?"

"A whole six hours."

"Wow, I got five. I couldn't get the case out of my head to relax enough to go to sleep."

"I get that." I sat down and leaned back in my chair. "I think we should dust the car for prints."

Zelina's eyebrow raised slightly. "We already dusted the cars."

"We dusted inside the cars. I think we should dust the outside. All four cars. The other two women's cars should still be there because no one was around to pick them up."

"So we should dust the outside of the cars because…"

"You remember being a patrol officer?"

"It was so traumatic I blocked it out. But continue."

"Most cops touch the back of a car they are stopping just in case something happens during the stop." Most cops did this as a precaution. A way to protect themselves in case something goes wrong during a routine traffic stop. "You touch either the trunk or a taillight."

"Oh, yeah. I didn't do that a lot." She picked up the phone. "So if we dust for fingerprints on the trunk of the car or the taillight, we might find the killer's fingerprints."

I nodded. "I think that might be possible. I mean, he was careful with the body, but maybe he forgot when he initially did the stop."

"It's worth a shot. I'll take any leads at this point, even if they lead nowhere."

"Yeah, me too." I sent a text to Keith. If it was a cop we were looking for, I didn't want any of the patrol officers doing it. There was no way we could get away with using a police lab for this investigation.

He confirmed he'd get a team on it immediately, and then I noticed the time. "Let's head to the morgue anyway. Her brother should be there to identify the body."

The brother was there at the morgue waiting for us when we arrived. "Thank you," he whispered. "For all that you did to find her. We appreciate it. You were determined even though I think we all knew she was dead."

"It's our job."

A small smile kissed his lips. "Thank you for not half-assing it."

I smiled regretfully and nodded, acknowledging the compliment. "Let me check on the coroner. I'll be right back." I walked out of the waiting area and entered the morgue. Keith stood by the body, shaking his head. He looked up.

"Is he here?" Keith asked.

"Yeah, are you ready?"

"Help me pull the table to the window." We moved the body and I went back outside and stood with her brother.

"Are you ready?"

He drew in a shaky breath. "Yes. I'm ready."

I tapped the window three times. The blinds rose, and Keith pulled the sheet down just enough that her face was the only thing he could see.

His bottom lip quivered, Tears streamed down his face. He nodded. "That's her. That's Delilah," he said as he turned away from the window. The blinds were lowered.

"I'm so sorry for your loss."

A sob tore through him. His shoulders shook. A few minutes later, he drew in a shaky breath. "I need to go."

"Okay. I can drive you home."

"No. Don't trouble yourself. I can get home. It's not far from here. I'll be okay." He hurried out of the room before I could utter another word.

"Okay, if you say so." I stuck my head into the morgue. "Thank you. He confirmed the ID."

"Okay."

"Get some sleep. There's nothing you can do right now," I told him. I was lucky enough to have a day off due to my ankle injury, but Keith had been working around the clock for nearly a week.

"I sent my techs to print the outside of the cars. I should wait until they come back."

"You have an assistant. Go home or at least go back to your office and get some sleep."

He sighed. "Okay. That I can do."

"We'll hang out here until you get your results."

We took seats in the lobby, setting up our laptops and doing a deep dive into all four women, trying to see what they had in common. But only a couple hours later, I got a ping on my phone.

"The prints came back." I stared at the screen on my phone. "Keith wants us to come down to his office."

We headed down the hallway to his office, and Zelina glanced over at me as he hurriedly shut the door behind us. "You found something, right?" she asked.

Keith's face was almost rigid. As if he were quelling some emotion.

I looked at Zelina, and then back at Keith.

He lowered his voice. "The last three cars were wiped clean. But the first... there was a match."

My feet carried me forward without even having to think about it. "Who is it?"

He took a deep breath. "It's a cop." He turned the monitor so we could see it. A picture of the officer was front and center. "Officer Stephen Blaese."

CHAPTER TWENTY-FOUR

Jamie Washington

"Hello?" Jamie stood in the doorway, wondering if she was dreaming. Or maybe hallucinating. She hoped he was a hallucination.

"Hi, honey." Chris wrapped his arms around her and squeezed. "I know you said not to come, but I missed you, and I wanted to know how you were doing." He moved past her into the house.

"I told you I was okay. You don't have to worry about me." She closed the door behind him.

"I know. I know. But I missed your face." His thumb brushed her cheek as he lowered his lips to her.

Jamie rolled her eyes internally. She didn't want to kiss him or see him. His presence wasn't necessary. It was never necessary. She thought she had kept him at bay. Talked him out of visiting her during their last conversation. She thought it worked.

But clearly, it did not, and now she was stuck with him.

"How long are you going to be here?" She tried to sound upbeat. A smile painfully etched into her face. It was painful.

"A day or two. Got to get back to work."

"Where are the children?" She sat down on the sofa.

"They're with your mom."

Jamie bristled at the comment. She didn't want her mother anywhere near her children. She didn't want her mother near anyone in her life. The woman was toxic. She smiled tightly. "You thought that was a good idea?"

"She seemed eager to have them," he said as he sat down next to her. "They were eager to go. All parties seemed happy."

"Okay. Well, that's nice. They get to spend some time with their grandmother and she with her grandkids."

"Yeah, they don't really get to do that too much. It's nice to have a break. Some time to ourselves." He grinned.

She smiled tightly. "Of course."

"How are things going?" Chris wrapped his arm around her. She tried not to grimace at his touch.

"I don't know yet. I'm waiting to hear back from my lawyer. She said she was working on something."

"Oh, well, that's good. Maybe it will be over soon. We need you home," he said, and she nodded slowly.

For the next few hours, Jamie felt like she was having an out-of-body experience. Desperately trying to distance herself from his touch. He was her husband, but she didn't like him. But he was also rich, so he came in handy. While he slept in the bedroom upstairs, she slipped on her nightdress and a robe and went into the bathroom. A long hot bath later, she heard the doorbell.

"More uninvited guests?" she said to herself. She slipped on a pair of pajamas and ran downstairs. Her lawyer was waiting for her there. "Oh, I thought you were going to call with news, not come by."

"Well, I'm in town, so it seemed like a good idea." She craned her neck to see inside the house. "Is now a good time?"

"Of course. Come on in. I hope you have good news."

"Well, that depends." She walked over to the sofa and sat down. She set her briefcase on the coffee table and opened it. "His lawyer wants to do mediation."

Jamie sat down. "What is that?"

"It's where both parties sit down and talk through their differences. The idea is that you two could work through it without the courts getting involved. This would be ideal for everyone. Once a judge gets involved, you can't change your mind."

"I'm not sure I like that idea."

Her lawyer sighed. She knew Jamie wasn't going to like the idea, but it was her job to approach her client with any offer made. And she had done her job. "I figured you weren't going to like it."

Jamie sat with the offer for mediation in complete silence. Her mind rolled over the thought again and again. How would mediation be good for her? How would it allow this situation to work out in her favor? Jamie was a simple woman who thought mostly of herself and her sister. But mostly herself. If something did not benefit her, then she would not do it. But if it did, then she would try to make it work.

The mediation was more for Logan than for her. He wanted a chance to talk her out of this. But she knew better. She knew that this was what was best for both her and Dani.

Maybe she could show him that he wasn't thinking about Dani or what best for her. He was the only one thinking about himself. Even if he didn't agree, she would have witnesses to his delusion. Witnesses that would side with her once she explained the facts.

"Maybe it would be a good idea," she finally said. "Maybe we could lay out all the facts and talk him into handing over custody before we have to get the law involved."

"That's possible. Are you willing to share custody?"

Jamie bristled at the question. She wasn't. In no way did she want Logan to be in her life. She wanted him far away from her and Dani, and he didn't deserve her. He wasn't taking care of her; Bonnie was. Dani needed attention; she needed love. She needed a mother. And Jamie needed Ma—she needed to be the one to take care of her. She could be her mother. She wasn't willing to share custody, but she would say she would if it meant the proceedings would go by faster.

"I guess. If it would make it easier."

"It would. He might be more amenable to it." She stood up and closed her briefcase. "I'll let them know you agree to mediation. And when it's scheduled, I'll get with you and go over how things are going to work and how we can bring up our points."

"Okay." She walked toward the door and then spun around. "Your husband... will he be there?"

"Should he?"

"It's a good thing to have on record what a great mother you are and how much your children love you and are loved. That would help get our point across."

"Chris is upstairs sleeping. I'll ask if he can take some time off work and be there. Let me know the date as soon as possible."

"Sure thing."

When the door closed, Jamie sat back on the sofa, annoyed. She didn't want her husband there. She didn't want him in town in case she did get custody of Dani. He would want to spend time with her and then take them both back, but that wasn't her plan. She'd ask if he could be there if it would help. But she'd have to make a plan so he couldn't follow her.

After her lawyer left, she had time to think about her request. Chris was a heavy sleeper, so he didn't hear her coming or going. This was a relief to Jamie because he hadn't heard her request. The more Jamie thought about it in the hours she waited for him to wake, the more she thought it was a horrible idea.

Sure, he could tell everyone what a great mother she was because that's what he believed. But he would also hear things. Things she had never told him about herself. These are things Logan probably knew because of Marie… or his lawyer might have done research on her.

For her plan to work, it was better if he didn't come. He had to get back to the children anyway. He couldn't stay for a lousy mediation that would probably never work. The mediation didn't matter as much as her lawyer thought it did. But she'd go along with it for a little while.

"You're awake?" She pulled her lips into a smile when she saw him; it was like pulling teeth, unwelcomed and painful.

He returned her smile. "I've been awake for a little while. Just dealing with emails on my phone. Most of the other stuff can wait until tomorrow. How long have you been awake?"

"Only a little while. Are you hungry? I could order something. Not a lot of options in town this late, though."

He shook his head. "Not really. I think I'll be okay. I have to leave tomorrow morning."

"Really?" Jamie feigned interest as she was known to do. She had gotten good at it over the years. She had learned what to say and how to say it to make him happy. It wasn't difficult. Instead, it was something she had been doing all her life. Changing herself to fit what someone else wanted her to be. He wanted the happy, always smiling housewife, so that's what she was. Interested in his work, even though she didn't know nor understand what the hell he was saying when he talked about his day.

Jamie had transformed herself into a tool at a young age. Ready to be whatever the person holding her wanted her to be. It had become her camouflage. She learned to mimic emotions and actions that matched what he wanted.

She leaned forward and pouted like she was sad he was leaving so soon. This brought a smile to his lips as it often did.

"Yes, honey. I have an important meeting tomorrow afternoon that I can't miss. I tried to reschedule, but the other parties couldn't agree on a time or day. It's just better to go ahead and get it over with." He sighed. "I wanted to be here for your mediation, but I'm afraid I can't."

She waved a hand dismissively. "That's fine. You have more important things to do, and my lawyer says this mediation is really just a formality. A way to show that we tried to present him with reasonable terms before getting the police involved. She said that if he doesn't agree to hand over custody for a short period of time while social services check everything out by the end of the mediation, then we are going to the police and then social services. She said we should file a complaint with both."

"Why?" He twisted his body so he could look at her head-on.

"Well, he has some friends in the local police department. She believes that because he is the town doctor and people know him, the police might be reluctant to take our complaint seriously. I don't know what he's told them about me, and that might cloud his judgment. So if we file a complaint with them both, social services will help keep them in check and take it seriously. That is the hope anyway."

He nodded solemnly. "I'm so sorry you have to go through this alone. I wish I could be here for you."

"It's okay. It's almost over anyway. And then we will be back home and start a new life with our growing family." It hurt her to smile as wide as she was.

He grinned and wrapped his arms around her.

She was eager to start her new life, with her niece. As far away from him as possible.

CHAPTER TWENTY-FIVE

Riley Quinn

MY JAW DROPPED, AND THERE WAS A PERSISTENT RINGING IN MY ears as I stared at the screen. I couldn't believe it. "Blaese? Are you sure?" I stumbled back. My back hit the table behind me.

Keith nodded grimly. "I ran it through several times, and it came back the same way every time. His prints were on the car. It could be a coincidence, but I know we all don't believe in coincidences, so here we are."

"Yeah." The words squeezed out of my mouth. He worked on the case with us the whole time. He found one of the bodies. How could he do that? How could he look at what he did to those women and not show an ounce of remorse? Was he a psychopath?

Or was it really just a coincidence?

But if it was, why would he not have mentioned it in the investigation at all?

I ran out to grab my laptop and quickly checked the paperwork, and my heart sunk. "He definitely recorded a traffic stop of this vehicle on the day she went missing."

I looked back at Zelina, who shook her head.

"I can't believe this," she hissed. "That—"

"Okay." Captain Williams interjected, having come down once he'd been notified. He folded his arms across his chest. "We need to do this gently. Don't spook him or let him know that we are on to him. So how can we do that?"

I shrugged. I didn't care if he knew we were on to him. I had so much shit I wanted to say to him. So many questions that I wanted to ask him. How the hell could he do this? My blood boiled in my veins. "We could bring him in. He was the first on the scene, and he might have some insight that we haven't put together yet. He might have seen something that might have been a small detail that he saw. We could say that we just want to pick his brain about the case." I spun around and faced them. "Maybe getting him to talk about the case might get him talking. Might get him to open up. It'll be difficult because he knows all of our angles. He knows how we operate, so we have to broach the subject without him getting suspicious."

"That sounds difficult," said Keith. "I do not envy you three. But I've done my job."

"Oh, so you're just throwing in the towel?"

He smiled. "No, but I am passing the baton. My part of this race is done." He bowed curtly and then handed me the file.

I laughed. "Okay. So what are we going to do?"

No one had an answer. Interrogating fellow officers was the worst. It was difficult not to feel betrayed by them and keep it from showing up on your face. I wasn't sure it was possible at the moment. But aside from that, they knew the game plan. They knew how we spoke to suspects so an officer would be able to spot it.

The trick was to not speak to him like he was a suspect. And to say that was going to be difficult was an understatement. Neither of us knew how to approach it. Zelina and I left the morgue, went back to the station, and sat at our desks in silence. I didn't know what to say, and neither did she. She stared at her computer screen, her eyebrows slowly knitting together.

"I don't know what to do," I said.

She sighed. "I still can't believe he had something to do with this. There has to be some kind of explanation. Maybe she had a problem with her car, and he stopped her."

I leaned back in my chair. "Okay. Maybe, but if that was the case, then why not say anything when the body was found? Why not bring up that he stopped her that same day?"

"You remember everyone you stop?"

"If one of them was found dead, I think I would have remembered. I mean, look at the evidence. All the victims' licenses and registrations were missing. Why else would that happen?"

She shrugged. "I know. I know. I just can't believe it was him. Of all the people here, I don't see him as this monster. I really don't."

"We could say the same thing about Craster. I never would have thought he was a killer either, but look at what he did. Look at the monster he was hiding. Anyone is capable of anything. That's what he taught me."

Zelina nodded slowly. She knew I had a point, even though she didn't want to admit it. It was hard to believe because Stephen had been working the case with us since the very beginning. I couldn't understand how you could look at the body and the parents and the family and not feel an ounce of remorse. That was impossible for me to understand. For either of us to understand.

"So what... how are we supposed to approach him and not give anything away? We shouldn't do any searches on our computers because he might be looking for that. Keith isn't going to upload anything into the database until we arrest him, just in case."

"I say we do your plan. Ask him in and ask about the cases. He was first on the scene, so he might have seen something that we missed."

She shrugged. "That might be the right angle." Zelina glanced at her screen. "But first, I want to learn more about him. Now, I feel like I don't know anything about him. Is he married? Divorced? Does he have kids?"

I leaned forward. "Huh. Good questions!" She had made another valid point. What did we really know about Stephen? Was he married? In the back of my mind, I thought he was. I could have sworn I heard something about him getting married a couple of years ago, but I couldn't remember if it was his first or second marriage. "'You know what, yeah, we should look into him before we call him in. And maybe we should try to do it off our servers."

Zelina nodded. She pulled out her computer from her tote bag underneath her desk. It was amazing how you could work with someone and see them every day and not really know them. I stared at Zelina for a long moment. Did I know her? Or was she hiding something, too?

I sighed as I pulled my computer out of my bag. I pointed to the conference room, and she stood up.

I wanted to do my research where no one could sneak up on me and see my screen. I sat facing the door, and so did she. Instead of using our internal system, we did a deep dive on public social media. Stephen Blaese had been an officer for the past ten years or so. He never moved up in the department or showed any interest in doing so. He liked being an officer. There was nothing wrong with that, but it was something I hadn't known before.

He had been married before and had no children. "Huh," I said as I stared at the picture on the screen. I turned my computer slightly so Zelina could see. "She look familiar?"

Her jaw dropped. "I can't believe it."

On the screen was a picture of Stephen's first wife, who looked almost identical to Delilah and the other women who had been killed. He had a type. It was clear that he was killing these women because they looked like his wife. "I want to talk to her." I wrote down her address.

"Yeah, we should go meet her instead of inviting her to the station."

∽

Isla Blaese eyed us from the small opening in the door. I could only make out half of her face, and her voice was so low that I could barely hear her. I leaned forward as I repeated why we were there. "We want to speak to you about your husband. Well, your ex-husband."

"Why?" Her eyes darted past us like she was expecting someone to walk up.

"Can we come in?"

She blinked. Her eyes were watery as she stared at us for such a long time. Seconds ticked by slowly until she drew a deep breath and inched out of the way. When we entered, she closed and locked the door behind us.

"What is he saying I did now?" She shuffled past us. We followed her down the hall until it opened up into the kitchen. "I haven't done anything wrong."

I sat at the breakfast bar near the stove. She took the tea kettle off the stove. Steam billowed in the air. "This isn't about you, this is about him. We want to know more about him."

She paused. A slight hesitation while she poured the hot water into her cup. She set the kettle back on the stove. "Him? What about him?" She stared at me, rheumy brown eyes searching my face.

"What was your husband like when you two were married?"

Her right eyebrow lifted. "Why? Why now?" Her head darted toward Zelina. There was a panic in her voice that hadn't been there before. "Is it about the women you found?"

My back straightened immediately. "Why would you ask that?" I leaned forward, resting my elbow on the counter. "What do you know about your ex-husband that we don't?"

"Anything you can tell us might help with our investigation. We won't say anything to him about who told us. Just trying to get to the truth," explained Zelina.

Isla took a deep breath. Her hands shook as she brought the hot cup to her lips.

"Maybe you should sit down," I gestured to the round black table with the bright yellow chairs around it. She followed me to the table, and we all sat down. Zelina took out her notepad and pen.

"He's a horrible man with... certain appetites that I just couldn't live with anymore." She squirmed in her chair, the thought making her uncomfortable. Immediately, my mind flashed to Tory and his wife and what she probably had to deal with.

"Can you be specific? Why did you think we were here about the women?"

She sighed. "I saw them... pictures of them on the news, and I immediately thought they looked like me. Which made me think of him. He hates me."

"Why?"

"I got away. I had to. If I didn't, he was going to kill me. The beatings just kept getting worse and worse. Like every time I opened my mouth, he got angrier and angrier. I couldn't even speak in my own home unless I agreed with him, and sometimes that didn't even work."

"Took a lot for you to get away from him," said Zelina.

She nodded. "It took a lot of planning. A year's worth, if not more. Carefully putting all my ducks in a row so once I was gone, I'd never have to come back."

I wanted to ask her why she didn't come to the police, but I knew the answer. We took care of our own. If my husband was a cop and beating on me, I wouldn't go to the station he worked at either. I would have moved so far away from this town that he would have never found me.

"Why didn't you move?" I asked.

"I tried. I really did, but he always knew where I was. It felt like I could never get away from him. He was everywhere, even when he wasn't there. He called me one day. I had moved to Denver, and he told me what I was wearing that morning and what I was doing. Where I went and who I talked to, everything. It was like he was there. Right there next to me. He was following me. I didn't know how; I wasn't posting anything on social media. I didn't have an account. So I figured if I couldn't get away from him, I might as well come home. Plus, my mom was sick. She died last year from cancer."

"I'm so sorry for your loss," I said. "So he was following you, and you came back. Have you had any contact with him since you've been back?"

She rolled her eyes. "I see him sometimes. He drives by my house. He came to my mother's funeral uninvited. My mother hated him. He makes his presence known."

"And his hatred for you is why you believed he killed those women?" asked Zelina.

"Yes. They looked just like me when I saw them on the news. Same hair and eyes. It was uncanny. I thought he was still mad at me. Working through his anger issues."

"By killing them." I leaned back in the plastic chair and folded my arms across my chest. "It makes sense. He knows he can't kill you, so he takes it out on the women who look just like you. It's the next best thing to ensure he doesn't get caught."

"Think he might have miscalculated on something, because here we are," said Zelina.

"He's not a good person. Never was. I just couldn't see it back then. He was so kind when we first started dating. I was nineteen; he was just starting out as an officer. But I guess these stories always start this way. Nice in the beginning, hell toward the end."

She looked up, seemingly lost in thought, and her fingers tightened around her mug. "I wanted kids. I've always wanted children. Stephen would not have been a good father, but early in our marriage, I hadn't seen that side of him until I got pregnant. He beat me so terribly that I lost the baby. And then every time I got pregnant after that, he beat me. He beat me so bad the last time I was told I could never get pregnant again." She blinked back tears. "He smiled when the doctor said it. Not because he never wanted children but because I was devastated and started crying. He just wanted to hurt me."

Tears pricked the corner of my eyes, but I blinked them back. I had to stay strong for her. For all those women. "Thank you for speaking with us. I really appreciate your insight into what your husband was like. We thought… well… who would know him better than you."

Isla nodded. "Glad I could help. Especially if you put him away."

Zelina stood up and tucked her notepad into her back pocket. "Still trying to get all our facts together. Gather as much evidence as possible before we make the arrest."

"Please hurry," she said. "If he finds out you've come here, I don't know what he might do."

"We can protect you," I offered.

She gave me a look so hard and so cold that it sent chills down my spine. "No, you can't."

I never would have thought Stephen was capable of that kind of cruelty. How could he keep that side of himself hidden from all of us? How was that even possible? I couldn't picture it, and I didn't really want to.

While I walked to the car, I wondered how many times he had stopped a woman that looked like his wife and strangled her. How many times had he done it?

CHAPTER TWENTY-SIX

Logan Elwood

My heart stuttered in my chest when I opened the door. I knew she was coming, but I still found myself unprepared to see her. My mother-in-law never liked me, and that feeling did not get any better since Marie had died. Especially since I was the one driving. If anything, Marie's death made it worse, but at least she never tried to take Dani away from me.

"You look good. Healthy. I guess that's one of the benefits of being a doctor." She stepped inside, and I closed the door behind her. She wasn't very enthused about being there, and I wasn't enthused to see her, but it wasn't about us. It was about Dani.

"I guess it is. I can't tell my patients to eat right and exercise if I'm over three hundred pounds. I don't think they'd believe me."

"I wouldn't," she said brusquely.

"I'll keep that in mind."

She walked slowly to the living room. Inch by inch, glancing around like she didn't think the house was safe. I was used to it by now, so it didn't bother me. She did the same thing at our house whenever she came to visit Marie. I sat down on the sofa. Once she inspected the cushion in the chair across from me, she sat down, too.

"Seems like a nice town."

I hate small talk. "It is. People have been really nice and welcoming to us. Dani loves it here. She's already made friends at school."

She smiled. "That's so good. Marie was great at making friends, too. She would talk to anyone, as I'm sure you remember."

"I do. Never met a stranger."

Her smile slowly deflated. "Yeah. She never met a stranger."

The front door opened. Seconds later, Dani burst into the living room, grinning. She paused in front of Everly. "What are you doing here, grandma? I wasn't expecting you to be here." She wrapped her arms around Everly.

I smiled. Dani loved her grandmother even though she didn't see her often. She always lit up when she did, and so did Everly. I stood up and went into the kitchen to give them some privacy. When Dani was excited, she talked fast. Words spilled from her mouth like a geyser. I didn't know how Everly kept up with her, but she did. I made iced tea while Dani told her all about her day, talking a mile a minute, and Everly understood enough to ask questions.

I smiled and nodded but none of what she was saying stuck. After thirty minutes, Dani kissed Everly on the cheek. "Got to go do my homework now. You should stay for dinner. Uncle Sac is cooking, and he's really good at it." Without saying anything else, she grabbed her bookbag and rushed out of the room.

"Your brother stays here now?" Her eyebrow lifted slightly. Last she heard, I didn't speak to my brother. And when I was married to Marie, I didn't. Not really. We were never in the same room together long enough to have an actual conversation.

"Yeah. He wanted to see Dani, so he just stayed. He got a job at the local diner, and he's doing really well. Dani loves him being here. She likes spending time with her favorite uncle."

She smiled. "That's good. She seems to be adjusting well, and it looks like you are taking great care of her. She looks happy." She glanced back at the entryway.

"Thank you for saying that. I can't tell you how great that is to hear. I really appreciate it."

"The truth is the truth. I can't believe Jamie stayed here with you and then decided she would take better care of Dani. I just can't believe it, but then again, she always had a screw loose." She leaned forward and placed her hand on my knee. "You know she's telling people you're abusing Dani?"

"What?" I leaned forward, too. Rage pulsed in my veins, red and hot. "Who is she telling that to?"

She sighed. "I think everyone or anyone that will listen. When she told me, I figured she just wanted to get people on her side. And that accusation was the best way to do it. I didn't believe it for a second because I know her, but others might."

I leaned back. I figured she might have been doing something, but not that. She was too quiet. I hadn't seen her in a while. Isaac saw her at the diner, but she didn't stay to eat. I shook my head. "I don't know what to say."

"When Jamie wants something, she's determined to get it. No matter who she hurts. I'm sorry she's doing this to you. I know we haven't always seen eye to eye on anything, but even I know this isn't right."

"She's going to use that," I said quietly.

Everly's jaw twitched. "Use what?"

I sighed. "The accusation of abuse. She's going to try to use it against me to get what she wants."

"I'm still not following."

I took a deep breath. "I'm a doctor. An accusation of child abuse would ruin my career."

"But it's not true. We know that."

I nodded slowly. "I know. But just a mention of child abuse, true or not, will ruin me. That's why she hasn't gone to the police yet. Or involved social services. It's her ace in the hole. If this mediation doesn't work, then she can go to the police on suspicion of child abuse. Social services do home visits. And this is a small town, word will get around, and when it does..."

"No one wants a doctor who might be abusing his daughter," she said quietly.

"Exactly. Even if it's proven not to be true, people will always have something to say about it. It will always be on their minds when they see me. And that means still no one will want me to be their doctor. I'll probably have to move to a... different town. Not a neighboring one because they all talk."

"That conniving little bitch. She's cunning and utterly ridiculous," she said in a harsh whisper. "I can't believe her."

"Yeah, me either. I don't know where this is coming from all of a sudden. She never showed this much interest in Dani before. And then she showed up unannounced, and then all this shit happened."

Everly shook her head. "She never mentioned anything to me. I heard about it from her husband. She told him that you were abusing Dani. Even he said he couldn't imagine you hurting Dani. But she told him she had seen it with her own eyes. If she hadn't witnessed it, she wouldn't have believed it. I still couldn't believe it. That's why when you called, I felt like I had to come. If you need me to speak during the mediation, I will. Bear in mind I've never been able to talk that girl out of anything, but it might help show her lawyer that she's out of her mind."

"I'd really appreciate you being there."

"Of course." She ran a hand through her long, dark hair. "Marie would have been so upset about this. She might have finally confronted Jamie if she was here and saw what she was trying to do."

"If she was here, this wouldn't be happening." I stared at the black screen of the TV. I felt her eyes on me.

"I know."

The rest of the day was spent talking and finally getting to know each other. Bonnie and Dani joined us after she had finished her homework, and Isaac joined us when he got off work.

"Everly?" He threw his arms open. "Well, look at you, all beautiful and golden."

Her cheeks turned rosy as she smiled. "Marie said you were a charmer."

He grinned. "I have my moments. They don't happen often, though."

I laughed. He was better with women than he thought.

"What do you guys want for dinner?"

Dani tapped her forefinger on her chin. "Hmm.... what do you feel like making, Uncle Sac?"

He joined her in tapping her chin. She giggled. "Well, I'm not sure, Niece Dani. I'm thinking something with shrimp."

"That will work!" We said in unison and then laughed.

For dinner, Isaac made shrimp tacos with a tangy pineapple salsa. It was delicious. Even Everly had good things to say about it. After dinner, the three of them played until Dani went to bed. Everly read her a story before coming back downstairs. Isaac was nursing a beer while I was almost done with mine. He had been drinking less. He hadn't cut it out completely, but it was less than what I had known it to be.

At one point, once he got going, he didn't stop. Couldn't stop. I smiled as I watched him take small sips, glad that he was taking it slow.

"She's such a sweet girl. In some ways, she reminds me of Marie and, in others, you. Perfect combination of both of you," she said as she sat down. "Marie would be so proud."

"What about your other daughter? Was she always crazy?"

I glared at Isaac. Sometimes, he could be so blunt it made you want to hit him in the mouth. A smile tugged at the corner of her lips.

"I don't know what she's got going on. And yes, she has always been a little crazy and a little too obsessed with her sister."

I sputtered. "A little?"

She looked at me and smiled. "Okay, maybe a lot. I know I wasn't the best mother, which caused them to cling to each other, but Marie grew out of that. Jamie could never let go of her. I never understood her fixation on Marie. She had to know where she was, what she was doing, and who she was with. She tried her best to live as close to Marie as possible."

"And now she's gone," I said sadly. I never understood it, myself. I always thought it was weird, but Marie went along with it. She understood Jamie better than any of us ever would. She knew how to deal with her. How do I get her to back off for a little while?

"I always thought she was weird." Isaac sipped his beer. "I remember at one of the gatherings I was at, Jamie was sitting in the corner of the room, out of the way. She wasn't talking to anyone or engaging with other people, even though there were some around her. She just stared at Marie. Every move she made. I told Marie she had a stalker, and I felt like she knew who I was talking about without looking."

"What made you think that?" I asked.

"She said, 'Oh, she always does that. You get used to it.' and then walked away smiling."

I shook my head. "I guess she got used to it. What was Jamie like as a child?"

The slight smile on Everly's face soured almost immediately. "She was a handful.."

"In what way?" Isaac set his beer on the coffee table.

"Well... for example... Marie was given a dog. Well, a boyfriend bought the dog for the girls. It was cute and small and rambunctious. Marie loved it. Jamie didn't like the dog, and the dog didn't like her. He growled every time he saw her, or she got too close. She would try to pet it or hold it and one time, he bit her. But Marie and that dog went everywhere together. And then, one day, the dog disappeared."

"What do you mean disappeared?" Isaac loved gossip.

"One day, he was there, and one day he wasn't. I always thought—I don't have any proof of this-- that Jamie might have been jealous. I would catch her eyeing them. Staring at them while they played. Maybe she thought Marie was giving the dog too much attention. Once the dog was gone, Marie was so broken about it. She sat on the front porch, calling for him for days. Then there Jamie was, watching her. Pretty soon, she started giving her attention back to Jamie."

"Gave her what she wanted," I said. "Sounds about right."

"I could never prove she killed the dog, or let it out, but I think we all knew it. Deep down. We just never talked about it." She glanced down at her watch. "We did that a lot, and now I think we shouldn't have." She stood up. "I'll see you in the morning. Get some sleep."

"You too." I walked her to the door and closed it behind her. Isaac exhaled loudly, so I knew he had something to say. "Yes, little brother?" I went back to the sofa.

"She's nicer than she used to be."

"I guess that's what losing a child does to you. Makes you more empathetic."

"Sad it took that to change her attitude, but here we are. I wonder if Jamie knows she's here. I wonder if Jamie knows she doesn't side with her on this."

I told him what Everly told me about talking to Jamie and telling her this wasn't a good idea.

"Wow. And she's still going through with it. I'm surprised, and yet not, if that makes sense."

"Me too." I leaned back on the sofa. "Those shrimp tacos were incredible. You should add that to the menu at the diner."

"I was thinking about it. Might wait until it's a little cooler out. If that ever happens here."

I laughed. "It's hot all year round. Remember?"

"Hoped things had changed, but I guess not." He finally finished his beer. "Do you need me tomorrow? I can take the day off if you do."

I shook my head. "I appreciate the support, I really do. But right now, I think I'm good. Seeing you might just set her off before we even get started."

"I respect that. She really doesn't like me."

"I know."

"Let me know how it goes. I'm not kidding. Call me as soon as you know."

"Definitely will do. You'll be my first call." I stood up. "Now, get to bed so you can go to work tomorrow."

He laughed. "Will do."

I placed my hand on his shoulder. "See you in the mornin', Sac." I squeezed for a moment.

"Good luck, Log."

CHAPTER TWENTY-SEVEN

Riley Quinn

I TOOK A DEEP BREATH AND EXHALED SLOWLY BEFORE LOOKING AT Zelina, who was pacing next to her desk. Blaese agreed to come in and tell us what he saw that night when he found the body. We agreed it should be an easy conversation, not an interrogation. We should all talk to him and ask him questions like we would any other cop. In other words, pretending we didn't know what we knew. That was the difficult part, especially for Zelina. She had a very expressive face, her emotions woven into every crease. We decided she wasn't going to be part of the conversation.

Just me and him while Zelina was out chasing down a lead.

"You sure about this?" Zelina folded her arms across her chest. She rocked back on her heels, staring at me. "I mean... are you sure about this?"

A smile tugged at my lips. "I'll be okay, Z. I promise."

"I'm just not sure about it," she said. "I mean, I know what we agreed to, but this just doesn't feel right, you know."

"Yeah, Z, I know. But if we were all in there, he would get suspicious. This way, it's just us having a conversation about the case. Nothing more. I truly believe it will be better this way. And look around, building full of cops. Nothing is going to happen." I gave her my best reassuring smile. She was not amused.

"Okay. We'll do it your way." She grabbed her phone and keys just as Blaese was walking through the door. "I'll let you know what I find," she yelled back as she walked past him.

I met him at the front desk. "Sorry for ruining your day off."

He waved a hand dismissively. "No problem. We weren't doing anything. Just sitting on the sofa watching movies." He looked back at the front door. "Where is she going? You guys got a lead?"

"She's running down a lead. Don't think there's much to it, but we have to turn every stone, you know." I gestured toward the conference room. "Come on, we'll go in here and talk." I spun around. "Wait, let me get my case files and notes." I picked up the stack of files on my desk and then followed him into the conference room. "Okay. We know the cases are connected." I set the folders down. "We just haven't worked out how. But I know that when the body of Delilah Preston was found, you were the first on the scene. We've been talking to officers who were the first on all the scenes to see if they saw anything that might have seemed small at the time but could have been important. Your first thoughts when you got to the scene and all that. Anything you can tell us could be helpful at this point."

"Sure. I'd be happy to help. Just give me a moment to get my thoughts together. Do you have her file so I can refresh it?"

"Sure." I searched through the stack and found her file. I slid it over to him. "Take your time. You want some coffee?"

"I would love some, thank you."

I stood up. "Two sugars and one cream?"

"You know me."

I winced at the statement. I hoped he didn't notice as I walked out of the room. I returned with two coffees. "Here you go."

"Thanks." He took a long sip. "That's right. Scene was a mess. So many flies and mosquitos buzzing around, all over her body."

"What did you see when you first got to the scene? Anything jump out at you?" I took out my notepad and pen.

"Umm... not really."

"How did you find the body?"

He sighed. "Well... she was in the wooded area next to the road. I can't say what made me stop. I mean, we usually see trash on the side of the road. When I looked over there, I thought I had seen feet. Now, at first, I'm thinking it was a mannequin or something and started driving by, but then I stopped. Why the hell would a mannequin be on the side of the road? So I backed up, got out, and investigated, and that was when I found her."

"That's a good find. Was there anyone or anything in the area? Trash by the body?" He shrugged. "Not that I can remember. There was nothing. It was just her, which I thought was weird."

"Why?"

He leaned back and sipped his coffee. "I mean there... it was just her. No trash, nothing to try to obscure the body. Nothing around her. I was amazed that someone could dump her there and leave nothing else behind. I knew she had to have been dumped because there were no drag marks. It was weird. The person was careful."

"Which meant they might have done it before."

"Exactly. But the case never went anywhere."

My phone buzzed in my pocket. I glanced at the screen. "Seems like someone came in saying they saw Delilah the night she went missing. She wants to talk." I slid the folders over to him. "Look through the files and see if anything jogs your memory."

"Sure."

I walked out of the room, rounded the corner, and stopped short. A woman stood next to my desk with Zelina. She looked exactly like Stephen's ex-wife. Same dark hair and deep brown eyes. They could have been related. I walked over.

"I just walked in, and she was here looking to speak with us."

"Okay." I looked back at the hallway that led to the conference room. If we walked in that direction, Blaese would see her. I didn't know what she had to say but I didn't want him to see her at the moment. "Let's talk in the captain's office." We ushered her inside. He frowned in surprise.

"What's this, Detective?" he asked.

I closed the door behind me. "She has something she wants to talk to us about the case."

"Let's hear it."

The woman's eyes went wide. "Umm... was this a good idea?"

"Yes. We will take any information you can give us. It would be much appreciated," I said.

"Right. Well, I don't know if this is pertinent to your investigation." She glanced at the captain for a moment. "But I heard that you all believe an officer did this. To those women."

Zelina, Williams, and I traded glances. "Where did you hear that?"

"Rumor going around town. I was at the coffee shop and heard some people talking about it."

My jaw twitched. My mother loved to gossip, and while she may not have gotten that information firsthand, she sure helped to pass it around. I hadn't even talked to her about the case.

"Did you hear the name of the officer?" asked Zelina.

"No, I didn't. No one said his name. But... it made me think of something that happened a little while ago. I was pulled over and something weird happened."

"Weird, how?" I leaned against the door.

"An officer pulled me over. I didn't know why because I wasn't speeding or anything. I had a bad feeling, but I pulled over anyway. I grabbed my license and registration and got out of the car like he asked. I met him by the trunk and handed him everything he needed. He started talking like he was trying to pick me up or something. I asked him if we could hurry this up because my husband was sick in the car. We were out, and I think he ate something bad in Oceanway. I was trying to get him home before he threw up in my car."

"What did the officer say?"

"He looked startled. Like surprised my husband was in the car. He craned his neck to look into my car, but he was lying down. He walked around the side of the car and peered inside. When he saw my husband, he stumbled back, handed me my license and registration, and told me to get him home. He ran back to his car and then left."

"Wow."

"I got such a bad feeling about everything. I got back in my car and drove off. I wanted to call the police, but I didn't know what to say. I mean, what could I say? He didn't do anything. He was weird and cagey, and he gave me a bad feeling, but," she threw her hands up, "I mean, nothing happened."

She had a point. It wasn't like we could prosecute him for pulling her over. If he didn't do anything, there was nothing we could do. "Do you remember his name?"

She shrugged. "We didn't get that far. I remember what he looks like, but it was too dark for me to read the name on his shirt."

"I see." Zelina scrolled through her phone and then held it out to the woman. "Him?"

The woman gasped. "Yes! That's him. There was something about his eyes. They were so dark and emotionless. It was like he was looking right through me. Like I was nothing."

"Okay." Zelina shoved her phone into her pocket. "I'm going to take your statement, and I want you to describe everything in detail."

I opened the door and let them out. "Okay," I said, closing the door behind them. "Now we know. I feel better about interrogating him now."

The captain nodded. "Yeah. I still don't want to believe it, though. He was one of our best. What happened to him?"

"His wife left him, and then he snapped, I guess."

"Okay. Go back and keep him talking."

I left the office and headed back to the conference room. Stephen sat at the table, his arms folded, with a wide grin on his face.

"Did you find anything?" I closed the door behind me.

"How about we cut the shit?" he shrugged. "Tell me why I'm here."

"What do you mean why? I told you why already, didn't I?" I smiled as I sat down. His grin was unnerving. A shiver coasted up my spine. "Are you okay?"

"You think I did something to those women."

I blinked. "I never said that."

"I'm a cop. I know how you all operate. I'm not stupid. If you wanted to know about the case, you could have just looked at my notes. But you wanted to see how I reacted when I looked at the case files and the pictures. You were hoping I would open up."

I leaned back in my chair. "Where is this coming from?"

"You thinking you could play me? I was a cop before you bought your first training bra. I know what you're doing, so just ask me what you want to ask me."

It wasn't just the dark look in his eyes, but his voice. He was calm. His voice was light. It was creepy. "Okay. Since you brought it up, did you have anything to do with these missing women?"

"Of course not."

"Do you have an alibi for the dates and times these women went missing?"

"What are they?"

I looked through the folders for each case and told him when they went missing. He recounted his alibis before standing up. "Check that and come back to me and apologize." The smug smirk on his face made my blood boil. I watched him walk out and down the hall before relaxing in my chair. How was he on to us? I was careful, or at least I thought I was. I didn't say anything to tip him off.

My fingers drummed against the table while I replayed my time with him in my mind. Before I left, he was fine, but once I came back, it was like something changed. A switch had been flipped, and I just needed to know what flipped it. I stared at the files on the table. He had looked through them. Did something in the files tip him off?

"What happened?" Zelina burst through the doors. "Why did he leave?"

"He gave me his alibis for the times the women went missing, and then he left. Told me to check them and then apologize to him."

Z's eyebrow raised. "Are you serious? What did you say?"

I threw my hands up. "I don't know. I was just running it through my mind. Everything was fine until I got up and left the room. When I came back, it was like he knew what we were trying to do."

"Okay. Let's run down his alibis. We'll divide and conquer and see if he's telling the truth. I don't think he is, though."

We split up to check his alibis. The first place I went to was a convenience store, where he said he stopped by to get some snacks for the car. The owner could not tell me if he was there that night.

"I'm sorry. I don't know, and the tapes record over the previous footage every other day. I can say that Officer Blaese comes in a lot. At the start of every shift. He gets some sports drinks and some snacks. I'm always telling him to have a full meal. He says his wife cooks for him when he gets home."

"I see. Well, thank you for your time." Since that was a bust, I moved to the second place, a bar where he said he broke up a fight between two guys that started over a pretty girl. Patrol officers broke up a lot of fights, so it was plausible.

"Hello, I want to talk to you about a fight that had to be broken up by the police a little while ago."

The bartender stared at me for a long moment. "A fight?" He looked back at a waitress who was loading glasses underneath the bar. "Yo, Alice, did the cops have to break up a fight a while ago?"

She paused for a moment. "I don't think so. Not recently, anyway. We did last year, though."

"No, it would have been sooner than that. March fourteenth, to be exact."

They exchanged a look and then laughed. "Yeah, no one was here that night."

"Are you sure?" I leaned onto the bar.

She nodded. "Definitely. Some dumbass in the kitchen overloaded the fuse box, and everything shut off. The power went out, and we couldn't get it back that night. It wasn't fixed until the next day. That afternoon, actually. Regulars were pissed."

"Oh, I see. So there was no fight here to break up because no one was here." I nodded slowly as I inched toward the door. "Thank you for your time."

I hurried back to my car, eager to call Zelina. This just busted his alibi. It was just what we needed to pull him back in and begin the interrogation. If he had been anywhere near the bar that night, he would have known that it was closed. The lie was proof he was somewhere else.

CHAPTER TWENTY-EIGHT

Logan Elwood

MY HEART POUNDED AGAINST MY RIBS. IT HAD BEEN LIKE THAT all morning. No matter how many deep breathing exercises I did or how I tried to calm myself down, my heart never got the message. Bert sat next to me, reading something on his phone.

"Relax, Logan. No point in getting worked up about something until we know how it will turn out."

That was easier said than done. I couldn't stop thinking about all the things that could go wrong and how this could impact my working in the town. Jamie hadn't made a formal complaint, so that was a good sign. But if this mediation didn't go her way, that might be her next course of action.

Everly peered into the room. "Thought I was late." She walked in and sat on my right.

"You are, but she's later," I said.

Everly looked down at her watch. "That girl was never able to be on time for anything."

I sighed. "I guess old habits die hard."

Jamie was thirty minutes late. She and her lawyer strolled in like nothing was wrong and they were right on time. Bert made a point to check his watch. Her lawyer noticed.

"Sorry for the delay. We were hoping Mr. Washington could join us, but he had to go home and be with the kids. I'm sure you understand. But now that we are here, let's get started."

Jamie and her lawyer reminded me of each other. Both women were dressed to the nines. Her lawyer wore an expensive pantsuit with Louis Vuitton black heels. Jamie wore a dark blue dress that just looked expensive with black stilettos. Their jewelry was expensive. Everything about them oozed money.

"What are you doing here?" Jamie's eyes narrowed at her mother. I guess she really didn't know Everly was coming. She looked betrayed as she sat down. "Thought you weren't getting involved."

"I want what's best for my granddaughter."

Jamie rolled her eyes. "Then you are sitting on the wrong side of the table." Her tone was terse. She sounded like if she could, she would have had a lot more to say to her mother. But that would have made her look bad.

The mediator walked into the room, an older woman with graying hair around her temples and a no-nonsense look on her face. She stared at Jamie as she walked in, as if she didn't approve of her tardiness. She sat down at the head of the table.

"Are we all ready to get started?"

Both lawyers answered yes, and then it started. She explained the rules and made sure we both understood that we would not talk over each other. We were supposed to take turns speaking, and we were only supposed to speak when she called on us. I knew I could follow the rules; I wasn't too sure about Jamie.

"Now, as I understand it, this mediation is about the custody of Danielle Elwood. Is that right?"

"Yes, ma'am," said Bert.

"Okay. Mrs. Washington, since you are the one who started all this, you start. Why are we here?"

Her lawyer spoke first. "My client's sole interest in all of this is what's best for her niece. That's her main priority. Her only priority. We don't believe Dani is in a good environment living with her father."

My hands clenched underneath the table. *Who the hell was she to say that?* Bert placed a hand on my arm, signaling to me to calm down. I took a deep breath.

"Now, Mr. Elwood might be a good father. He might love his daughter, but his home is not the best place for her at the moment."

"What makes you say that, Mrs. Washington?"

Her lawyer looked at her, uncertainty rippling through her facial expression. I saw it. She wasn't sure if she should let Jamie speak. It was probably better if she didn't. I knew Jamie, and so did her mother, and I think her lawyer might have gotten a feel for what her client was really like.

"Well, Dani needs love and care and attention. Logan works all the time. I stayed with him when I first got into town. He gets home so late. By the time he walks through the door, she is already in bed. They can only spend time together in the morning, and that is stunted by both of them trying to get ready for the day. They have no time together. He's missing out on her growing up, and she's missing out on a loving parent." Jamie opened her mouth to say something else, but her lawyer clamped a hand on her forearm. She didn't want Jamie to talk too much and get off track.

"What do you have to say about that, Mr. Elwood?"

"Someone has to work, and I am all she has right now. Mrs. Washington is a stay-at-home mother, so yes, she can be there with her all the time. But she also has children of her own that she doesn't care for. She has two nannies that take care of her children. If she can have a nanny, why can't I? My nanny, Bonnie, loves Dani, and Dani loves her. She fills in when I'm not there. And I usually am home for dinner unless there is an emergency."

"What kind of an emergency?"

"The night Jamie was there when I didn't come home until late was because a patient of mine was having a hard time breathing and other complications. I suspected she had a deadly condition if left untreated, but the clinic didn't have the equipment to check. I had to drive her to the closest hospital so they could do the scans and then surgery."

"And you stayed with her after you got her there?"

"He did. But getting back to Dani should have been his main priority," said Jamie.

"It was, but this patient didn't have anyone else to stay with her. Her daughter was informed of her condition, and she was on her way. I stayed to explain things to her, and I wanted to see how my patient reacted to the surgery. I wanted to make sure she came through the surgery okay, and she did. I checked on her and made sure there were no complications, and then I went home."

"Where Dani was already sleeping."

"My daughter knows that I love her. And she knows that my job is to help people. To make them better. She understands that. She knows me… but she doesn't know you."

Jamie's jaw twitched. "She is my niece. She knows I'm her aunt, and I love her."

"She's had very little contact with you until very recently. That wasn't my choice, it was yours. And now, out of the blue, you want to take her from me."

"Okay." The mediator took off her glasses and rubbed her eyes. "Both of you believe you can give the girl a better home than the other. My question for Mrs. Washington is, why would you fight to get custody of your niece—using the evidence of the nanny—even though you would be bringing her into a similar situation?"

"I just think I can give her a better home. And I do spend time with my children. He doesn't know what he's talking about. I love my children. He's never been to our home; he doesn't know anything."

She turned her attention to Everly. "And you are?"

"I'm Dani's grandmother. Jamie's mother."

"I see. And what do you have to add to this conversation? Is your daughter correct?"

"No, she's not."

Jamie's eyes narrowed at her. Rage poured through her pores. If we weren't there, she would have slit her mother's throat right then and there.

"I'm sorry, Jamie, but I'm only thinking about my granddaughter's best interests. I believe she is right where she needs to be. I love my daughter, but uprooting Dani for no reason doesn't make any sense. She's happy where she is, and she is loved and cared for. Logan is doing a wonderful job raising her. Just what Marie would have wanted."

The scowl on Jamie's face grew deeper. Everly winced next to me at the sight of her.

"Hmm, that is something to think about. The best interest of the child. Move her from the only loving home she's ever known to someone who says they can give her more love and attention or keep her with her father?"

Jamie shook her head. "He is not a good father. He abuses his daughter."

"That's a lie!" I snapped.

She glared at me. "I saw it with my own eyes. You can fool everyone else, but I know what you are. You will never fool me, and Dani will not be safe until she is away from you," she spat.

"Those are serious allegations, Mrs. Washington. Are you sure you want to make them?"

"It's the truth. I know what I saw."

"Jamie—"

"Stay out of this, Mother." Jamie leaned forward, her dark eyes burrowing a hole through Everly. "You did not know what Marie wanted. You didn't know her. She didn't even like being around you. *I* was her sister. She told *me* everything. Not you. I know what she wanted, and she wanted me to take care of Dani."

"What about a compromise," I interjected, trying to quell as much of the hostility in the room as possible.

"Okay, what is the compromise?" asked the mediator.

"Dani can spend half the summers with her aunt and her cousins. She would like to get to know them. And that way Jamie could spend more time with her."

Jamie burst out of her seat. "The summer? I'm sorry, *part* of the summer? Are you serious? Why don't you take her part of the summer, and I have her full time."

"For Heaven's sake, Jamie!" Everly jumped up. "Dani is not *your* child. Why can't you see that? Why would you have more rights to her than her actual parent? How does that make sense? You are not owed her. She is not some rag doll you can pick up and play with whenever you want. She's his daughter."

The mediator cleared her throat. "Okay, let's all calm down. I know tensions are high, as they usually are during custody disputes. But remember, you all came here to let cooler heads prevail."

I took a deep breath. "What do you want, Jamie?"

She leaned forward, pressing her palm onto the table. "Dani. I want Dani. You can get visitation, but I want her full-time. It's either all or nothing."

"That is not a fair proposal," Bert said. "You are her aunt. There are no signs of abuse in the home. No complaints from the school or anyone else who comes in contact with Dani on a daily basis. There is no reason for you to take custody."

Jamie rolled her eyes. "Either I get it, or we go to court."

I couldn't help but notice how quiet her lawyer was now and how she looked up at Jamie. She stared at her like she was surprised Jamie was saying all of this and was this angry about the situation. It was clearly a side to her she had not seen before. She tried to reach out and grab her hand. Jamie jerked her arm out of reach. She would not be calmed.

"We need to think about Dani—"

"I am! What's best for Dani is all I think about. She is everything to me."

"Since when!" Everly mimicked her posture, leaning forward so she could hear her. "You have never cared about that child. If you did, where have you been? She's seven, why now? You are not good with children. We all know this, so why fight harder for your niece than you do for your own kids?"

Jamie looked like she wanted to scream. I braced myself for what would come next. My heart stuttered in my chest. Jamie's face contorted in such a way it surprised us all. The rage etched into every line, every crease was startling. The mediator stood up sharply. "There will be no further shouting in this room. This is mediation, where we talk about the problems calmly."

Jamie's eyes were fixed on her mother. It was like there was no one else in the room, just Everly. "Dani will be mine. We're going to court if we have to," she spat and then turned on her heel and rushed out of the room. Her lawyer lingered for a moment before gathering her briefcase and inching out the door. Everly collapsed into her chair.

Can't wait to tell Isaac about this.

❧

Bert followed me home after the chaotic mediation. We sat in the living room in silence for a long moment. It went about how I expected. Her lawyer, Diane, looked surprised by Jamie's outrage. She wasn't expecting it. I imagined them talking about their game plan and Jamie being calm and collected and telling her she wouldn't do or say anything that might make her look bad. And there she was. Screaming at her mother like she lost her mind.

"Were you expecting this?" Bert's voice snapped me out of my thoughts. I looked up at him, his eyes fixed on mine. "You were the only one in that room that didn't jump when she started screaming. Well, you and Everly."

"We both expected it. When Jamie doesn't get what she wants, she explodes."

"I see. Damn. She needs therapy, not another child to take care of." His phone dinged. Bert pulled it from his breast pocket. The blue screen lit up his face. "Do you know anything about St. Mary's School for Girls?"

My eyebrow raised. "What? Why?"

"I told you I was having someone look into her. She seems a bit unhinged. My investigator just found out she went to that school for a time."

"He can't ask them about it?"

"School's closed. Burned down, actually, while she went there. Thirty-three students and faculty died."

My jaw clenched. "Are you serious? I can't believe I didn't hear about that. Like it wasn't on the news."

"You would have been in high school, and I doubt you were paying attention to the news back then. And it was a Catholic school. If they can keep something under wraps that might make them look bad, they do so at all costs."

"It doesn't ring a bell." As soon as I heard the word 'fire', Jamie flashed in my mind. I didn't want to think she would have started that fire, but the way she acted today made it plausible. If there was something in the school she wanted and was denied, she would have done whatever she could to get it or punished the people who denied her.

"She might have gone there. Don't know who to ask as I assume the fire burned all the records."

"The entire building was burned down?"

He turned his phone so I could see the picture he had been sent. On the screen was a building utterly destroyed. Seventy-five percent was crumbled onto the ground. The rest was charred, uninhabitable. "Damn."

"He's going to keep looking into that. While he does that, I should tell you a social worker might show up in a couple of days. Jamie made a complaint of child abuse, and even though there is no evidence, it still has to be investigated. It has to be reported."

"Okay. I figured as much."

"It might be a few days or a week. They won't find anything." He stood up. "If anything else happens or she shows up, call the police and then call me. If someone comes here and tries to take her, call me and then the police. Understand?"

"Got it."

CHAPTER TWENTY-NINE

Logan Elwood

It didn't take a few days. The next evening, the doorbell rang.

"How can I help you?" I stared at the older woman with light, pink-rimmed glasses hovering in my doorway.

"Yes, I'm Peggy Lockwood, with social services. I'm here for a home visit."

I stared at her, my mind completely blank. I didn't know what to say or what to do. My throat felt dry and crawled out of my mouth. "What? We just had the mediation yesterday."

She smiled warmly. "I understand this might be a shock. Surprise home visits give us a better view of what family life is really about." She looked behind her and then leaned forward and whispered, "Maybe we should take this inside, so your neighbors don't get inquisitive."

I blinked. "Right. Come in." I moved aside so she could enter.

"Thank you. Now we have received a complaint about you and the home you provide for Danielle. So I'm here to get a lay of the land and see if the complaint holds water." Her voice was soft and cheerful. She was probably used to diffusing chaotic situations.

"By whom?"

"Well, I can't give out that information. I'm sure you can understand. I will say there was a complaint, and someone at the courthouse vouched for you, but I still have to check."

My mind immediately flashed to the mediator. She might have been on my side. "What do you need to see?"

"Well, first, I need to do a walkthrough of the house. Look at her room and the fridge, and then I need to speak with her and the nanny."

"Understood. I'll give you a tour."

She smiled again. "Lead the way."

I showed her around the house, even the rooms and bedrooms that had nothing to do with Dani. I showed her the kitchen and inside the fridge. She approved of all the fruits and vegetables.

"And she eats them?"

"My brother cooks. He even packs her lunches, and he has a way of fixing them in a way she eats them."

She laughed. "That sounds fun."

"He's a big kid, she's a kid, they get along perfectly."

"Well, it takes a village."

I sighed. "Yes, it does. Now I'll take you upstairs. Dani is in her room."

"Doing her homework?"

"She should be." I led her upstairs and knocked on her bedroom door.

"I'm doing my homework!" She yelled from the other side.

Peggy laughed. "Now she is."

I opened the door. Dani sat at her desk with her books open and a blank sheet of paper in front of her. "I see you're doing your homework."

She grinned.

I gestured to Peggy. "This is Mrs. Lockwood; she wants to talk to you."

The woman leaned forward with a kind smile. "You can call me Peggy."

Dani giggled. "That's a funny name."

"Be respectful to our guest, Dani," I said lightly.

"Oh, don't worry. It is a pretty funny name. That's why I kept it!"

I left them alone and closed the door behind me. I wanted to lean against the door and listen to what was being said, but if caught, that would have gotten me in trouble with Peggy and Dani. I walked downstairs and gave them their privacy.

"So what happened yesterday?" Isaac sat his phone and wallet on the console as he got home.

I shook my head. "Exactly what we thought was going to happen." I walked into the living room and sat down.

"Seriously? She snapped?" He collapsed next to me.

"Pretty much. She snapped at her mother. Jumped up and started yelling. Said Dani was hers."

"She's not a car. You can't own a person."

"I proposed a compromise, you know. As much as it pained me, I said she could spend half of the summer with Jamie and her family. She said no. She said she gets full custody, and I can see her for part of the summer."

"What kind of bullshit is that?" Isaac leaned to the side and looked at me.

"That's a good question. Even her mother was against Jamie's getting custody, and that only made her angrier. Like the way she was looking at her, if we weren't there, she would have slit her throat. You could feel the rage in the room. It was crazy."

"She and her mom ever get along?"

I shrugged. There might have been a time when Jamie and Marie were younger when they got along with their mother, but that was ancient history. "If they had, it's all gone now. But Everly stood up for me, and I was both surprised and really appreciative. She even thought I was raising her the way Marie would have wanted. Almost made me tear up."

"Aww!"

"Shut up." A chuckle bubbled up my throat as Mrs. Lockwood approached.

"Well, I've talked to both Bonnie and Dani." She looked at Isaac and smiled.

"Who's the old lady?" whispered Isaac. He never learned how to whisper. Peggy grinned.

"I take it, this is your brother?"

"His favorite brother," answered Isaac.

"Only. You are my only brother."

He smiled. "Again, who is this lady?"

"Isaac, meet Peggy Lockwood. A social worker. Jamie lodged a complaint, and they had to do a home visit."

Isaac straightened up. "I can't believe her—well, you know what, yes, I can." He looked at Peggy. "So what now?"

"Well, from what I can see, there is no reason to be concerned about Dani. She's adjusting well to her life here, and she doesn't look abused or malnourished. She's a happy, healthy seven-year-old girl. I don't see anything wrong here, and I will include that in my report. Now that a complaint has been filed, we may do another home visit in a few months, but I don't think this is anything you have to worry about."

Peggy turned around to leave. She paused. "Look... I shouldn't be saying this, and if anyone asks the words never came out of my mouth."

Isaac leaned forward, eager to hear whatever gossip she was about to lay down.

"The person who made the complaint is someone you need to watch out for. I can't get into particulars."

"But?" I watched her for a long moment. Her face twisted, and her mouth opened and closed several times before any words came out.

"Keep Dani close. Just keep her close, and don't let her out of your sight."

CHAPTER THIRTY

Riley Quinn

"I wonder what his second wife looks like." Zelina sat at the head of the table, staring at the folders on the table. They were open, crime scene photos scattered around the table. "The one he supposedly just got married to."

I paced back and forth near the whiteboard at the front of the room. "Has anyone seen her? Is she still alive?" I spun around and faced the room. Captain Williams sat at the far side of the table typing on his computer.

Zelina jumped up. "I'll go check on that. See if she has anything she wants to add to this conversation." She ran out of the room. Officer Rainwater walked in behind her. The captain jumped to his feet. "Rainwater, this is a private—"

He held up a hand to stop him. "I know you guys are looking at Blaese for these murders, and I want to know if there is anything I can do to help."

I stared at him. We hadn't told anyone that we thought Stephen was a killer. How did he know? "He's your partner."

"I understand that. But I don't think these accusations are unfounded."

"You think he did it?" Captain Williams inched forward.

He sighed. "I think that it might be possible he had something to do with it. I have no proof, just a hunch."

"And why do you have this hunch?" the Captain asked. I sat down at the table, and he followed suit. "What has he done to make you think that he might have been responsible for this?"

Rainwater took a slow, deep breath. "When his wife left him... when she finally divorced him, he became a different person. I wasn't his partner when they were still together. I came on a week or so after she left him. He was angry all the time. And he really didn't like women. I mean, when he pulled one over, it got nasty."

"Why didn't you say anything?"

"He was going through something. He was working through it and slowly got better. Really, after he met his second wife, I thought he was okay."

"When he used to pull women over, what did they look like?"

"Most of them have brown hair and dark brown eyes. Kind of petite."

I sighed. "You should have said something."

"I know. But I was a rookie, and he was my superior. He was just mad about his wife and was working through it. I tried to give him a little grace."

"You gave him too much." The captain's voice vibrated off the walls.

"I know." He leaned back. "I screwed up."

My fingers drummed against the table. "What made you come in here?"

He shrugged. "I don't know. I was thinking about Delilah's body. The way he looked at her on the ground, it... there was something evil there."

"What do you mean?"

"He didn't see me coming behind him when we saw the body. He smiled. He stared at her body before you guys pulled up, and he was just smiling at her. It was unnerving. I can't get the image out of my head. At first, I thought I was just making it a bigger deal than it was. Maybe he was happy we found her. But I heard you guys were looking at an officer for the murders, and he immediately entered my mind. As soon as I heard it, the image of him standing over her body... it was all I could see."

"Right." My forefinger tapped the table. "I guess we should bring him back in and start asking more questions."

～

Blaese and his attorney, a portly man with a trimmed beard and gold-rimmed glasses, sat in the interrogation room. He walked in with a smug look on his face, like he knew we had nothing concrete against him. My blood boiled in my veins.

"Hey, so I met with his wife, and she's in one of the interrogation rooms. She was eager to come down." Zelina set her phone on her desk. "You want to talk to her first?"

"Could always use more ammunition."

Sharon Blaese's eyes went wide when I walked in. "What has he done? Did someone make a complaint?"

"No." I sat down. "We just want to ask you a few questions about your husband." I ignored the fact that she immediately jumped to him being in trouble before we even had a chance to say anything. "How does he treat you?"

She winced. "What do you mean?"

"Well, we've spoken to his first wife, and we know how he treated her. The abuse. We just wanted to know if he did the same to you." I stared at her. She looked like the first Mrs. Blaese. Same dark hair and dark brown eyes. Petite frame. She was pretty, but her nerves were frayed. She looked jittery, like she was expecting him to walk through the door at any moment.

"We have him in an interrogation room. He doesn't know you are here, nor will we tell him. We just need to know more information. How has he been acting the past few days?"

Her shoulders fell slightly. Zelina's words seemed to help her relax. "I don't know. Same as always. Angry."

"He's always angry?"

She nodded. "Mad at me, mad at the job. He's just mad. All the time. He wasn't like that when I met him. He was kind and gentle, even. That all went out the window."

"Did he talk about the cases we were working on?"

"The missing women?"

I nodded. She tapped the table. "He watched the news a lot. I only noticed because he usually doesn't. But every night, when they talked about the case, he was watching. Eyes glued to the screen. He didn't even notice me." Her eyes drifted to the ceiling. "He had this weird smile on his face—more of a smirk—when they talked about her. That Delilah woman. I know that grin. I've seen it on several occasions. He only does it when he's about to hurt me. Every time."

My heart hurt for her. Tears pricked her eyes. She tilted her head up and blinked them away. "I don't know how I can help you. He doesn't let me go anywhere unless I'm with him. He doesn't like taking me places."

"Okay. I think that's enough for now," I said. The conversation went about as well as I thought it would. She didn't know anything more than we did. It was time to talk to Stephen. I walked into the room, Zelina trailing close behind.

His eyes met mine, and he smiled. "Thought you had forgotten about me."

"Not possible." I sat down across from him. Zelina stood by the door silently.

The lawyer cleared his throat. "My client is a decorated officer. The fact that he is accused of this crime is ridiculous."

"That's what I said." Stephen smirked.

"We have his fingerprints on the back of the car driven by one of our victims."

Stephen laughed. "All officers do that when they make a traffic stop. You know that. *That* doesn't mean I did anything to her."

He was right. The fingerprints weren't enough to arrest him. We didn't have much else in the way of evidence. Our best bet was to keep him talking.

"We met your wife—well, your wives, actually." The smile on his face disintegrated. Now, it was my turn to smile. "They both had a lot to say about you. I mean, a *lot*."

"And yet you still can't arrest me. I guess those bitches didn't have too much to say, huh?"

And there it was. The only button he had that we could press. His wives. The women who looked just like his victims. His Achilles heel. I stood up, grabbed Zelina by the arm, and led her out of the room. Closing the door behind me, I took her arm again and led her to our desks. Her face wrinkled in confusion.

"That's it?"

She stared at me for a moment. I went on to explain. "That's his sore spot. What's going to get him to talk? His wives. You think you could talk his ex-wife into coming down here?"

Zelina grabbed her keys from her desk. "I'll give it a shot and let you know how it goes."

While she was gone, I sat at my desk and started writing. Zelina returned with the first Mrs. Blaese in tow. "Hi. Thank you so much for coming down."

"She said it was important."

"It is. It really is, even though it will be difficult for you. I need you to talk to your ex-husband and get him to confess."

Isla took a large step back. I reached out and grabbed her shoulders. "I know you don't want to do it. And I understand why, but he killed those women because he was still pissed at you. And if we don't get some kind of evidence to send him to prison, he will do it again and again and again. Until he goes after the real thing."

She blinked back tears.

"I know this will be hard," said Zelina. "But we will be in the room with you. He won't be able to hurt you. We promise."

"We wouldn't ask if we didn't need you."

Her eyes flicked to my desk, where autopsy pictures of Delilah were front and center. That wasn't intentional. I had forgotten about them until that moment. Tears welled in her eyes. Zelina handed her a tissue. She wiped her eyes and drew in a shaky breath.

"What am I supposed to say to him?"

I smiled. "Thank you." I handed her the notepad I had been writing on. Questions for her to ask him. If this was to work, she had to be the only other person talking. I gave her a few minutes so she could regain her composure, then I led her into the room.

Stephen's eyes narrowed as soon as he saw her. I felt her body shaking next to me at the sight of him. I placed my hand on the small of her back. "It's okay."

I pulled out the chair. Slowly and reluctantly, she eased down into the chair. The notepad rested on the table. I followed Zelina, leaning on the back wall and watching him. Isla looked back at me, watery-eyed, bottom lip trembling. My heart sank into my stomach. Doing this to her wasn't right, but it was our only option at the moment. His second wife might piss him off a little bit, but the first one... this was where the rage started, why he killed those women to begin with. The main source of his anger. Just the sight of her should set him off. It wasn't something we wanted to do, but we had to try it. If it got too intense, we would step in.

"Did you kill Delilah?" I asked.

Stephen laughed. "You gettin' her to do your work for you. She's never been good at anything." He leaned forward, eyes fixed on her.

I watched her left leg vibrating underneath the table. My fists clenched at my sides.

"Why do you hate me so much?" Her voice was shaky. She sounded like her lips were quivering.

His eyes narrowed at her. "Who said I hated you?"

She slid the pictures I gave her onto the table. Moving them directly in front of him. "Then why do they look just like me? Why them?"

He rolled his eyes and leaned back. Arms folded across his chest. "I don't know what you're talking about."

She stared at the pictures. "You strangled them." It wasn't a question, nor had I written it down for her to say. "I remember how you used to strangle me with your gloved hands. Sometimes, with a small cord. Pull so tight until I passed out. I remember waking up..." Her leg shook violently under the table. "Waking up with you on top of me. Inside of me."

He grinned. "You deserved it."

"Why?"

She's going off-book.

"Because you were my wife. I had a right to do those things. You were mine!" He spat the words through clenched teeth. "You deserved everything I did to you."

"What about them?"

"They deserved it too."

"But they weren't your wives."

"Well, if you had stayed in your place, that wouldn't have happened. It's your fault, not mine. *You* left."

"I left you, so you had to kill women that looked like me?"

"Well, I damn sure couldn't kill you, could I? It would have been too obvious. I'd be the first suspect."

I looked at his lawyer, who sat next to him stunned. His mouth gaped open, eyes wide. I half expected him to interject at some point. Tell him to stop talking. End the interrogation. But he was just as engrossed as we were. Hanging on every question.

"I guess that makes sense. But they didn't deserve it. You strangled them and left them in the woods where no one would find them."

"I wish I could have left you somewhere no one would find you. I couldn't do to them what I wanted to do to you. I had it planned.

Written out and everything. But that would have left behind too much evidence. I would have cut up my hands and the *things...*"

He closed his eyes and smiled. "The things I would do to your mangled body... mmm. I would have had to burn you to get rid of all that evidence." He opened his eyes. "I went for the less risky option. Something that ensured I got away scot-free. But now... now I don't care."

Stephen jumped to his feet. He lunged for her, but before his hands could land around her neck, I grabbed his wrist, twisted it, and shoved his face into the table. I twisted his arm until it was behind his back. I placed him in cuffs. Zelina led him out of the room.

I wrapped my arms around her. She sobbed into my shoulder. His lawyer leaned against the wall, mouth wide open, hands trembling. It was a long while before the three of us left the room. My shirt was soaked with her tears, and he was still trembling. The station was so quiet when I walked her out to escort her home. Even quieter when I returned. Zelina sat at her desk filling out paperwork.

I collapsed into my chair. "Second time this year we've arrested someone everyone liked."

"Says a lot about everyone, doesn't it?"

CHAPTER THIRTY-ONE

Riley Quinn

I HAD NEVER SLEPT SO HARD IN MY LIFE AS I DID IN THE DAYS AFTER Stephen Blaese was arrested. Going off of a few hours of sleep was not healthy, as Doctor Elwood kept reminding me. I was instructed by both he and my mother to go straight to bed. My sister still had Luna. I missed her. Sleeping in bed wasn't the same without her snoring or her paws scratching me while she slept. She was an active dog even when she dreamed.

I slept in fits. Tossing and turning. A few hours here, a few hours there, the first night. Then, the next I didn't remember waking up to go to the bathroom until midnight. All twenty-four hours out like a light. I guess my body needed all the energy drinks and coffee to work its way out of my system before it could relax.

I still got the gossip from the office though. Mostly from my mother. *Who is feeding her information?* She told me about Stephen and his refusal to take a plea. We had his confession on tape, but he said it didn't count. His wife wasn't a cop. And while she wasn't, he still confessed while we were in the room in front of his lawyer.

The prosecutor was looking for a way to make it stick. Aside from that, the Prestons buried their daughter, and the other bodies were taken to their loved ones.

"I feel like we might have missed a few, you know? Those women couldn't have been the only ones that looked like his wife. I don't believe that."

I agreed with her. Zelina wanted to search for other bodies, but we didn't know where to look, and he wasn't talking.

"What happened with Cynthia's mother?"

"Oh! I forgot I hadn't told you about that. Well, she did what we thought she did."

"I thought so! What did she say?"

"Basically, she realized he had been molesting their daughter, and she was going to tell. He killed Cynthia in a fit of rage. She figured it out and killed him. Then she staged it to make it look like a suicide."

"Wow. I get it. I mean, it's wrong, but I get it. You turning her in?"

"No. Sending her to prison won't do anything. That woman is living in hell every day."

"Okay. So... what's up with you and the doctor? I heard you two were giggling and all huddled up at the movie—"

"Bye, Z." I hung up before she could utter another word. She sounded like my mother. There was nothing going on. That man was still in love with his wife and trying to raise his daughter. The last thing on his mind was dating someone even though Marie had been dead for years.

I stayed in bed for a long time. Then my stomach said it was time to get up. "What is in my fridge?" My stomach soured as soon as I opened the door. I hadn't really been home in a while, and everything in the fridge was bad. The smells of spoiled fish and rotten fruit mingled together. I slammed the door and ran outside.

"Guess I'm going out as usual." I could cook. I really could. I just didn't feel like it. I didn't feel like it most days. After putting on clothes and finding my keys, I walked to the diner. The lunch rush was about over with, so it should have been easy to find a booth.

As soon as I walked in, I spotted Logan in the back booth talking to one of the cooks. His eyes met mine. I waved, a small one so no one would notice. He waved me over just as the guy sitting in his booth stood up.

"This is my brother Isaac."

"Right. We've met." I smiled as I shook his hand.

Isaac grinned at his brother. "Nice seeing you again. I'll leave you two to your lunch."

"Don't say it like that," Logan yelled after him.

"I don't know what you mean."

I slid into the booth. "You two sound like my siblings and I."

"Glad to know it's not just us."

"Nope. It's a universal thing. How've you been?"

He sighed.

"Oh no. What did your sister-in-law do now?"

A smile tugged at his lips. "You think that is the only thing that's upsetting me right now?"

"Hmmm…. yep."

He explained about the mediation and how it did not go well. And how Jamie stormed out of the room and he had a bad feeling about it.

"Well, you have my number; if something goes wrong or she tries to start something, call me."

"He has your number?"

I looked up at Isaac. He had two glasses in his hands. "Interesting. He never mentioned that." He slunk away back into the kitchen.

I chuckled. "Your brother lives to embarrass you."

"Favorite pastime. Now, enough about me and my drama. Have you slept?"

I nodded. "And I haven't had any coffee or energy drinks. Mostly because I just woke up."

He chuckled. "Surprised you didn't stay in."

"I tried. There is nothing edible in my fridge. Going to have to clean it out with bleach."

"You're horrible at taking care of yourself."

I shrugged. "When I'm working on a case, I'm not the priority. I don't focus on what I need. I just don't. I do when I'm done, though."

"You need to find a balance." Logan stopped talking as soon as he saw his brother. He set two plates on the table, eyed us, and then walked away.

"I didn't order anything." I stared down at the plate in front of me. "Shrimp tacos."

"He's trying it out."

"I'm okay with being his guinea pig," I said as I picked up my fork. The shrimp was spicy, and the salsa was tangy and delicious. "'This is amazing. They need to let him add it to the menu."

"Yeah, I think today is like a test run or something like that."

"Look at him thriving in our small town. What about you?"

He shrugged. "I'm trying. I do like it here, though."

"Well, that's something."

"What happened with the case? I heard rumors, mostly from your mother."

I dropped my fork onto my plate. "I don't know who is feeding that woman information."

"Everyone from the station stops there at some point during the day."

"Cops. Can't hold water." I told him how the investigation ended, the confession, and everything else we found out. I left the part out about Cynthia's mom. He didn't need to know that. I mentioned Larry's death as well as his lawyer's. His eyebrow rose.

"That was the suicide you were looking into. That's really suspicious."

"I know. I'm really anxious to figure out what the hell is going on."

"Well, perhaps I can be of assistance in that..."

"Perhaps you can," I replied with a grin. My first one in days.

CHAPTER THIRTY-TWO

Logan Elwood

For the first time in a while, things felt pretty normal in Pine Brooke. The crazy search that brought the whole town out was over. Pine Brooke seemed like a small town until you started looking for someone. There was more town than I thought. Dani and I hadn't really explored it yet.

I learned there was a hiking trail near the outskirts of town that took you along the lake and through a beautiful forest that the town shared with Oceanway. It was like a preserve with tortoises, deer, and other animals.

"I'm really thinking about putting something together to get this town moving," I mentioned to Nicole as we finished for the day. "Something to get people out, help lower blood pressure, and just get people moving."

"Sounds interesting," Nicole said as she packed up her bag. "Like what, though?"

I slung my pack over my shoulder. "Well, I was thinking twice a month we could have a hiking club. We walk the trail and see what animals we can find."

Nicole smiled. "That would be a great idea. A lot of our patients would love that."

"And then maybe a gardening club. We could set up a garden area in the main park area. Studies have shown that touching and handling dirt can help people dealing with depression and anxiety. And it's good exercise. I figured that could be geared more toward our older patients; it would get them out of the house and allow them to meet up with different people and get some Vitamin D. I think it would work toward the overall wellness of the town and people might get to see other residents that they don't see often." I opened the door.

"Hmm, gardening club... I like it. You'd have to go to the town council and ask them whether they approve or not. I'll check when the next town meeting is. I can't imagine anyone saying no to this, though."

"Glad to hear it." I closed and locked the door behind me. "I'll write up a proposal for how it would work, and maybe that would help persuade them." A smile pulled at my lips. I was relieved to hear she liked my ideas. If she was on board, chances were that others would too.

"You coming to movie night?"

I clapped a hand to my head. "Oh, crap, that's tonight?"

"I thought you remembered; now that the search is over they're putting it back on tonight."

"Right."

Dani wanted to go; she expressed her feelings several times a day with a ferocity I didn't know she had in her. I hated to disappoint her when I told her it was postponed. She'd be so happy to come out and see everyone. We'd even take Bonnie and Isaac and make a night of it. Once I got home, I started prepping the cooler with snacks and drinks and getting our blankets together. We left the house around seven, opting to walk to the park where the movie would be streamed. We weren't the only ones who had the same idea of getting there early.

We passed families and couples, each one with a smile on their face and a curt head nod in our direction as we walked by.

"I don't think I will ever get used to how people are so happy here," whispered Isaac. "It's a little unnerving."

As two city boys, the constant smiling was a bit weird for us. I didn't think they were happy all the time; they were just polite, which was nice to see and would, in fact, take some getting used to. In the city, a smile was a sign of weakness and was often misconstrued in a negative way. Here, it was warm and inviting.

The park was large and equipped to handle a large group of people. People had already started putting down blankets and opening their coolers in front of a large screen.

"Doctor Elwood!"

The loud and shrieking sound of my name startled me. I looked to my left and saw April Quinn, owner of the coffee shop, and Riley's mother, waving us over.

"Come sit with us."

Dani ran over to greet her before I could say anything. We all followed, except Isaac, who had broken away from the group in search of Nicole. He didn't actually say she was who he was searching for, but she was about the only person in town I had ever seen him talk to, so it was a good guess.

"Hello, Mrs. Quinn." I went to shake her hand. She smacked it away and pulled me into a hug.

"So great to see you." She leaned forward and whispered in my ear, "Thank you for upping his blood pressure meds. Big improvement."

I smiled. "I'm glad."

"Well, put your stuff next to ours. We don't bite."

Dani laughed. I laid out our two blankets to sit on while Bonnie opened the cooler and handed juice boxes to both Dani and Riley's niece—at least I assumed it was Riley's niece. She looked like Riley, but I wasn't sure if she had any children. She had her same piercing blue eyes and rich brown hair.

Bonnie and Dani sat next to Mrs. Quinn. The women talked and laughed like they had known each other for a long time. I sat on the other side with Dani. My head spun, looking for Isaac. When I spotted him, the movie was just starting. He was on a red checkered blanket with Nicole whispering in his ear.

Hmm... I hoped that ended well.

"Well, look at you."

I felt her leg brush against mine before I saw her face. I turned, and she smiled sweetly.

"I'm more surprised you came. Don't you need to finish up your case?"

"It's mostly taken care of. I'm still exhausted, though." She sipped her coffee. The smell of coffee beans and caramel wafted up from the cup.

"How many of those have you had today?" I whispered.

Her blue eyes sparkled with mischief.

"More than you'd recommend. But no energy drinks."

"I guess that's an improvement."

She chuckled. "Enough about me. How's the medical business?"

I told her what I wanted to do with the town. Her eyes lit up. "That's a great idea. It would really help so many in town who are struggling with their weight and other health issues. Have you talked to the town council?"

I shook my head. "Not yet. I think I want to get a proposal together first. Cover all my bases."

"Tell my mom about it. She's on the council, and she'll tell you whether it is something they will approve or not. I'd be up for going hiking. Not sure about gardening, though."

"We could have a town garden right here in the park. Everyone contributes, and everyone gets to receive some of whatever is grown. Or it could teach you how to start a garden at home. Grow your own food."

"Not sure if that is really something I *want* to do. Getting it from the grocery store is so much easier. And I'd hate to take all that business away from him."

A chuckle threatened to bubble up. I pushed it down as I shook my head. "I'll grow a garden, and you are more than welcome to it."

"Don't say that. I'll be like one of those rabbits, constantly eating your carrots and lettuce."

"So, like a pest?"

The corner of her lips curved into a slight smile. "Rabbits aren't pests. They are cute, lovable creatures that like carrots and lettuce."

I had to laugh. "If they're messing up the garden, they're pests."

She looked offended. "How dare you."

Before I could answer, I felt something vibrating against my leg.

"I really hope that's your phone."

Riley cackled so loud everyone's head jerked back to look at us.

"Sorry," I whispered. Riley's quiet laughter was only evident by the way her shoulders kept bouncing up and down.

She pulled her phone out of her pocket. "Hello?" she whispered, a laugh on the edge of her voice. "I'll be there in a minute."

"Sherlock's back on the case," I said when she hung up and slid the phone back into her pocket.

"The work never stops." She stood up gingerly as if she were avoiding putting too much pressure on her right knee. "Now you can enjoy the movie."

"Won't be the same," I whispered. She stalled for a moment and then continued walking. When I turned my head, Bonnie was staring at me, a playful grin on her face. "What?"

She shook her head before turning her attention back to the screen. "I didn't say anything." She didn't, but she did, and we both knew it.

The movie was a lot longer than I anticipated, and it was full dark when it finally ended. Adults groaned as they tried to get off the ground. Bonnie leaned on me to get to her feet. In turn, she helped pull me up. "Bonnie, we're getting old."

She shook her head. "There is no *we* in that."

I couldn't tell if that was a dig at me or her way of telling me I wasn't old. She grinned as she folded up one of the blankets.

"What are you doing for the rest of the night?" Mrs. Quinn bounced over to me with a big grin on her face.

"Umm..." I looked at Bonnie, who shrugged. "Nothing, I guess. Why?"

"Come have dinner with us. We can gossip about the town, and I can tell you everything you need to know."

I grabbed the handle of the cooler in one hand just as she wrapped her arm around mine and pulled me forward. Clearly not taking no for an answer. Dani was excited as she didn't want to let go of her new friend just yet. So we followed them home.

Before we left, I looked for Isaac. He was so wrapped up in whatever Nicole was saying that he didn't even notice the movie was over. I shot him a text on the way, telling him where we were.

Mrs. Quinn's home was decorated beautifully. It smelled like roasted meat, butter, and a hint of something sweet.

"It smells good in here," said Dani.

"It really does," added Bonnie.

"Thank you." She closed the door behind me. "My husband is an excellent cook. You are in for a treat."

Her home was warm and inviting. Pictures all over the walls of her family. My eyes lingered on Riley's graduation picture. She looked exactly the same in her light blue cap and gown.

"Well, it's all ready." A large man with the same eyes as Riley emerged from the kitchen with a roasting pan. The lid was on, so we couldn't see what it was, but I could smell it. If I had to make a guess, it would be a pot roast.

"Hey, Doctor Elwood."

"Nice to see you again, Mr. Quinn."

Dani and her new friend scurried upstairs, giggling.

"Come back down in five minutes!" Mrs. Quinn laughed and pointed at a chair. "Sit down, you two. Make yourselves comfortable."

Bonnie and I sat at the dining room table, followed by Mrs. Quinn and Riley's sister. She stared at me for a moment before sitting across from me.

"So you're the new doctor... What were you and Riley laughing about during the movie?"

I shrugged. "Something to do with the case she's working. I can't remember exactly what it was."

Her lips curved in a sly smile. She didn't believe me. "Right, something about her case. Makes sense. Missing woman found dead is a laugh riot, right?"

"Depending on the punch line, I guess it can be."

Judging by the look on her face, she did not like my response. The girls came back down, and Mr. Quinn came out of the kitchen with two more pans and a bowl stacked with buttery rolls. My mouth watered.

"Alright, dig in." He sat at the head of the table.

Riley's niece's hand shot up. "Should we leave some for Aunt Riley?"

"Don't worry about her. That girl doesn't eat," Mrs. Quinn. We laughed. "I doubt if Riley has any solid food in her fridge except what she gives to Luna."

"Luna?"

"Her dog," said several voices.

"Ah... the dog eats, but she doesn't?"

Mrs. Quinn laughed. "Yup."

"That sounds like Riley."

"Oh, very funny," came a voice from the doorway. Riley wasn't really upset, though. Her eyes sparkled as she came into the house.

"We weren't expecting you back," her mother said. "We would've waited."

"Don't worry about it," she said. "Now, for your information, I'm starving. Move out of my way, Logan."

She bustled in between me and her father. Someone pulled up a chair from somewhere in the house and she immediately started filling a plate. We talked, we laughed, we had a few drinks, and Dani and her new friend even showed off some cool new dance moves they had learned from each other.

It was a good night. A really, really, good night.

And for the first time since I can remember, it really felt like home.

EPILOGUE

Jamie Washington

Jamie hadn't slept in days. Her phone rang next to her head. She heard it, but it was distant. Muffled. Like when your head was underwater, and someone was talking to you. You knew they were there, but you just couldn't quite make out the words. She didn't care to speak to anyone.

The mediation hadn't gone as she had planned. Well, it did, and it didn't. She knew Logan would refuse to give her what she wanted, what she deserved. But she let herself get angry. So angry, she spoke without thinking. She knew better than to do that. She avoided it whenever possible.

Jamie knew how she got when she was angry. The rage boiled inside her until it had to come out. It had to be released in some not-so-healthy ways. She felt it even now. Even though she yelled at them and screamed when she got home, the rage was still there, pulsing in her veins.

Logan acted how she expected him to… but her mother? She hadn't expected her mother to be there.. Why hadn't she mentioned it? She wanted to blindside her. Make her look bad in front of everyone. That was the only thing Everly ever wanted. To make Jamie look bad. She had been doing it all her life. Ever since she was a child. To her, this was one more example of how much her mother hated her.

Jamie tossed and turned all day and all night. Marie's voice echoed in her head.

"You shouldn't have let yourself get so angry. Why do you let her bait you like that? You know what she's like."

"I know. I know. I can't believe I let her win. She knew what she was doing." Jamie rolled over on her side for the millionth time. "How could I be so stupid?"

"You're not stupid. She just knows how to push your buttons. You need to call her. Invite her over, and finally, work through your issues together."

Jamie was reluctant to agree with her sister. She and her mother had never gotten along. Being in the same room together was probably not the best idea. But Marie sounded so sure about the idea.

"Trust me. She will come around. You two just need to talk… alone. Everything will be fine."

Reluctantly she felt around her head and found the phone. At first, she didn't think her mother would answer. When she did, Jamie knew she would say no to meeting her.

"Text me your address. I think we need to talk, too."

Her mother had surprised her twice in five minutes. *Perhaps Marie was right,* she thought. First time for everything.

Everly arrived at her daughter's home against her better judgment. She could never deal with Jamie when she was angry. It was always Marie's job. It was too much to put on a child, but the girl seemed to be the only one alive to calm her sister down. Marie just knew what was wrong when no one else did. Maybe if she had paid more attention to her daughters, she would have understood them better. But it was a different time, and she was a different person. She wanted to be a better mother. A better grandmother. She just needed the opportunity.

The door opened. For a long moment, which felt like an eternity to both women, they stood there staring at each other. Both waiting for the other to make the first move. Jamie relented and stepped inside to let her mother enter. She closed the door behind her.

"You don't have a car?"

"Everywhere in this town is practically walking distance. I just walked over. Figured I could use the exercise."

Jamie eyed her mother. If there was one thing Everly did without question, it was take care of herself. She exercised daily, ate healthy meals, and took supplements. She kept herself in *finding a husband* shape. Just in case she wanted another one.

"You were always trim," said Jamie.

Everly smiled. "A lot of work not to end up like my mother, three hundred pounds and dying alone."

Jamie sat on the sofa. Everly followed.

"This is a nice house."

"Thanks. Better than staying in a hotel for an extended period of time."

Everly swallowed hard. She was never one to coddle her children. She didn't coddle anyone. She was a straight shooter, and that was one thing about her that would never change. "You wouldn't have to rent it if you went home to your husband and children. They must miss you."

"This again?"

"Yes. And again. And again. Until you leave Dani and her father alone and go home to your family."

"Dani is my family. She's my sister's daughter."

"She's dead! Marie is dead... she is not coming back. As much as I wish she could. She was the only one that could deal with you. But she's gone. Raising Dani is not going to bring her back. Let it go!"

Jamie barreled out of the room, but Everly wasn't done talking to her. She followed after her, and they ended up in the kitchen. Everly by the kitchen table, and Jamie using a melon baller on a watermelon.

"She's not coming back. You don't get to ruin that little girl's life because you miss your sister."

"How would living with me ruin her life?" Jamie kept her back to her mother. She didn't want her to see the tears pricking the corners of her eyes. "Marie loved me. She loved spending time with me. I was her best friend. It would be the same with Dani."

"Marie hated you," Everly said quietly. It was something she had known for a while but never brought it up because Marie never mentioned it. But it was something they both knew.

Jamie spun around, melon-baller gripped tightly in her hand. She inched closer to her mother. "You have no idea what you're talking about."

Everly, believing that Jamie was still in the position to see reason, thought that if she finally told the girl the truth, she would let go of this fantasy of the perfect sister. She would come to her senses.

She took a deep breath. "You ruined her life. You ruined everything. Marie was twelve when you were born."

"No she wasn't."

"Yes, she was. I had sent her to some Catholic school so no one would know."

"Know what?"

"...that she was pregnant."

Jamie's heart stalled in her chest. "What?"

Everly thought things would be easier if she just said everything as quickly as possible. Rip the Band-Aid off. "She had the baby. And when she returned, I told people I had adopted you from a sister who couldn't take care of you. No one knew. Marie didn't want anyone to know. And neither did I."

Jamie stumbled back. "What are you saying?"

Everly clenched her fist at her sides twice before shoving her hands in her pockets. "I had a boyfriend once... I didn't know he was that kind of man, and by the time I figured it out, it was too late. He ran away. We never saw him again."

Bile coated the back of her throat. Jamie felt like she was floating, her body moving all on its own. A weed in the wind. "Marie was my mother?"

"Yes. It was hard for her to look at you, but she persisted. She became your big sister, and she protected you. But you ruined her life, Jamie. A constant reminder that just wouldn't let her go. You followed her everywhere. You always had to have all of her attention. It was exhausting. She never complained because that wasn't her nature. But—"

Jamie lunged at her. She struggled to get her hands out of her pockets before cold metal slid into her eye socket. The melon baller wrapped around her eyeball in one swift motion.

Everly screamed. She placed her hands on Jamie's chest and shoved. Jamie stumbled back, Everly's eye going with her. Blood oozed down her cheeks. Everly screamed, her hands clutching her eye socket. Jamie lunged forward, knocking Everly onto the floor. Blood sprayed into the air and pooled on the ground as Everly shrieked in pain and terror.

Jamie dropped that tool and went looking for another. The knife she used to cut up the watermelon was still on the edge of the cutting board.

She grabbed it. In one swift, practiced motion, the knife slid across Everly's throat. Blood sprayed into the air as she gasped, struggling to breathe. Her mouth filled up with blood.

Jamie stood up. She stared down at Everly. Her eyes were wide, her hands clutching at the wound on her neck. Slowly fading. Each spurt smaller than the one before.

"Dani is mine!" Jamie's breaths were shallow and fast. Beads of sweat coated her forehead.

"She's mine! Dani is mine!"

She dropped the knife on the floor next to her mother.

"Marie gave her to me. She is mine!"

AUTHOR'S NOTE

My dear reader,

Thank you so much for picking up *Murder in the Pines* and continuing this journey with me and Riley! After hearing your feedback on The Girls in Pine Brooke, I was buzzing with ideas! The collective enthusiasm sparked a late-night brainstorm that inspired me to weave in another layer of mystery to this story. I feel it deepened the suspense and made Riley's investigation even more intricate, and I hope you enjoyed experiencing it all! It truly feels like we're piecing together these mysteries as a team, and I couldn't be happier about it. That excitement is driving me as I'm already busy crafting the next one, and I will work tirelessly to get it into your hands soon!

Your support truly means the world to me. As an indie author, living my dream of crafting these tales is all thanks to wonderful readers like you cheering me on. If you enjoyed this latest mystery, I would be incredibly grateful if you could share your thoughts in a review or tell your friends who love these types of stories. Word of mouth and your feedback are my lifelines, helping me continue Riley's journey and reach even more readers. Even just a few lines about what you enjoyed can make a huge difference!

If you're enjoying exploring Pine Brooke, I think you'll also love the adventures of Emma Griffin and Ava James! These series feature female detectives with big hearts and fierce determination, just like Riley. Each story is filled with an entertaining cast of characters and plenty of twists and turns to keep you guessing until the very end. I'd love for you to dive into their journeys and see what exciting mysteries await!

With endless gratitude and excitement for all the adventures still to come, I'm so glad to have you along for the ride. See you in the next book!

Yours,
A.J. Rivers

P.S. If for some reason you didn't like this book or found typos or other errors, please let me know personally. I do my best to read and respond to every email at mailto:aj@riversthrillers.com

P.P.S. If you would like to stay up-to-date with me and my latest releases I invite you to visit my Linktree page at *www.linktr.ee/a.j.rivers* to subscribe to my newsletter and receive a free copy of my book, Edge of the Woods. You can also follow me on my social media accounts for behind-the-scenes glimpses and sneak peeks of my upcoming projects, or even sign up for text notifications. I can't wait to connect with you!

ALSO BY
A.J. RIVERS

Emma Griffin FBI Mysteries

Season One

Book One—The Girl in Cabin 13*
Book Two—The Girl Who Vanished*
Book Three—The Girl in the Manor*
Book Four—The Girl Next Door*
Book Five—The Girl and the Deadly Express*
Book Six—The Girl and the Hunt*
Book Seven—The Girl and the Deadly End*

Season Two

Book Eight—The Girl in Dangerous Waters*
Book Nine—The Girl and Secret Society*
Book Ten—The Girl and the Field of Bones*
Book Eleven—The Girl and the Black Christmas*
Book Twelve—The Girl and the Cursed Lake*
Book Thirteen—The Girl and The Unlucky 13*
Book Fourteen—The Girl and the Dragon's Island*

Season Three

Book Fifteen—The Girl in the Woods*
Book Sixteen —The Girl and the Midnight Murder*
Book Seventeen— The Girl and the Silent Night*
Book Eighteen — The Girl and the Last Sleepover*
Book Nineteen — The Girl and the 7 Deadly Sins*
Book Twenty — The Girl in Apartment 9*
Book Twenty-One — The Girl and the Twisted End*

Emma Griffin FBI Mysteries Retro - Limited Series
(Read as standalone or before Emma Griffin book 22)

Book One— The Girl in the Mist*
Book Two— The Girl on Hallow's Eve*
Book Three— The Girl and the Christmas Past*
Book Four— The Girl and the Winter Bones*
Book Five— The Girl on the Retreat*

Season Four

Book Twenty-Two — The Girl and the Deadly Secrets*
Book Twenty-Three — The Girl on the Road*
Book Twenty-Four — The Girl and the Unexpected Gifts*
Book Twenty-Five — The Girl and the Secret Passage*
Book Twenty-Six — The Girl and the Bride*
Book Twenty-Seven — The Girl in Her Cabin*
Book Twenty-Eight — The Girl Who Remembers*

Season Five

Book Twenty-Nine — The Girl in the Dark*
Book Thirty — The Girl and the Lies
Book Thirty-One — The Girl and the Inmate

Ava James FBI Mysteries

Book One—The Woman at the Masked Gala*
Book Two—Ava James and the Forgotten Bones*
Book Three —The Couple Next Door*
Book Four — The Cabin on Willow Lake*
Book Five — The Lake House*
Book Six — The Ghost of Christmas*
Book Seven — The Rescue*
Book Eight — Murder in the Moonlight*
Book Nine — Behind the Mask*
Book Ten — The Invitation*
Book Eleven — The Girl in Hawaii*
Book Twelve — The Woman in the Window*
Book Thirteen — The Good Doctor*
Book Fourteen — The Housewife Killer

Book Fifteen — The Librarian

Dean Steele FBI Mysteries
Book One—The Woman in the Woods*
Book Two — The Last Survivors
Book Three — No Escape
Book Four — The Garden of Secrets
Book Five — The Killer Among Us
Book Six — The Convict
Book Seven — The Last Promise
Book Eight — Death by Midnight
Book Nine — The Woman in the Attic
Book Ten — Playing with Fire

A Detective Riley Quinn Pine Brooke Mystery
Book One —The Girls in Pine Brooke
Book Two — Murder in the Pines

ALSO BY
A.J. RIVERS & THOMAS YORK

Bella Walker FBI Mystery Series
Book One—The Girl in Paradise*
Book Two—Murder on the Sea*
Book Three—The Last Aloha*

Other Standalone Novels
Gone Woman
* Also available in audio

Made in the USA
Monee, IL
23 December 2024